HOMEWARD WITCH

HOMEWARD WITCH

THE WITCH NEXT DOOR™ BOOK EIGHT

JUDITH BERENS

DISRUPTIVE IMAGINATION®

LMBPN Publishing
PMB 196, 2540 South Maryland Pkwy
Las Vegas, NV 89109

First US edition, January 2020
Version 1.01, December 2020
ebook ISBN: 978-1-64202-710-5
Print ISBN: 978-1-64202-711-2

THE HOMEWARD WITCH TEAM

Thanks to the JIT Readers

Veronica Stephan-Miller
Peter Manis
Debi Sateren
Diane L. Smith
Dave Hicks
Jeff Goode
Dorothy Lloyd
Deb Mader
Larry Omans

If we've missed anyone, please let us know!

Editor
SkyHunter Editing Team

DEDICATIONS

From Martha

To everyone who still believes in magic
and all the possibilities that holds.
To all the readers who make this
entire ride so much fun.
And to my son, Louie and so many wonderful friends who
remind me all the time of what
really matters and how wonderful
life can be in any given moment.

From Michael

To Family, Friends and
Those Who Love
To Read.
May We All Enjoy Grace
To Live The Life We Are
Called.

ONE

A long, warbled bellow echoed through the silence of the woods. Trees snapped and cracked beneath the thunderous footsteps of one of Mabayn's perilous creatures. The ground shuddered, and Lily Antony woke with a start.

"What was that?" Wide awake now, she turned toward Romeo Stephens beside her in the king-sized bed that would have been impossible to fit in a regular tent. But here in this dimension, the impossible seemed the new normal. A few more trees fell only a few miles away with tortuous groans. "Romeo."

The werewolf's green eyes opened the second her hand settled on his shoulder. He jerked, then turned his head toward her with a tiny frown. "Oh, man. I had the weirdest dream, Lil. Something was attacking us, and it made this sound like a foghorn, only—"

The bellow rang out once again, and the ground trembled enough to swing the lantern hung from a hook in the tent's ceiling violently from side to side. She whipped her head toward the tent's closed entrance flap. "Okay, is that loud and way too close?"

"Yeah, I'd agree with that."

They shared a quick glance before she tossed the thick comforter off her lap and slipped out of the bed. "We need to go."

"I'm right behind you." He darted out of the bed and snatched his clothes up off the floor as she yanked the ridiculous emerald-green velvet dress over her head again. "Didn't your mom say we were safe here?"

She rushed toward the tent's entrance on bare feet and paused to listen for more frenzied chaos from outside. "I'm not sure that applies when something that sounds like an exploding skyscraper is headed directly toward us. Don't tell me you feel like waiting around to find out."

"I won't and definitely have no problem with moving." Once Romeo jammed his feet into his sneakers, he skirted the huge bed in the tent that didn't look nearly as roomy from the outside and stood beside her. "Maybe it stopped, huh? Or changed direction?"

Right on cue, another warbled cry blared from the creature outside.

"I very much doubt it." She grimaced. "Come on."

She tossed the entrance flap aside and ducked beneath it before she moved quickly into the clearing Greta Antony had called Kahara. The iron brazier was dark and empty, although the basket of exotic Mabayn fruits still rested beside the tree stumps. Rays of pink light from the sky above the forest canopy streamed through the branches as the young couple darted toward the second tent Greta had chosen for her use.

Before Lily could open her mom's tent, the heavy footfalls pounded the forest floor again, this time much more quickly. Trees splintered and cracked, and she and her friend both stumbled sideways over the trembling earth. The young witch regained her balance and lunged toward the tent entrance. When she pulled the flap aside, fully ready to drag her mom out of bed, Greta Antony already stood a few inches in front of her.

"Mom!"

Her mother glanced quickly from Lily to Romeo before her gaze darted toward the woods around the tents. "That's a heck of a wakeup call, isn't it?" she quipped as she pushed past her daughter and scanned their surroundings

"I think it's coming right toward us. So we—what are you wearing?" She scrutinized her mother in surprise and noted the loose white blouse, the tight beige trousers that looked more like riding pants, and the black, calf-high boots.

Romeo cocked his head and grinned. "Did you find a horse in that tent too?"

Greta shot him an exasperated look before the creature that approached uttered another vengeful, earsplitting cry. All three magicals in the clearing ducked instinctively and covered their ears with their hands before the enormous, unknown beast's roar faded into an ominous echo.

The woman nodded at her daughter and the young

werewolf, her eyes wide with determination. "This is the part where we run."

She almost knocked Lily over as she darted fully out of the tent and raced past the second one toward the brazier on the other side of the clearing. Romeo managed to catch Lily before she stumbled too much off balance and they stared after the older Optatus witch intent on setting an example of what she'd meant.

"Keep up and do exactly as I say," Greta called over her shoulder.

The forest barely a few dozen yards behind the woman's tent rustled with movement and a few more trees split and were flung aside with a scattering of blue bark and a burst of purple leaves.

"That's your plan?" Lily shouted but her mother didn't slow.

"Running sounds good to me." Romeo caught her hand and jerked her forward across the open space after Greta.

The young witch lurched across the ground on her bare feet as he pulled her along. She stumbled constantly over the soft purple moss underfoot and when they reached the edge of the forest, she jerked her hand out of his and stopped.

The older woman finally stopped, rolled her eyes, and glanced across to the other side of the clearing where the forest seemed to be systematically shredded by the gargantuan beast that approached. "Do I need to tell Romeo to carry you?"

"You know, there actually is such a thing as a stupid question." Lily pointed at the tight, restrictive skirt of the velvet dress she'd been forced to wear at the Black Heron Society's High Seat, and a bright yellow light erupted at her fingertip. She drew the razor-sharp spell down the skirt from the middle of her thigh all the way to the hem and felt much better slicing a giant slit through the stupid garment. "Okay. That's much better."

Two huge blue trees toppled on the other side of the open space, and the party whirled as a mottled green fist on an arm the size of a school bus thrust through the opening created by the destruction.

Without another word, Greta launched into a sprint between the trees. The young couple followed and Lily had no problem keeping up with the pace her mom set this time. The trunks very quickly grew closer and closer together the farther they moved. The monster behind them cried out again, but the sound cut off in mid-bellow before the pounding footsteps increased to surprising speed.

"Stay away from the red," the older woman shouted and turned sharply left through the thickening forest.

"The red what?" Romeo glanced around them quickly before he and Lily followed the new path.

"Anything. Basically, anything that is the color red."

"Like that giant red door in the middle of the forest?" Lily pointed as they ran past.

"Especially that! Hurry."

The young witch cast a fleeting glance at the red door through the trees. It seemed to hang suspended without hinges or a supporting wall while glittering flecks of gold light sparkled around its stark outline. Something behind it beckoned her to come in and take a look for herself but the next tree she passed blocked her view. She shook the odd sensation out of her head and continued to run.

Greta hurdled a few fallen tree trunks covered in purple moss. Romeo had no issue getting over them either, but the shreds of Lily's emerald dress snagged on the jagged edges of broken limbs and slowed her. "Wait!"

He spun and saw her stuck on the fallen trunk immediately before he saw the trees they'd passed seconds before knock against each other. Most of them fell where they stood, but one of them sailed through the forest and lodged itself in the higher branches of its fellows.

The werewolf bounded back toward the log, caught her by the waist, and lifted her up and over. The dress tore with a loud ripping sound before he settled her on her feet and they raced away after her mom.

On their right, tiny orbs of red light floated in a dispersing stream like bubbles from a bubble machine. Lily found the source—a brilliant, blood-red flower the size of a basketball that opened to release the tiny spheres of light.

At least they're not heading toward us. Yet.

Thick purple vines draped from the dense growth ahead. Greta ducked under them first and had to slow to slip beneath the dangling creepers that looked more than easy to get tangled in and strangled by in seconds. Directly in front of her, a huge, glistening black spider with way more than eight legs lowered itself on a massive cable of bright-yellow thread.

"Mom, stop!"

The woman froze in her crouch and glanced at the spider-like creature that scuttled on a direct trajectory toward her. Lily delivered a hasty round of her favorite sparking-red attack spell and caught the would-be attacker easily. The creature uttered a hissed shriek as it was launched into the trees with a wet thump, and Greta pushed herself to her feet and flung globs of bright-yellow sludge off her arms.

"And that's the best reason to not like spiders right there," Romeo muttered as he and Lily ducked under the vines.

The older woman extended her hands toward each of them and helped pull them through before the huge, destructive beast roared again. A gust of hot, acrid air pummeled the group from behind. She glanced through the vines with wide eyes. "Keep moving."

Her daughter and the young werewolf sprinted after her again and now, Lily was acutely aware of the change from soft moss to crunching purple pine needles and prickly undergrowth beneath her bare feet. They continued their run as the rage-maddened creature thrashed through the vegetation in pursuit.

Finally, they all but fell into another clearing beside a rise of rolling orange boulders on their left. Greta stopped short and extended an arm for the others to stop with her. "Damn."

"What is it?" Lily leaned forward a little to catch her breath.

Romeo turned to check the status of the giant that blundered through the woods behind them. "I don't know if we have much time to sit and take a breather."

In reply, Greta pointed at the far right edge of the

clearing where the purple grass, clover, and underbrush looked much darker and almost burnt. Searing red lines snaked across the ground and ejected sporadic bursts of steam. "That's off-limits."

"I wouldn't have opted to try to walk across that anyway." The werewolf scratched the back of his head and the mop of dark curls there. "It looks clear up ahead, though."

He started to walk forward but the woman snatched a handful of his shirt and yanked him back. "I told you to do exactly as I say because it is not clear up ahead."

"But there's nothing—"

She released a rapid burst of red magic toward the open ground of the clearing in front of them. Where her spell struck, the ground erupted in plumes of thick, white-gray smoke that smelled way too much like rotting vegetables.

"The mushrooms are tiny," she said, released his shirt, and gestured to the purple ground now studded with thousands of small blue dots. "But they're absolutely everywhere and their spores will eat through you in under a minute. If you stumble into that, you will not make it out."

Romeo took a step back and shook his head. "Great. You took us to a dimension that's one giant deathtrap."

"It's simply the way Mabayn is."

Behind them, the trees shattered in an explosion of blue splinters and cascading purple leaves. The same nasty-looking green arm punched through the branches, and the creature's next blood-curdling bellow almost brought Lily to her knees.

"The only way to go from here is up." Greta turned to their left and the mountain of orange boulders piled high through the trees.

"What?" her daughter shouted over the ringing in her ears.

"Let's go." The woman began to climb and wedged the toes of the black boots she hadn't brought with her to this plane into the crevices between the rocks as she scrambled over them. "Hurry!"

"Barefoot rock climbing." Lily shook her head. "This place has everything, doesn't it?"

"Seriously, Lil, I'd take this over flesh-eating fungus." Romeo raised his eyebrows at her, then pulled himself onto the closest boulder.

A splintered tree hurtled through the air from behind them and bounced a few times over the field of tiny blue mushrooms. Thick streams of what looked like white smoke billowed from the soil and in the next moment, the monster thrust another arm through the tangle of branches and broke free into the clearing.

The brute was tall as a three-story building, covered in dark-green boils, and flung its arms wildly in every direction. Its huge mouth opened for another howl that transformed into an earsplitting roar as it stumbled forward. The shuddering footsteps jostled a small avalanche of orange pebbles and loose rocks to tumble down the rocky hillside Greta and Romeo were already scaling.

No wonder it's crashed around like this. It can't see.

Where the creature's eyes should have been was only

more mottled flesh covered in boils without even the shape of eyes.

The spore clouds rose even thicker from the mushrooms and shredded the thrown tree hungrily with each passing second. Lily found a firm handhold in the closest orange boulder, ignored the rocky edges that cut into her bare feet, and started to climb.

TWO

The first few yards up the orange cliffs were the most difficult because every time the sightless monster took another step across the clearing, every boulder shivered and threatened to come loose from the mountainside. Lily had to stop and cling to the jagged rock with her entire body held motionless to reassure herself that she wouldn't be thrown loose either.

It didn't help when another blue tree impacted with the cliff barely inches below her last foothold and pelted her with shattered bark and chipped rock fragments. By the time she reached her companions at a ledge eroded into the boulder-strewn mountain, she was high enough to see the clearing stretched out below them and the creature that had stumbled blindly into a natural Mabayn trap with danger on every side.

Romeo helped her onto the ledge with a firm hand and the three magicals sat above the forest floor to watch the creature that was either still looking for them or seeking a way out without being able to see.

"Do you have any idea what that is?" Lily asked and crossed her legs beneath the ripped and tattered remains of her velvet dress.

"Not really." Greta sniffed and wiped the thin sheen of sweat from her forehead. "Only that it's best to avoid it."

"Did anyone else notice that it doesn't have any eyes?" Romeo paused when both Antony witches turned slowly to fix him with incredulous expressions. "I mean...because it wasn't immediately obvious, at least not to me."

"It's probably some kind of mutation." Greta peered over the ledge. The green-skinned creature—whose head bobbed half a dozen yards below the ledge—now uttered a series of much quieter whines and grumbles. "Most things on this plane keep a certain type of balance. This whole world works together in harmony to keep the cycles moving seamlessly."

"Acid rain and giant spiders and whatever that is"— Lily pointed at the charred earth across the clearing streaked with flaming red veins—"don't really seem that harmonious, Mom."

The woman raised her chin as she studied the clearing, then rested her head against the orange stone behind them. "Not for us but remember, we don't belong here. The life in Mabayn was created to sustain the life in Mabayn and maybe even to shelter a few foreigners like us who pop in for a brief visit. That aberration, though, is one of the outliers."

"Or part of the balance." The young Optatus witch

glanced at her mother, but she had her eyes closed with her head still leaned against the rock wall. "Do you think maybe now is a good time to answer my question?"

The corners of the woman's mouth twitched in a small, weary smile. "You asked a number of questions around that brazier, Sweets."

"This question. How do you know so much about this place if you've never been here before?"

With a long, slow sigh, Greta raised her head and glanced at the creature that now shuffled in slow, hesitant circles across the clearing. "I was taught, Lily. It's as simple as that."

"By wh—"

A puff of thick white clouds gusted from the field of flesh-eating mushrooms, followed by the blind creature's choked coughing and an agonized wail. It thrashed across the tiny blue fungi, which merely released more clouds of spores and exacerbated its situation.

"Come on." Romeo wrinkled his nose in disgust and pity. "It should be put out of its misery."

Greta tilted her head, then huffed a wry laugh and looked at her daughter. "You know, you might be right about the balance part."

"What?"

"When you said it's part of the balance. That pitiful creature might hold the key to some kind of balance somewhere else in this world. That's how things work here. One creature's misfortune is another's saving grace, et cetera, et cetera."

"Mom."

The older Optatus witch gave her daughter a blank, expectant look.

"You didn't answer my question."

"No? I thought I had."

The werewolf leaned forward to peer at the hapless monster that continued to struggle and flail among the deadly mushrooms with low, keening noises. "I thought you said those spores would eat through flesh."

"Seriously?" Lily slapped his arm with the back of her hand. "You're not helping her focus."

"Sorry." He nodded toward the clearing. "But the spores ate that tree. So...why hasn't the giant melted into a screaming puddle of sludge right now?"

"Gross."

"That is interesting." Greta's face lit up with excitement and she folded her arms. "It looks like a creature that can't see is the only thing with an immunity to the deadly forest."

"Or it's simply so big that it takes a whole field of mushrooms to bring it down." Lily closed her eyes and tried to bring her anger down too. *The beast that chased us here isn't the most important thing now that we're out of its way. You know she's only trying to deflect. Don't give up.* "Can we table the whole spore-resistant creature subject for a minute? Please? Because I really—"

"It's still going." Romeo's jaw had fallen open as he watched the creature trudge through the mushroom field, barely visible through the thick curtain of released spores. "Is it trying to crush them all or is it simply totally confused?"

"Hmm. That's an interesting theory." The woman drummed her fingers on her opposite arms folded over her chest. "It may be confused. If it was hunting us for one reason or another, it might have lost our scent, given that we're all the way up here. Maybe it's trying to find our trail again."

"Okay, Mom—"

"But if it were trying to destroy all the spores in that field, that raises a completely different set of questions, why being the most prevalent. For whom? Itself, or us, or maybe other creatures of Mabayn—"

"Forget about the mushrooms!" Lily shifted on her crossed legs to face her mother and grabbed Greta's shoulder. "I get that you have this insatiable curiosity for everything except what needs to be addressed right now. I've spent six months without you and I would really like to not have to pull every single answer out of you like a rotten tooth."

Romeo snorted and lowered his head to hide his smile.

The older woman pressed her lips together in an effort to fight her own smile and looked at her daughter with a mixture of embarrassment and amusement that made Lily feel like she was twelve all over again. Finally, she patted the girl's hand on her shoulder and nodded. "Okay. I can't walk away from you and tell you to ask me later. So, in the interest of not being thrown off this ledge by my own daughter, remind me of your question."

She sighed and removed her hand. "You said you were taught about this place. By whom?"

"Right. By my mentor."

When her raised eyebrows and silent staring didn't prompt her to continue, the young witch had to do it vocally. "You have a mentor?"

"Had, Lily. He was my teacher once, a very long time ago. And now I like to think of him as something of a friend. Maybe even my equal." Greta smirked. "Even though we both know I surpassed his knowledge and ability in the end."

Romeo chuckled, then cleared his throat when the Antony witches sent him questioning looks. "Sorry. It's funny to picture Greta as someone's student. And kinda hard to imagine, actually. Or were you, like, an apprentice?"

Lily laughed a little and waited for her mom to answer.

"Not the way people think of apprentices these days. But maybe I was. Sure."

"Huh. Greta Antony as some other witch's apprentice." The girl grinned.

"Oh, please. It shouldn't be that surprising. Did you think I woke up one day and suddenly had the knowledge of everything I taught you?"

"No..." Still smiling, she glanced into the clearing but instead of seeing the creature and the clouds of flesh-eating mushroom spoor below, she was caught up in the mental image of her mom being trained exactly like she'd trained her. "But it's weird to think of you learning from someone else."

"Really."

"Or maybe it's weird to think of you taking orders from someone else."

Greta scoffed. "Well, you and I are still so similar that way, too. I was not very good at following instructions without knowing exactly why I had to follow them. It got me into far more trouble than I like to admit."

"That sounds like you." The young witch smirked at her mother. Beside her, Romeo fiddled with the orange pebbles beneath his crossed legs. "So who was he?"

"Oh, he's still around. Very much alive and kicking. Actually, you've met him, Lily. A few times." The woman shrugged and seemed to think that was enough of an answer.

"Mom, don't make me try to guess. You know tons of people and I've met more of them than I can count."

Greta took a deep breath. "Brast."

"What?"

Romeo glanced from one to the other in confusion. "I'm the only one who doesn't recognize that name."

"Hmm. Well, no. It makes sense that you wouldn't." Rather than explain, the woman gave him a sympathetic smile and turned away.

"And why does that make sense?"

Lily nudged his thigh gently with the back of her hand. "Alexander Brast sits on the Council of Magic, Romeo. Remember when I told you about meeting him at that gala in Boston?"

The werewolf's eyes widened. "That Alexander Brast?"

"So you have heard the name," Greta muttered.

"Yeah, Lily mentioned him for a split second. Werewolves don't really spend all that much time memorizing the names of magicals on the Council."

"I guess not." The woman smoothed the blonde hair away from her face and scanned the treetops surrounding them on the ledge. "The Council doesn't spend that much time on understanding werewolves, either. It seems fair."

"Mom, you were trained by a member of the Council." Lily cocked her head with a small frown. "You didn't think that was an important thing to tell me?"

"I trained with Alexander before he became Councilmember Brast. A long time before. He was a powerful witch even then and he had considerable knowledge to pass on, including his study of this place." She closed her eyes and leaned back against the orange rock again. "Telling you about my relationship with him didn't ever make it to the top of my priority list."

"But if I'd known about it, I could have gone to him for help." Lily swallowed the thick knot of discomfort in her throat and tried to stay calm. "I wouldn't have had to spend two months trying to get someone—anyone—to listen to me after you disappeared. I could've gone straight to Brast and told him you were still alive. He taught you and would have at least wanted to make sure I was right—"

"It's a little more complicated than that, Sweets." Greta patted her daughter's thigh.

"How is that complicated?"

"Because I went to the Council two weeks before my disappearance. I told them everything I'd found on the Black Heron Society and how detrimental the Transference spell would be for magic across the world if those people succeeded." She clenched her jaw and her nostrils flared as she drew a long, deep breath. "They didn't believe a word of it."

"You're kidding."

"I'm really not." Greta scoffed. "That would be the worst joke I've ever made."

"But they'll listen to you now."

Both witches turned to look at Romeo, who merely shrugged under the attention.

"What makes you think that?" the older woman asked.

"Well, they all think you're dead. The whole world thinks you're dead except for us and the Black Heron."

"And Bentley," Lily added.

"Bentley..." A nostalgic smile settled on Greta's face.

"He's right, Mom. That's where we need to go when we get out of here. Set up a meeting with the Council and tell them everything. You're obviously not dead. And we have proof of what the Black Heron was doing in that stupid castle."

Her mother blinked and licked her lips. "What proof?"

"Carmichael's stone. We simply have to find it first, then we take it and you to the Council and explain everything. Someone has to stop him from trying the Transference spell all over again. He doesn't seem like the kind of messed-up magical who would give up and move on. Especially when you were the one who brought it all crashing down around him."

"Don't give me all the credit for that, Lily. I couldn't have gotten out of that mess without you."

Lily rolled her eyes but she couldn't help a tiny smirk.

"Fine. I'll take some of the credit. But the Council has to believe you after we walk in with a witch who's supposed to be dead and a stone full of magic from who knows how many different magicals. Brast won't turn you away again— as long as you're still on good terms, right?"

Romeo grimaced. "I really hope you guys are still on good terms."

"Oh, we're fine."

"Then that's what we'll do." Lily gazed at the forest of blue bark and purple leaves, needles, and fronds that made up the plant life in this totally weird dimension. "Once we get out of here."

Her mom's smile looked more pained than resolute. "It sounds like you have everything decided. Exactly like I taught you."

Something's wrong. She still looks like she's hiding something. She decided to ask why her mother wasn't more excited about the idea of getting the entire Council of Magic on their side to put Carmichael away for good. Before she could open her mouth, however, a shrieked howl rose from the clearing below their ledge.

The blind creature had finished its rampage through the mushroom field, which had subsided to only a few stray puffs of white clouds. The ground that used to be covered in mushrooms had been trampled to a blue, sludgy pulp. And now, the blind golem pounded across the deep-purple earth marred by all the blazing red cracks. A spray of steam hissed up beneath the creature's every step, and it couldn't quite work out how to escape the ground that literally seared its huge stump-like feet.

"Balance or not," Romeo muttered, "I don't think it's smart enough to escape this one."

"Do you still wanna put it out of its misery?" Greta asked with a wry smile.

"Kinda, yeah."

The eyeless creature bellowed again, raised its huge, gnarled fists into the air, and thumped them both onto the fractured red earth beneath him. The ground trembled and triggered another flurry of orange pebbles and loose slag onto the three companions. A frustrated growl burst from the creature's throat before it strode away through the woods again and destroyed trees or threw them in every direction. It seemed determined to rampage across Mabayn with no apparent purpose at all.

"Well." Greta pushed herself to her feet and dusted her hands off. "All that running and climbing and conversation made me hungry. I wouldn't recommend trying to forage for anything in the woods—"

"I don't think we would have suggested that," Romeo cut in and stared with wide eyes at the trail of destruction left behind the enraged creature as the sounds of its furious retreat faded away.

"That's smart of you." The woman nodded and studied the edge of the cliff. "But I do know where we can find an overflowing basket of exotic fruits that are perfectly safe. Are you ready to head back?"

Lily stared at her mother. *How does she switch like that from serious conversation to thinking about food?* But when her stomach rumbled in response to not having eaten for who knew how long—especially in this place—she really didn't have a reason to argue.

THREE

Greta led them on a different path through the woods than they'd taken to the dead-end clearing and the orange boulders. They didn't come across any more flowers that spewed red bubbles or giant spiders intent on catching a witch for its next feast. Lily saw two more red doors much farther away through the trees and a huge insect like a cross between a beetle and a centipede clamped hand-sized pinchers around the hem of her ripped dress. Her legs had far more breathing space after that.

"Here we go." The older woman nodded curtly and swerved around a few more blue trees before she stepped out into the clearing she'd called Kahara.

They'd gone in a large circle to double back to the open ground, the tree stumps around the brazier, and the two tents behind it. Surprisingly, it all looked as undisturbed as it had been when they'd found it the first time.

"Wait a minute." Lily glanced into the thick forest

behind her and frowned. "This is where that monster came from."

"Yep." Her mother headed toward the ring of tree stumps, saw that the baskets of fruit had moved, and stuck her hands on her hips.

"But it destroyed all these trees before it reached us. And it followed us that way." She pointed across the clearing.

"I'm glad to see your observational skills haven't diminished any, Sweets." Greta chuckled and headed toward the tent on the left that she'd claimed as her own. "That's a little too obvious, though. Especially for you."

Romeo scratched the back of his head and turned in a few slow, confused circles. "Yeah, but a whole forest of broken trees putting themselves back together like nothing happened isn't normal."

"Like I said, everything in Mabayn works together to keep the cycles moving. It looks like we've completed at least one—maybe even two since we slept for...huh. I really don't know how long."

He snorted. "What is this? The Hunger Games?"

Lily nudged him gently with her elbow and he flinched with a small, confused smile.

"It's exactly like that, Lil."

"Everything here must have been reset too." Greta approached her tent and extended her hand toward the flap. "And that means completely restocked—"

The canvas was whipped aside from within and the woman froze. Inside the shelter stood a man who was easily six and a half feet tall. A huge, bushy beard covered his face and hung to his breastbone, matched by a thick mustache and wiry brown eyebrows. His long hair was pulled back and held in place with a leather thong that might or might not have been pulled from the fringe dangling off his brown leather jacket.

"Oh." She took one step back and grinned at the stranger. "Hi."

His dark-gray eyes studied her for a few seconds before his gaze flicked aside to take in the young couple who stood on the tent side of the circle of tree stumps. "I knew someone had touched my stuff."

"Your—" Stepping aside quickly to avoid being bowled over by the giant man's barrel-shaped chest and bulging shoulders, Greta blinked rapidly and frowned after him. "Since when did Kahara belong to you?"

"Since I came here. Alone." The man headed directly to the brazier and the circle of stumps with a massive, wickedly honed ax swinging in one hand beside him. "And I assume at least one of you knows what that means."

Lily pried her gaze away from the weapon that looked like it could chop any one of these trees down with one swing and glanced at her mother. Greta's lips were pressed into a thin line and her face had paled considerably. "Mom?"

"Excuse me." The stranger stopped in front of Lily and Romeo, who both stepped quickly aside so he could get where he was going. He thumped the head of his ax into one of the tree stumps and sat on another beside it with a groan to face the empty brazier. "You're here for a reason and as far as I know, the price of that is a story. So, let's get it over with."

He sat with his back to the three who'd apparently arrived and touched his stuff. The young friends exchanged a confused glance and the werewolf mouthed, 'What's going on?'

"Right." Greta cleared her throat. "Stories. Yeah. You don't mind if I grab one of those baskets of fruit, do you? To keep us occupied while we talk?"

"You didn't need my permission the first time." The man leaned forward and propped his forearms on his thighs. "But go ahead. Be my guest."

She gave her daughter a reassuring nod and raised a finger to tell them to wait. They stood motionless as the woman jerked the tent flap aside and vanished. When she emerged, she carried another huge basket like those they'd found when they first arrived, this one also overflowing with all manner of oddly colored, weirdly shaped, and unpredictably flavored fruits—despite how much they'd eaten of it before they'd gone to sleep. Both Romeo and Greta had put a dent in the food.

She adjusted the basket in her arms and crossed the clearing swiftly before she nodded to her daughter. "Come on. The man wants a story and I have no doubt we'll hear his too. Let's go."

Without hesitation, she stepped into the circle of stumps and stopped in front of one beside the burly man's ax. She set the heavy basket next to the buried ax head and took a seat, crossing one of her borrowed boots on top of the opposite knee.

The man straightened enough from hunching over his own lap to reach out and snatch what looked like a blue orange from the basket. He rested his forearms on his thighs again and peeled it silently.

Lily and Romeo walked around the entire semi-circle of tree stumps. He leaned down toward her and whispered, "Where did he come from?"

Her only response was a quick shrug before they stepped into the circle. She sat on the man's left and the werewolf sat on her other side. A short silence settled as they all waited for someone else to say something first.

The stranger peeled the blue orange methodically in one long, winding strand, then flicked it into the purple grass where it landed with a muted thud. "I've only done this once, mind, and it was from where you're sittin'. So I'm gonna follow tradition that way and start this by telling my tale first. Does anyone have a problem with that?"

The three companions shook their heads.

"Nope."

"Go for it."

"The circle is yours." Greta gestured to the brazier with a wide sweep of her hand, which then hovered over the basket and finally selected a soft, squishy pink fruit that looked like a miniature gourd sprouting orange hairs. She bit into it and closed her eyes in appreciation.

"Okay." The man peeled the light-blue segments of his fruit apart exactly like a regular orange and popped each of them into his mouth one at a time. He didn't say another word until he'd eaten the whole thing. "The name's Mac."

"Nice to meet you, Mac. I'm Greta. That's Lily and

Romeo."

Mac raised his head, sucked the blue juice off his fingers, and scrutinized the young couple on his left. His gaze lingered on Lily a few seconds longer than could be called comfortable consideration before he nodded toward Greta. "Is she your mom or something?"

"Yeah." She managed not to avoid his gaze as he studied her, and Romeo slid his shoe over the purple clover until it pressed up against the side of her foot.

"Huh. And you're a werewolf." Mac raised one wild eyebrow at Romeo.

"Well, yeah. Mostly." Romeo wrung his hands and shoved them between his knees to keep from accidentally releasing the magic he'd been given as part of the Black Heron's backfired torture techniques.

The man's thick eyebrows twitched together, then he returned to leaning on his thighs and stared at the purple-covered ground. "The fire—"

Greta pointed at the brazier and a green light seared from her fingertip before all the freshly laid wood on the iron platform burst to life with a whoosh of air and a sharp crack. She folded her hands, looped them over her crossed knee, and grinned. "Ready when you are."

The man grunted. "I told you my name. And I've called Kahara home for the last...twelve years, give or take." He scratched his wild beard with a harsh rasp of finger-nails on skin and hair.

"Really?" The woman said it with as much enthusiasm as if she'd found a new magical artifact she could use to further her career even more.

And we all know how that turned out for her. Lily pleaded silently for her mom to stop getting so overly excited about anything before they knew all the facts.

"I've been keeping track," Mac added. "For whatever that's worth. Two meals, maybe three before the sky dims. Two resets in that whole time. I decided I'd call that a day and count 'em that way."

"So a little over four thousand days, huh?" Greta took another bite of the fuzzy pink gourd but didn't take her eyes off the man.

"I said give or take. There's a running tally, but I don't really spend much time countin' 'em anymore. This place is—"

"I have one more question."

"Mom." Lily leaned forward and widened her eyes at her mother, who seemed completely unfazed by her own lack of etiquette in not letting the man say what he wanted to say.

"If that's all right with you, Mac." Greta sent the same exasperated look at her daughter, then replaced it with her eager grin again.

Mac continued to stare at the ground. "Go ahead."

"When exactly did you step through the doorway? Into Mabayn, I mean."

He puffed out a long sigh through loose lips, tipped his head back, and looked for his answer in the rustling purple leaves of the canopy overhead. "September 12th, 2019."

"You don't say." The woman leaned back on the tree stump, her hands still clasped around one knee crossed over the other.

"Um…" Lily frowned and glanced from her mom to Mac. "That was only a week ago."

"Maybe for you." He nodded and shrugged his massive shoulders. "Time plays by its own rules here. And I've spent much longer than a week trying to understand them all. Or not trying, in the end."

"A different dimension where everything's trying to kill us, and you could spend your whole life here without anyone in our world noticing you left." Romeo snorted. "I'm surprised more people don't pop in for a visit."

"It's never only a visit. I hope that's not what any of you expected when you showed up."

Greta grimaced and actually looked a little embarrassed. "Honestly, we didn't expect anything. It simply kind of happened."

"Passing through the doorway doesn't simply happen, and you know it." Mac straightened fully on his tree stump and set his hands carelessly in his lap. "I spent a long time waiting for the next person to pass through and offer me a ticket out. So long that eventually, I stopped hoping for it. So I bet you can imagine how surprised I was to see my things moved and upturned and searched through like the three of you wanted to rob me of all my riches."

"I was told Kahara belongs to every traveler who passed through."

He turned to fix his dark-gray gaze on Greta and inclined his head. "You spend twelve years in one place without another living soul around and tell me that place and everything in it doesn't become your home."

The woman nodded in acknowledgment. "Well, no. I don't think I'd be able to tell you that."

"And now you three are here. So which one of you gets to stay behind?"

"What?" Lily almost lurched forward off the tree stump. The pressure of Romeo's calf pressed against hers tethered her to the present and what not to do if she didn't want to upset the giant man with a very sharp ax who'd played *Castaway* in an uninhabited dimension for the Mabayn equivalent of twelve years. She took a deep breath and released it quickly. "None of us will stay behind."

"Hold on, Lily." Greta lifted a finger to signal her daughter to wait.

"No. We're not about to sit around a mystical fire in a non-existent dimension and start making deals about who gets to go home and who has to stay behind. That's ridiculous."

Mac turned his head slowly to look at Greta and his long ponytail fell across his opposite shoulder. "You didn't tell them."

The woman grinned pertly at the man as if they'd known each other for years and he was now spilling all her secrets. "Of course I haven't told them. Yet. I was trying to find the best moment for it. Like after we found a way out of here. So thanks for blowing that right out of the water."

He didn't react at all to her vocal disappointment.

Lily's stomach sank. "What didn't you tell us, Mom?"

"Oh, boy." Her mother exhaled a huge sigh and bit into the fuzzy fruit in her hand. "Here we go."

FOUR

"Do you remember when I told you that this would be my first and last trip to Mabayn?" Greta asked.

Lily licked her lips and fought her cynicism to remain unvoiced. "Because a person can only open the doorway once."

"Right. There's a little caveat I may have neglected to mention when we first arrived."

"Yeah, that's made itself fairly clear right now." She scoffed and frowned at her mother. "Just say it."

"Anyone who opens the doorway themselves is bound by the laws of this place, Sweets. I merely want you to know that this wasn't part of my plan."

A cold chill raced up the young witch's spine. "Now you're scaring me."

"No, I'm not." Greta grinned at her daughter from the other side of the circle around the brazier and leaned forward. "You've been through enough to scare some of the bravest magicals I know out of their boots. And you'll be fine even after this. We both know that."

"What's the caveat?" Romeo sounded equally as annoyed and wary as Lily felt. She pressed her calf a little harder against his.

The older woman cleared her throat. "The person responsible for opening the doorway into Mabayn pays a toll, of sorts. There most definitely is a way for the two of you to leave this dimension and get back home again. But because I brought us here..."

When her mom shrugged and let the rest of the sentence hang in the air, Lily thought she might be sick. "You have to stay."

"That's the gist of it, Sweets."

"That's not gonna happen." Her fists clenched in her lap and she stared at her mother and Mac in turns. "There has to be a way to get you out of here."

"There is," he muttered, but he didn't offer anything else.

Even Greta looked surprised to hear him say it, and she uttered a little laugh. "By all means, Mac. Do enlighten us. I think now would be the right time for that."

The huge man ran a hand over his wild beard before he stroked the end of it. "She can leave when someone else opens the doorway and comes to take her place. Which now, apparently, is what you did for me."

Mac raised his head and sent her a sideways glance but somehow, he didn't look very happy about the whole situation.

"Well." The woman slapped her thighs and rubbed

them a few times. "There are plenty of people who pop in and out of here all the time, I'm sure. It won't take me that long to skip out of here after the three of you leave."

"Mom…" The words lurched and Lily had to drag in a deep breath before she could continue. "This man's been in this world for twelve years. That's way too long."

"He opened the doorway a week ago, Lily. It'll be a piece of cake."

Mac grunted, and although his bristly beard hid most of his mouth, it looked like he might have been smiling.

"I won't leave you here." She shook her head and wanted to do something else besides sit there and talk about what she wouldn't let happen. "We'll find a different way. Or we'll wait here with you until someone else comes in."

"Oh, no you won't." Greta's lighthearted smile faded. "You don't have a week to waste, Sweets. Whatever's left of the Black Heron won't stop simply because we brought that fortress crashing down around their backfired spell. Carmichael won't stop."

"She's right, Lil," Romeo muttered. "I was lucky but there are too many other magicals out there who don't happen to have an Optatus witch to protect them from everything Carmichael's gonna keep doing if no one's there to stop him."

Lily turned toward the werewolf with wide eyes. "You're not helping—"

"Excuse me." Greta's sharp outburst cut across their conversation and caught everyone's full attention. "Romeo understands, Lily, and I know you do too. You're merely too stubborn to admit it."

"I'm not—"

"There's no arguing this, Sweets. You and Romeo will go home. With Mac, I guess." Greta nodded at the giant man seated a tree stump away. "You're welcome," she told him but he made no response. "And then, the two of you will find that stone and take it to the Council. Tell them everything you've seen and everything that will still happen if they don't help you do something about it."

"If we don't have you..." Lily flung her hands up with visible irritation and willed her mom to get the whole picture without her having to spell it all out for her. Greta didn't offer to fill in the blanks. "Mom, you're the proof. That stone isn't gonna convince the Council any more than you did the first time you asked for help. And they know you. I can't convince them of what's happening unless I bring Greta Antony back from the dead."

"Don't sell yourself short, Lily."

"Well do you see another way? 'Cause I don't."

Mac cleared his throat and brushed the sleeve of his brown leather jacket off. "You're both forgetting something."

Both women glanced at him and shouted, "What?"

Romeo leaned away on his own tree stump and watched the building tension without a word.

"We're trading stories around this fire, aren't we?" The huge man gestured toward the brazier and the green flames that roared inside it. "You've tossed around all kinds of confusing pieces like Black Heron and fortresses and backfired spells. It's been a long time since I've had anyone to talk to, let alone tell me a story. So I'd really like to hear what the hell kinda story the three of you lived to get here."

The Antony witches stared at him in surprise but neither of them said a word.

"Okay, so..." The werewolf spread his arms with a little shrug and glanced from Lily to Greta and back again. "I guess I'll start?"

The older woman's eyes narrowed a little as she studied her daughter's friend, but a tiny smile quirked her mouth. "Take it away, Romeo."

"Right. Feel free to jump in if I miss anything important."

Lily put aside her frustration with her mother—and the fact that everyone seemed to think they had to leave Greta behind—to turn toward him with a reassuring smile. "I don't think you will."

It turned out he was a fairly good storyteller and needed no help at all. He started with Lily knocking on his door in Charleston so many months before and skimmed over the less important parts of their road trip in a Winnebago through a dozen countries and now four different continents. A little more time was spent on the details of the Black Heron Society, what Carmichael's followers were trying to do by essentially socializing all forms of magic, and what the three of them had to do in order to finish what they'd started when they destroyed his High Seat fortress and let him loose on the world.

"That probably gives you a better idea of why we actually need Greta to come back with us," Romeo finished. "And I guess that's about it."

Both women and Mac stared at him in complete silence. The green fire spat and crackled in the brazier, and the werewolf's gaze darted uncomfortably around the clearing. "Did I mess that up?"

"Not even a little." Lily finally managed to overcome her surprise. Hearing the epic tale of the last few months of their journey to find her mother was entirely surreal, especially from his perspective. A surprised chuckle escaped her. "That was incredible."

"I'd even go so far as to say you might have uncovered a new skill," Greta added. "That was very well done."

"Thanks." A small flush Lily hadn't seen since she'd knocked on his door after not talking to him for seven years crept up Romeo's neck, mostly hidden by the green tinge from the fire. He turned his attention to the flames with a confused grin.

"There you have it, Mac." Greta nodded at the burly man in their circle and clapped her hands sharply. "Do you have any questions?"

Mac didn't reply for a few seconds and continued to stroke his beard the way he had through the entire retelling of a particularly unlikely—but completely true—story. Finally, he turned toward the werewolf slowly and muttered, "You can cast spells now?"

Greta barked out a laugh and rocked on the tree stump. "Out of all the questions, that's the first?"

Her amusement was infectious, at least to her daughter. Lily pressed her lips together and tried to stifle her own laughter but the ridiculousness of so many conflicting truths one right on top of the other finally got to her. She snorted and couldn't keep the smile off her face.

Romeo eyed them, then raised an eyebrow at the man. "Yeah. And I can do it on purpose about half the time."

A low, rumbling chuckle escaped Mac, although it lasted for only a few seconds and didn't get much louder than any of his grunting. The man nodded and took a deep breath as he turned his attention toward the green fire in the brazier. "That was far more of a story than I expected."

"Okay, I thought I might have talked too much. And I skipped a lot." Romeo rubbed the back of his neck. "Why didn't either of you stop me?"

"That would have interrupted your flow, kid." Greta winked at the werewolf and laughed again.

"I'm glad they didn't," Mac added. "You painted quite a picture. Thank you."

"Yeah, no problem." He sighed and wrinkled his nose at Lily. "It's simply part of the deal in front of this weird fire, right?"

"I guess so." She smiled and gave his knee a little reassuring squeeze.

"I suppose that brings us to the end of our little powwow in Kahara." Mac slapped his hands on his thighs and pushed to his feet. "Come with me. I want to show you something."

He didn't wait for any of the newcomers to respond and he didn't slow his large strides either. The huge man headed toward the forest beneath the pink sky with long, slow steps. Greta watched him for a few seconds, then leaned toward Lily and Romeo.

"I don't think that invitation is something we should refuse. It's time for another walk through the woods, right? We're coming, Mac. Don't walk too fast." She stood quickly and hurried after him.

The young couple stared after Greta, and Lily grabbed Romeo's hand before she stood and almost pulled him to his feet beside her. "Come on."

"Do you really wanna go back into that forest, Lil? We just came outta there."

She stood on her tiptoes and gave him a quick kiss on the cheek. "The guy's been here for twelve Mabayn years. This is probably the first and only time I feel safer with someone else than with my mom."

"Good point." With a sigh, he let her lead him past the tents in the clearing toward Mac, Greta Antony, and the woods of a different dimension.

FIVE

Carmichael Cantus emerged from Mabayn and into the Sahara Desert. The silver disk in his hand that had been his quick ticket out of that disconnected dimension burned in his palm. With a quick, hissed breath, he shoved it into his pocket, shook his hand, and looked at the wavering orange wall of his own concealment wards rising in front of him. With a few muttered words and a quick flick of his wrist, the leader of the Black Heron deactivated the wards before he stepped through to the other side.

What had once been the glory of the society's High Seat—the culmination of his personal hard work, sacrifice, and no small amount of heavy spellcasting—now lay in ruins. The black stone of the sanctuary he'd created for himself and the magicals who followed him had fractured along the very earth itself. Although the high walls still stood and the heat of the Sahara on the other side of his wards was counteracted by the chill in the air, that was all that remained of the empire he'd built.

The outbuildings along the wide avenue toward the main fortress—and the fortress itself—had collapsed into heaps of black rubble. He walked quickly down the avenue, his back straight and his fists clenched at his sides. Instinctively, he slid his hand into the interior side pocket of his smoking jacket before he recalled that the stone he'd kept on him for decades was gone. Margaret Antony and her duplicitous brat of a daughter had taken it from him.

"That traitorous bitch." He stopped at what used to be the entrance to the main building and rubbed a hand over his mouth simply to keep his rage in check. High towers and long corridors of black stone piled before him in the general shape of his home. A few columns of smoke spiraled into the air on his left. *Those were the potions labs. There won't be anything in there I can salvage. Nothing in this whole cursed place I can—*

A few large slabs of black stone toppled from the pile of one of the collapsed towers. He tilted his head and listened for the source of the echo. It came from the right side of the High Seat, where his ritual chamber had been before the whole structure crashed down on him and all his highest-ranking members. When a muffled shout followed, Carmichael darted around the perimeter of the ruins of everything he'd built.

He turned the corner toward the north side of the fortress and the shouts grew clearer.

"Get it off her!"

"I'm trying, you idiot."

"Yes, thank you. A rescue by morons is exactly what I hoped for."

With a low, guttural curse, he strode toward the voices where a few of his members struggled to remove some of the rubble that had fallen onto more of their people. He raised both hands and cast a compulsive force spell over the largest of the fallen chunks of stone. It elevated sharply and released a cascade of smaller pieces to rain on everyone. The other magicals ducked and shouted in surprise before he hurled the huge piece of debris aside with his magic. Black stone cracked against more black stone, and the surviving Black Heron members turned where he stood behind them with a scowl.

"Well, what are you waiting for? Get her out of there."

Theon and Leif managed to overcome their surprise and leapt into action. The woman they helped from the wreckage was none other than Ingrid, one of Carmichael's most valued necromancers. She accepted Theon's hand and he hauled her out of the hole that had kept her alive by pure luck. The woman limped as she stumbled over the rubble toward their leader.

"That was a goddamn disaster, Carmichael."

"Yes. It was." As she brushed the dust and glittering slivers of stone from her black robes, he settled a hand on her shoulder. The necromancer stopped and looked at him. "Who else survived the goddamn disaster?"

She brushed the skirts of her robe off and turned toward the depression from which the other society members had rescued her. "There wasn't anyone else in there with me if that's what you're wondering. Not alive, anyway."

Carmichael studied the woman's grimace of disappointment and regret, which he thought accurately reflected the way he felt himself. "All right. The ritual chamber took the worst of it, I'm sure." He nodded toward the two men—both of whom were smeared with black dust, bruised, and bloodied—and added, "Go find whoever else there is to find. We'll leave the rest."

"Really?" Theon frowned and glanced at the ruined High Seat fortress. "Carmichael, they deserve to be—"

He unleashed a stream of green crackling energy at what remained of his ritual temple and bellowed with rage as his spell shattered the larger fragments into smaller pieces. Shards of black stone erupted in every direction. Theon and Leif ducked and turned away. Ingrid raised a shield in front of her and the Black Heron's leader. When the flying fragments stopped and the echo died away, the necromancer lowered the shield and he straightened his smoking jacket around his hips. "The only thing of value left in this place are those of us who remain. I won't waste my time with the rest of it. Do you understand?"

"Yes."

"Got it."

Satisfied, he nodded, his nostrils flaring, and licked his lips. "Now, go see who else was strong enough to not give up the ghost under an Optatus attack and bring them to the front gates. We'll leave in an hour."

The two men made no protest and ran toward the side of the building.

Carmichael smoothed his dark hair away from his face and shared a glance with Ingrid. "We're not finished. Don't worry."

A small smirk bloomed on the necromancer's lips. "I'm not worried. Do you know where they went?"

"I do. They may have all the time they need to try something else but we have much less." With that, he turned and headed toward the front of his ruined fortress and the wide avenue leading to the High Seat's front gates. The necromancer followed in silence.

A low, mournful howl rose from the wreckage, followed by a few tumbling pieces of broken stone. A moment later, a white shape bounded toward them over the mound of the shattered fortress, followed by two more. The trio of stark-white wolves with blazing red eyes moved swiftly over the debris, one of them with blood matted in his fur. They skidded down the other side and stopped in front of Carmichael.

"That's all of you, then?"

The alpha of what had once been the Black Heron's warlock-werewolf hybrid pack licked her jowls and didn't break away from his gaze. The other two behind her panted, their tails hanging low between their hind legs.

He clenched his jaw and took a deep breath. "I'm glad you made it."

His posture stiff and angry, he strode toward the wide avenue with the necromancer and three remaining hybrid wolves in tow.

An hour later, he passed his gaze over what remained of the Black Heron Society—those who had remained loyal and hadn't turned against him in their own foolish attempts to reproduce his work on their own.

Things would have been so much simpler if the mutant

faction had been buried beneath those walls. I'll deal with them later.

"Our home is gone," he told the remnant of society members—one necromancer, three warlock-werewolf hybrids, a little over a dozen witches, and another dozen made up of fairies and warlocks. "But we can do what we set out to do from anywhere we choose. So, it's time to get to work."

The ruined High Seat of the Black Heron Society fell into complete silence as Carmichael turned away from his people and stepped through the warded wall he'd created to hide and protect them. The survivors followed without a single word uttered among them.

The desert heat hit him hard when he stepped into it, but he only squinted and kept moving. Scattered across the sands were the bodies of the rebel, mutant magicals he'd killed without any remorse whatsoever when Lily Antony and her werewolf pet had knocked at his gates. With a snarl, he stalked across the sand with the evening sun at his back and walked toward the Winnebago parked off the desert road to and from nowhere.

Ingrid stepped up beside him and her robes fluttered in the hot wind and the blown sand. "We can start on the teleportation spell now if you like."

"Yes. Do that." He glared at the side door of the RV and fought the urge to run toward it.

"Destination?"

"Make it Valencia."

She nodded and turned to face the gathered society members who now talked in low tones. Their voices were all carried away by the wind that whipped across the desert.

When Carmichael reached the vehicle, he jerked the side door open, took a deep breath through flared nostrils, and walked up the two steps into the place Lily and Romeo had called home for the last few months.

A person's home says more about them than they do. So what does this say about you, Lily?

The interior of the RV was stiflingly hot. He slipped a finger under the collar of his shirt beneath the smoking jacket, then snapped his fingers. A silver flash encompassed him and replaced the sweltering temperature with the equivalent of an air conditioner left on high for two hours.

He went to the front first and gazed at the empty driver and passenger seats. Two cell phones rested in the cupholders of the center console. Then, he turned and surveyed the outdated upholstery of the couch and armchairs, the neat but somewhat stained Formica countertop in the kitchen, and the tiny kitchen table with booth space for only two. He moved down the narrow hallway and stopped to slide the bathroom door open a few inches before he rolled his eyes and left it well enough alone. He did notice the large red pot beneath the table with a healthy plant bearing purple flowers.

"Hmm. How domestic of you."

The bedroom in the back should have held far more information, but there was nothing revealing about it other than that two children in their twenties who called themselves adults had lived in it. Carmichael stopped in front of the wardrobe across from the bed and studied his reflection in the long mirror—matted hair, a trace of dust on the lapel of his teal smoking jacket, and his one glass eye glinting at him in the low light that spilled through the bedroom window. Overall, he'd come out of this much more unscathed than his society members but no less furious.

With a flick of his fingers, he whipped the wardrobe doors open with a compulsion spell, only to find the young witch's clothes inside, a few scattered items that had to belong to the werewolf, and nothing more. He exhaled a sigh of disgust and frustration, then turned to examine the rest of the room. "How did she make it so far in a piece of junk like this?"

His gaze fell on the low shelf against the wall at the head of the bed. The only thing on it was a small wooden box, intricately carved. Carmichael's good eye twitched, and he raised a finger toward the box to summon it across the room and into his hand. The piece was heavier than he expected and intricately carved on every side with the shape of a lily blossom on the lid. "How cute."

When he undid the latch and lifted the lid, though, he found the box completely empty. "And useless."

He tossed the item onto the unmade bed and turned on his heel to head back through the RV. When he stepped outside under the desert sun, his remaining society members had gathered in some semblance of a ritual circle for Ingrid's proposed teleportation. He fully intended to step into the circle and give his necromancer the go-ahead to take them the hell out of here, but he caught a flash of something bright, metallic, and copper-colored that glinted in the sun.

Ingrid turned to look over her shoulder as he passed her and strode toward the shining metal fragments. "We're ready."

"Give me a moment." He didn't stop to look at her, his gaze focused intently on what he didn't dare hope to think he actually saw. *She couldn't have.*

His shiny leather shoes stopped in the sand in front of the long rod of copper half-buried in the sand. An eager, predatory smile spread across his lips as he squatted in the desert to retrieve the rod. Despite having laid out here under the Saharan sun for days, the metal was cool in his grasp. "But she did."

Carmichael pulled it from the sand and stood, but his smile faded when he saw the jagged, fractured end of his new discovery. It only took him a few seconds to scan the surrounding desert outside his fallen fortress before he located the other half only a few yards away. Quickly, the Black Heron's leader went to the other piece, removed it from the sand, and held a broken end of the full artifact in each of his hands.

It wouldn't be so easy, would it?

He brought the two ends together experimentally. While the fractured edges matched perfectly and didn't seem to be missing any pieces, the copper rods didn't react in any way to their proximity. He tightened his grasp around the pieces of metal and turned toward his gathered followers.

When he stepped into the circle beside Ingrid, whose

hands were raised toward the circle's center to lend her magic to the others', she glanced at the metal in his hand and frowned. "Is that what I think it is?"

Carmichael smirked. "That girl brought the Varelos to my doorstep."

"It's broken."

"Yes. And if anyone can fix it, I know who that would be. Forget Valencia. We'll go to Kingston instead."

The woman nodded and turned to face the center of the circle and their coalescing magic before she led the Black Heron's survivors through the rest of the spell.

SIX

Mac guided Lily, Romeo, and Greta through densely growing, huge blue tree trunks and purple foliage. Romeo tried to shake off the green sludge splattered across his arms and chest.

"This stuff comes off, right?"

Lily gave him a sideways look and choked back a laugh. "Probably. He said it wasn't toxic. You'll be fine."

"Yeah, but my definition of fine doesn't include walking around with a mess of four-headed snake guts all over me." He pulled a glob of it off his chest and flung it onto the purple leaves at their feet, then glared at Mac's back. "He also didn't say what that was or how to get rid of it, did he?"

"Well, that's what happens when you fling spells around first and think later."

"I reacted, okay?"

"That was definitely a reaction."

He glanced at her where she walked beside him,

frowned, then nudged her with his green-slime-covered elbow.

"Hey—actually, if I wore anything but this stupid dress, I'd probably care that you did that. So nice try."

"You know, it's almost the same color as that stupid dress. You can hardly tell it's there."

She snorted and stepped over the thick blue roots that protruded from the ground in front of them. Up ahead, her mom walked shoulder to shoulder with Mac, but neither of them said a word. *It's like they're already in cahoots. That doesn't help our little situation at all.*

A round of squawks rose from the forest floor somewhere on their left, and their guide paused. Both he and Greta scanned the forest in the direction of the sound, which gave the young couple an opportunity to catch up by a few yards.

Romeo squinted through the trees. "What's—"

Mac shushed him and slipped the giant ax from its loop at his belt. He grasped the handle in one hand and held the other out at the ready. "Try to keep them off you," he whispered. "And don't run."

"Fantastic," Romeo whispered. "Thanks for the vote of confidence, man. It's a good thing we've had tons of practice not running."

The man turned barely enough to cast the werewolf a sidelong glance. "Not from these."

The squawking sounded again and now came from two different directions in the forest but definitely moved toward the party of magicals. A harsh, scattered flapping—like thousands of quickly beating wings—joined the odd sound. Moments later, a bright orange shape flitted between the trees. It uttered a little warble and darted between Romeo and Lily before it disappeared behind them.

"That's it?" The werewolf looked over his shoulder at the place where it had disappeared. "A butterfly?"

"First of all, they're seeds," the bearded man muttered and squinted into the forest where the squawks and hurried flaps approached steadily. "Call it aggressive pollination."

Greta chuckled. "That's a good one."

Her laugh cut off when he sent her a warning look. "There's nothing good about it. These aren't your garden-variety weeds, either."

The calls rose even louder when a few more of them fluttered closer.

Lily took one step to reach Mac and leaned slightly toward him. "Do you care to tell us what we're—"

A swarm of fluttering orange bodies—apparently seeds—burst from the thickly crowded trees ahead and aimed directly toward the four companions. The squawks rose in pitch and before anyone could move, they were surrounded by the orange cloud.

Tiny floral wings buffeted the air and made it almost impossible to hear anything else. Lily raised an arm to shield her face and felt the sting of dozens of the flying seeds as they pelted against her. "Try to keep them off, huh?"

"And don't run!" Mac shouted. "That makes them worse."

Romeo swatted frantically at the orange blurs that whipped around his face. "How are we supposed to—"

Greta released a burst of searing blue flame through the oncoming swarm. The squawks turned to tiny, high-pitched screams, and a handful fell to the forest floor, where they twitched and spasmed.

Lily took her mom's lead and released a magical attack at the attacking seed army. She chose the blue fire that was particularly hard to put out. Dozens burst into flames and fell around her while those that escaped her spell tugged at her hair and whipped their sharp edges against her neck and cheek.

Mac added his own spells to blow the seeds up and over him with a compulsive force before he delivered a spray of glittering projectiles into the swarm. The ax swung up and down in his other hand and hacked more than one of the relentlessly attacking seeds in half.

"What the—ah!" Romeo hopped up and down beside Lily and stared with wide eyes at the attackers that had landed on his forearm and attached themselves with claw-like barbs to his flesh. "Get 'em off!"

"I'm a little busy," she shouted in response and continued to burn seeds in every direction with both hands.

The werewolf swiped furiously at the orange invaders on his arms while he swatted at others as they tried to stick to his neck and shoulders too. "This is the worst— Why would anyone—"

Frustrated, he whipped his hands out in front of him and roared more in startled irritation than anything else. A blast of shimmering silver light erupted from his hands and spread across all four of the magicals who battled the aggressive pollination. The swarm splattered against his spell like bugs on a windshield until the remainder took the hint and flew over the party and into the trees beyond. Lily and Greta held their own spells in check, and Mac simply lowered his ax hand to dangle the terrifyingly sharp weapon at his side again.

When the last of them had vanished, Romeo grimaced sheepishly and lowered his hands. His accidental shield dropped too, and the damaged seeds drifted onto the ground all around them. "I did that. Right?"

Lily glanced at the orange remains that littered the forest floor—a few of them still twitching or burning beneath the last few tongues of flame—and nodded. "Yeah. That shield was definitely yours."

"Very nice, Romeo." Greta nodded slowly and gave the werewolf another wink. "Are you sure you haven't had time to train with your new magic? Like in secret, maybe?"

He returned her grin and shrugged. "I guess I'm a natural."

Lily snorted and patted him on the shoulder. "That's one way to put it."

"A werewolf casting spells..." Mac frowned, opened and closed his mouth a few times, then shook his head and resumed his trudge through the trees.

"Yeah, you're welcome," the werewolf muttered, speaking to all of them as he rolled his shoulders and watched Greta turn to follow their stoic, bearded guide.

"Thank you," Lily said cheekily, and he turned that grin on her, too.

"You know, Lil, I might actually have something good to say about being stuck in a totally different dimension with messed up creatures and flying plants and all the wrong colors."

"Oh, yeah? What's that?" They set off again after Greta and Mac.

"I have time to practice all this weird new magic. And more than enough targets, too."

A final, lingering orange seed fluttered toward them and moved in a slow, lazy pattern that kept it separated from the rest of the swarm. It squeaked a little as it darted between the young couple. The werewolf smacked it out of the air with the back of a hand, then nodded for her to keep moving.

They were only attacked by two more unlikely enemies within Mabayn's flora—a silver-barked tree that opened a hole in its trunk like a giant mouth and tried to swallow Romeo's shoe, and two purple bushes that bolted up on blue roots like legs and waddled after the group. Mac buried his ax head into the silver tree, which was how Romeo managed to keep his shoe—and his foot. The werewolf was able to practice shooting yellow sparks at the purple bushes before they shivered and ran off in the opposite direction.

Finally, their guide stopped at a thick curtain of draped purple vines hung in front of a cluster of massive trees with trunks at least five feet in diameter. He looked over his shoulder at the others and his beard twitched with the tiniest hint of a smile. "We're here. Try not to blow anything up, werewitch."

As the man swept the curtain of vines aside and stepped through, then paused to hold them open for Greta, Romeo scowled after him and muttered, "Why does everyone automatically land on werewitch?"

Lily took his hand and gave it a little squeeze before she walked forward with him toward the vines. "It only shows a serious lack of imagination on their parts. That's all."

He snorted. "I'm still not a fan."

"We'll come up with something better."

His grimace was telling as he let her step through the opening in the vines first and followed. The bearded man released the curtain to drape again behind them, and they stopped to take in where they were.

"Wow." Lily smoothed the hair away from her face. "This is incredible."

"I thought you'd appreciate it." Mac circled the perimeter of this new clearing he'd led them to, which was more like a large dome created by dangling purple vines and branches densely packed with purple leaves.

The light of the pink sky was almost completely blocked by so much heavy foliage, although a different kind of light issued from the pool of glowing pink water in the center of the space. Tiny specks of shimmering light floated everywhere around them, unaffected by the travelers' presence, and definitely did not try to attack them.

Greta grinned as she studied the drifting lights and the

glistening pink pool in front of them. "I would love to know the story behind this place."

"This is the way out," their guide said and gestured toward the pool with his ax. "Even for those of us who opened the doorway on our own to get here—provided someone else takes our place."

SEVEN

L ily jerked her gaze away from the mesmerizing pool and glared at Mac. "You said you wanted to show us something."

"Yes."

"What? You wanted to make sure all three of us watched you leave Mabayn before we have to leave my mom here by herself?"

"Lily—"

"No." She batted Romeo's hand away, still seething at the bearded man who seemed unperturbed by her animosity. "We haven't even tried to find another way yet. I won't leave until I find out how to get her out of here—without having to wait another twelve years for someone else to open that stupid doorway."

Mac slipped the handle of his ax through the loop in his belt, folded his arms, and raised his chin to stare at her with no expression whatsoever.

"You don't scare me." She shook her head and folded

her arms to mirror him. "And if you leave before we find out how to get all of us back to our world, I'll find you."

"Lily. That's enough." Greta looked from Mac to her daughter with a concerned expression but she didn't attempt to get involved yet.

"I tracked my mom across four different continents, Mac." Lily jabbed a finger at him, completely unaware of the curling tendrils of black smoke that sifted slowly from the fingertips of both her hands. "I'm very sure it won't be any harder to hunt you. After all, you're only a lumberjack in a bad leather outfit."

Greta stepped toward her daughter and caught her wrist to lower it again. "Careful, Sweets."

Blinking furiously, her nose and eyes burning with the angry tears that hadn't yet escaped, she turned away from the man and met her mother's gaze. The blue eyes shared by the Antony witches for generations reminded her how important it was to get a grip and keep her emotions under control. Especially when Optatus magic leaked out of her hands like that. "I'm fine."

"Are you sure?"

"Yeah, Mom. I got it."

"All right." The woman studied her daughter, nodded slowly, and took both her hands in her own. "Listen to me. I have to stay."

"No, you don't—"

"And you have to go. Those are the rules, my love, and as far as I know, there isn't a way to so much as bend them, let alone break them."

"There has to be." Lily swallowed and gritted her teeth. "I won't leave without you."

"You have to." Greta squeezed her hands. "I have no problem staying here. It's been a long time since I've had a little peace and quiet. I have my own private dimension now, so that'll give me a break."

The weak attempt to turn this into a lighthearted joke —like always—only made it more difficult. "That's not gonna happen."

"Oh, come on. Give your mother a little space, will ya? You followed me all over the world, Lily. The least you can do is leave me here for a few days."

"It won't be only a few days for you, Mom."

"I know. And that's fine. You and Romeo need to go home, find that stone—wherever you sent it—and take it to the Council. Use whatever you can to make your case as convincing as possible. And while you're at it, go ahead and tell Brast his spell worked."

"What?"

Greta grinned. "His spell to open Mabayn's doorway. I'm fairly certain I'm the only other person who knew he was working on that. That's probably because I'm the only Optatus witch he knows and he thought I'd be able to give the spell a little extra juice."

Lily snorted and closed her eyes.

"That's as much proof as you'll have to convince him I'm still alive. Once you've done that, he can do the rest of the work on the Council." With a shrug, the woman swung their arms out to the side and chuckled. "Then, if you happen to find a little extra time, you can find out how to get back here and take me home with you."

"Greta." Romeo stepped toward them. "We did all this to get you out of the High Seat in the first place. There's no way we can leave you here."

"We got each other out, didn't we?" Greta raised her eyebrows at him, then looked at her daughter and nodded firmly. "And now, Sweets, I'll get you out of here before the only other window we have closes and Carmichael finishes his idiotic spell. Got it?"

The young witch's lower lip trembled, but she kept herself together enough to give her mom a nod. "I'll get you out of this too. I promise."

"I know you will." Her mother pulled her in for a hug that crushed the breath right out of her lungs. They hung onto each other like that for a few seconds—which wasn't nearly long enough—before Mac cleared his throat.

"Lily. Romeo. Step over here for a second."

She removed herself from her mom's embrace, swiped quickly at the few tears that had trickled out against her will, and gave Greta's hand another squeeze before she turned with Romeo toward where Mac pointed to a position in front of the pool. The werewolf brushed the back of his hand against hers, and she fumbled with his fingers before she entwined hers between them.

"Do you already have an idea for how to come back and get her?" he whispered.

"Not yet. But I'll think of something. I have to."

The older man walked with slow, lumbering steps

toward Greta, his arms folded again. "I'm not very good with parting words. Never have been."

The woman chuckled and leaned toward him with a conspiratorial grin. "How about any tips for surviving a decade in another dimension?"

He rubbed a hand over his chin, then tugged on his beard a little. "Yeah. Try holding your breath."

"What—"

Mac lunged forward and seized her by the shoulders. The older witch reacted immediately and jabbed her forearms against the insides of his elbows. His grasp slipped, and she ducked away from him.

"Come on, Mac. If you want a hug, just say so."

"This is how it works." He reached for her again and took a firm hold of her arm.

"What are you doing?" Lily shouted and darted around the pink pool as her mother struggled against the huge man in the leather jacket.

"You'll thank me for this," the man growled. "Whenever you happen to think of me—stop fighting!" He jerked Greta toward him and picked her up by the waist.

"Hey!" Romeo lunged forward.

"Put her down!" Lily summoned her red attack sparks in both hands and tried to get a good shot at the crazed lumberjack that didn't include injuring her mom at the same time.

"Lily." Greta stared at her with wide eyes. "Jump into the—"

Mac tossed the woman with more strength than seemed possible, even for his huge size, across the clearing and into the pool of glowing pink water. There wasn't so much as a splash when she broke the surface—merely a muted pop and then she was gone.

Romeo skidded to a stop a second before he would have barreled into the bearded man and grimaced when the swinging ax bumped his leg. He lost his footing on the soft purple moss beneath their feet and almost went down. Mac jerked a hand out to grasp the werewolf by the forearm and he helped him stay on his feet.

The sparks died in Lily's palms. "What are you doing?"

The large man clapped a hand on the werewolf's back and nodded at the young Optatus witch. "Honestly, I've always preferred being alone. After all this time, this place has grown on me. It's my home and I wasn't really trying to leave it in the first place. Plus, you need that woman to help you finish that...unbelievable story you told me."

His face scrunched and he actually laughed. The sound reverberated through the clearing as he shook his head and slapped the leather jacket over his stomach.

Romeo stuck out his hand again, this time to shake Mac's hand. "Believe it or not, it's all true."

"Oh, I'm sure it is, son. It's merely not my story."

Lily stepped toward them and extended her own hand to him as well. "Thank you."

"We all get what we want this way."

"If we ever do find out how to get you out of here without leaving someone else behind—"

"We can have that conversation then, can't we? Although at that point, I might be already gray around the beard." Mac nodded and pointed at the pool. "You'd better go after her. I wasn't kidding about holding your breath, either. Just in case."

She gave a disbelieving laugh and stepped toward the pool. "Thanks for the advice."

Romeo stepped beside her and slid his hand into hers again. "That was literally the last thing I expected."

"Sometimes, that's the best thing that could happen, I guess. Are you ready?"

"You have no idea."

"One...two...three."

Together, they each took a huge breath and jumped into the calm, glowing pink water. The doorway out of Mabayn accepted them as easily as it had accepted Greta with nothing but another muted pop behind them before they were gone.

Mac stared at the pool for a few seconds longer, then chuckled again and shook his head as he walked toward the curtain of purple vines. "I might've reached my good-deed quota for an entire lifetime with that one. Still, that was some story."

EIGHT

Half an hour after Carmichael Cantus and his surviving group of Black Heron Society members teleported out of the Sahara Desert, Greta Antony dropped onto the sand with a soft thud. Two seconds later, the young couple landed beside her, holding hands, the breath shoved out of them after their not so gentle reentry into their own world. She stared at them with wide eyes for a moment before she threw her head back to howl with laughter.

Lily responded with a wry chuckle, then winced and leaned over to rub her sore back. "Ow. That's really not a safe way to hop across realms."

Puffing out a huge sigh, Romeo tossed himself onto his back in the sand and let the blistering heat of the desert bathe his upturned face. "But it worked."

The older woman's laughter died down a little, and she wiped her eyes with the back of a hand and shook her head. "Oh, man. Yes, it did. That damn lumberjack..." She chuckled, froze, then burst out laughing again.

"Only you would laugh at something like this." She stared at her mom, and when Greta met her gaze, they both exploded into another fit of unrestrained amusement.

"You're both nuts." The werewolf smirked and wiggled into a more comfortable position on the sand, his eyes closed.

"You'd like to think that, wouldn't you?" She slid her leg out to kick his thigh gently, then sucked in a breath. "Ouch. The sand gets hot out here."

"So, let's get you out of that ridiculous costume and be on our way." Greta pushed to her feet, slipped a little on the side of the dune, then dusted herself off and offered her daughter a hand. "We have so much to do and not nearly as much time as I thought I would have in Mabayn."

"Oh, right. Like you're disappointed by how things turned out. Ow." Lily hopped on her bare feet, reoriented herself out there in the middle of nowhere, and felt a huge wave of relief wash over her when she saw the Winnie exactly where she and Romeo had left it who knew how many days before.

"Hmm. Maybe a little." With another laugh, her mother stepped out of the way to avoid Romeo who leapt quickly to his feet. "Now how the heck did you two get all the way out here?"

He scooped Lily into his arms and nodded across the road toward the RV. "The Adventuremobile can literally go anywhere, Greta."

Lily gave him an amused frown and ran her fingers

through the dark curls at the back of his head. "You like being able to finally carry me to safety somewhere, don't you?"

The werewolf gave her a lazy half-smile before he focused his attention on the vehicle. "I've kinda waited a long time for this, actually."

Greta stepped carefully around the fallen bodies of the Black Heron Society's wayward members but paused after a few steps. With her hands on her hips, she stared at the wavering wall of orange wards that shielded the Black Heron's High Seat from the rest of the desert. "What the heck is an Adventuremobile?"

"Mom!"

She spun quickly to see her daughter pointing across the road that led nowhere through the desert and at the Winnie on the other side. "Great, you found a van. Give me a second, though. Or two." She turned toward the orange wall again, gestured with her hand while she muttered a few words, and leaned forward to poke her head through the wards.

Lily shook her head as she and Romeo approached the RV's side door. "She stopped paying attention."

"It's not that weird for her, though. We're out of danger so her busy mind looks for things to focus on. Could you..."

"Yep." She stretched her hand out to pull the latch on the side door and held it open while he lowered her onto the first step. When settled, she leaned back and gave him a quick kiss. "Thank you."

"That's it?" He titled his head and regarded her with a playful frown. "That's all I get for sweeping you off your feet and saving you from certain burn-by-desert-sand?"

She pressed her lips together and glanced over his shoulder. "Well, my mom's with us. So yeah. That's all you get. For now."

He puffed out a sigh and shook his head. "Greta..."

The older woman withdrew her head from the wavering orange wall of the Black Heron's wards, paused as if in thought, and turned to stride across the sand toward the Winnie. "Guess what I found on the other side of those wards."

Lily walked up the RV's two steps to make room for her two companions to join her inside. "Hmm. Let me think. The entire High Seat has collapsed on itself, everything's turned to rubble, and no one survived."

Her mother let the side door click shut behind her and paused on the last step. "So that's a wild guess, huh?"

"No." She folded her arms. "I had a dream about it."

"Why am I not surprised?" Greta chuckled. "I wouldn't say no one survived. Or if they did, I'd bet the clothes on my back that Carmichael came back for them when he hopped out of Mabayn and has now taken his people somewhere else."

"I wouldn't take that bet anyway, Mom. And I already have enough clothes here, so I don't need yours. Speaking of clothes..." She glanced at the torn, tattered, and stained green-velvet dress Carmichael's lackeys had put her in and grimaced. "I'll be right back."

"Sure. Go change. I already had my opportunity." The older witch waved her daughter off and she headed into the bedroom at the back. The minute the door slid shut, Greta finally seemed to realize where she was. "Hey. This is Bentley's Winnie, isn't it?"

Romeo ran a hand through his hair and slumped onto the couch with a sigh. "Good ol' Adventuremobile. Yep."

"Wow." The woman gave a low whistle and studied the bamboo floors, the front passenger seat with more than enough extra legroom, and the plastic of the center console that had replaced the full-cover carpeting. "This is not how I remember it."

"Yeah, we made a few upgrades." The werewolf smirked and kicked his legs out in front of him to cross one sneaker over the other. "There are a few downgrades too, though. People tend to really enjoy targeting an old Winnebago. Or maybe it's only the 2002 Adventurer model."

With a wry chuckle, Greta made another sweeping glance around the RV's living area and shook her head. "And you two traveled all the way from Charleston to Libya in a few months?"

"With a number of detours." Romeo reached back and gave the interior wall behind the couch a loving pat. "We went to Canada first. That was when we called this a road trip—before we knew what we were getting into. Or what you'd gotten into."

"Le Chapeau Magique, right?" Her eyes lit up in excitement, and he fought not to shy away from her. That look always meant a crazy idea was brewing in Greta Antony's head.

"Yeah. And the invisible cabin. From there, we went down through the US into Mexico and found—"

"Melissa Bore." Lily's mom nodded and lowered herself into the armchair behind the passenger seat. "How was she?"

"Uh...making wards for an illegal fighting ring of were-wolves in exchange for protection from a pissed-off vampire who burned her house down." Romeo swallowed and pushed aside the memory of being strung up by his neck with chains and drugged with both magical narcotics and a curse for good measure. "I can't really tell you much more than that. Chihuahua was weird."

"It certainly sounds like it. And you almost caught up with me in Greece, didn't you?"

He laughed. "Almost, yeah. We chartered a freighter from South America to France. Off the books, of course."

Greta crossed one leg over the other. "Naturally."

"Then drove from France all the way to Romania and the Black Sea. Lily found you in Greece with the heron coin—"

"Right. I hope she used that sparingly."

"She did. But a handful of times is a handful too many if you ask me."

"You guys do realize I can hear everything you're saying, right?" Lily called from the bedroom. The rumble of drawers being shut and the thump of the wardrobe doors closing followed.

"I'm sure it's nothing you haven't already heard," her mother replied and looked toward the back of the Winnie with an expression of amusement. "Or experienced."

"It's still weird."

Greta smiled at Romeo and refocused her attention on him. "And how in the world did you get this RV from Greece to Libya so quickly?"

"Oh, right. You basically went dark from that point." He scratched his head as he thought back. "Or, at least, we didn't see your shadow bird anymore and Lily couldn't find you without bringing a whole horde of mutant society members racing after us. Those people are insane."

"They had to be a little insane to choose to do what they did, even before the mutations." The woman folded her arms and pressed her lips together in disapproval. "And that kind of magic no doubt made it even worse."

He exhaled an exaggerated sigh. "Much worse. One guy turned himself into a bomb by accident."

The two stared at one another before they both laughed. He sobered quickly and grimaced.

"It wasn't fun at the time, though."

"Oh, I'm sure you still managed to find some kind of humor in it. You continued to follow the trail, after all. But you still didn't answer my question." When he gave her a blank look, she added, "Getting the RV to Libya."

"Right. Yeah, we ran into the Vatra in Greece, and they told us they'd get the Winnie across the Mediterranean in half an hour if we brought them the Varelos."

"They what?" Greta's eyes widened and she leaned forward in the armchair.

"You know, a giant copper rod that talks in your head and has enough power to be the most destructive magical weapon ever." He frowned. "I'm surprised you haven't heard of it."

"Romeo, I know what the Varelos is. Please tell me you didn't give it to these Vatra. Whoever they are, that artifact is not a bargaining chip—"

"Don't worry. We didn't give it to them. Lily got it out of the God of Dreams' temple and made a copy."

The woman looked dumbfounded. "She made a copy."

"It was convincing enough to make the Vatran Royal think she'd handed him the real deal. Yeah." Romeo folded his arms in a mocking reflection of her posture and nodded. "That's how we got the Winnie into Libya. The Vatra carried it in this... I dunno, maybe waterproof bubble is the best way to describe it, and it took half an hour like they said."

The bedroom door slid open again and Lily stepped toward the living area in a pair of dark-gray joggers, a turquoise tank top, and an old pair of silver sneakers she'd found buried in the back of a drawer. "Even when we encountered a little extra trouble."

His eyes widened at the memory. "Yeah, those siren things. What did the Vatra call them?"

"The seirí, I think."

"That's right. Those things were awful."

She smirked and sat beside him on the couch. "They weren't that bad."

He puffed out a breath and rolled his eyes. "Okay."

"Lily." Greta hadn't lost her expression of wary inter-est, even though her daughter and the young werewolf joked about their adventures. She leaned forward. "Do you still have the Varelos with you?"

"I did, yeah. We brought it all the way here until we finally found that glowing tree you left me. By the way, that was a nice touch. Maybe next time, give that giant yellow beam stretching from my chest an off button. I didn't sleep for...well, it seemed like forever."

"That's merely the way it works. And it prepared you for a few more nights without sleep."

She laughed at her mother's way to describe Black Heron torture so lightly, then stopped when she noticed that the woman wasn't smiling at all. "What's wrong?"

"The tree outside is gone, I noticed."

"Yeah, I kind of had to destroy it to get inside those wards." Lily frowned.

"That's fine. It served its purpose." Greta pressed her lips together and stared at her daughter, then took a deep breath. "Where's the Varelos?"

With a hasty glance at Romeo, who looked as confused as she felt, she nodded across the Winnie and the desert at the warded wall beyond. "I kind of had to destroy that too."

"You...destroyed the Varelos?"

"Yeah, Mom. I couldn't take it with me or leave it here for whatever insane magical might think it a good idea to root through our stuff. It was part of the deal."

"What deal, Lily?"

"The deal I made with the Varelos. To get you out of that place." She shook her head and gave her mother a side-long glance. "I don't see what the problem is. I did what I had to do and hit two birds with one giant, exploding stone.

No one else can get their hands on it. That's all that matters."

"What did you do with the pieces?"

"Seriously?"

"I'm not playing with you, Lily." Greta raised her hands to either side of her face and brought them down slowly in controlled frustration before she caught and held her daughter's gaze. "Where are the pieces?"

"Out in the sand."

"You left them out—" With an irritated grunt, the woman leapt from the armchair and down the Winnie's stairs and almost broke the side door off its hinges in the process of her hurried exit.

"Mom, wait a minute." Lily followed her outside, and Romeo rolled his eyes before he stood slowly to join the Antony witches again out in the desert.

"Where? Was it here?" The woman pointed to two different places in the sand and picked her way through the bodies littering the area in front of the vehicle, ignoring them completely. "Or over here? Did you bury the pieces?"

"Calm down." She hurried toward her mom and grimaced at the cloying scent of decay that now wafted on the still air once the wind had died down. "They're here, okay. I told the Varelos to destroy itself and the thing blew up. We heard it break."

"So where did you leave the broken parts?" Greta yelled, whirled in circles, and looked far more frantic than her daughter remembered seeing her in high-stakes situations.

"I don't know!" Now, Lily felt the contagious strain of

her mom's concern without having any idea why. "It's not like I had much time to notice, okay? The minute it exploded, all these idiots"—she gestured toward the scattered bodies—"came out of nowhere and attacked us."

"Of course they did."

"Then, Carmichael stepped out from behind those wards with a small army behind him and didn't even bat an eyelid when he slaughtered his own people."

"They turned against him, Lily."

"How does that make a difference?"

Greta stopped her search, took a deep breath, and tipped her face to the sky with closed eyes. "And he took you both into the High Seat."

"Yes. That's exactly what happened." Lily's hands dropped against her thighs in exasperation. "But I swear, the Varelos is destroyed, Mom. No one can use it."

Slowly, the woman looked at her daughter, and the fiery glint in her eyes made her stomach drop. "Unless they know someone who can put it back together again."

NINE

"What?" Lily couldn't even begin to wrap her mind around her mother's words.

"Is that even possible?" Romeo stopped beside her, took a quick step away from the closest body, and stared at Greta.

"It's highly unlikely and even more costly," the older woman muttered. "But yes. It's possible."

"Oh, my God." She smoothed her hair away from her face and turned toward the Winnie. After two steps, she stopped again and jerked a hand out toward her mom. "How was I supposed to know that?"

"You weren't, Lily. Taking the Varelos from one of Morpheus' temples wasn't part of my plan."

"Please. You can't honestly say that everything Romeo and I went through to get to you was part of your plan."

Greta stormed past her to the RV and paused long enough to lean toward her and shout, "It was loosely calculated, okay?"

When the woman strode away again, she spun and followed her. "No, it wasn't. Not until we got to Greece. After that, you really fell off the face of the earth and I had to do everything else by myself."

Romeo jogged to catch up with them. "Hold on, Lil."

"Okay, yeah. With Romeo. But we did the rest all on our own. And if the Varelos happened to be something that brought us to you that much faster, how could I not have taken that opportunity?"

The woman jerked the Winnie's side door open again and stormed up the stairs.

"Mom."

"I'm not blaming you, Lily. Stop being so defensive."

"Stop walking away from me!" The young witch leapt up the stairs, and Greta whirled to face her daughter.

They glared at each other, and the werewolf stopped on the bottom step and waited for the next outburst and his cue to duck.

Finally, the older witch sighed. "You did exactly what I would've done if I were in your position, Sweets. Please believe me, none of this is your fault."

"I know." Lily folded her arms but the fight seeped out of her now by the second. "So what do we do?"

"The plan doesn't change." Her mother nodded firmly as if to convince herself of this fact and stared blankly at the back of the driver's seat. "We head home. Find the stone that contains the Transference magic, and set up a meeting with the Council. This time, we know I'm coming with you."

"That sounds like a plan to me." Romeo jumped up the

last step into the living area and moved toward the driver's seat.

Lily ignored him and raised her eyebrows at her mom. "And what about Carmichael?"

"What about him, Lily? The man's ambitious and vengeful at the same time and that makes him stupid. If he thinks he can pay the price of restoring an artifact like the Varelos and get what he wants out of the deal, he'll take care of himself soon enough."

"We should still try to stop him."

"We will. Or he'll do it for us. Either way, trying to stop him is like chasing a ticking timebomb down a hill. You might catch it before it reaches the bottom, but then what?" Greta gestured toward the couch and nodded. "Now, take a seat."

"What?" She glanced at the couch, then turned to look over her shoulder at the empty passenger seat beside Romeo. "Oh, no. This is my house."

"On wheels," he added.

"This is my house on wheels. Right now, you're simply along for the ride. You take a seat." Without waiting for her mother to reply, she went to the front, slipped into the passenger seat, and stared ahead at the desert through the windshield. "Let's do this."

The werewolf stared at her for a moment and tried not to look at Greta Antony, who still stood in the middle of the living area with a ridiculously smug look on her face. He leaned toward Lily and lowered his voice. "If you wanna drive, Lil, I don't mind sitting the first leg out—"

The older woman snorted. "No one's driving anywhere."

"Mom, we're in the middle of the desert in an RV."

"I know where we are." Her mother clapped her hands together and grinned. The sound made the girl turn in her seat. "I left you clues scattered across an entire continent so you'd be prepared before you found me. But we most definitely don't have to go that route again on the way back."

"So you're what? Gonna teleport us and the entire Winnebago into the middle of Charleston and hope no one notices?"

"Sure." Greta grinned. "With a few pitstops along the way."

Romeo scratched the back of his head and finally turned to look at the older woman. "You know, Greta, I'm not exactly the best at—"

The woman's hands jerked outward toward either side of the RV, and a blinding silver light encompassed everything. Lily's stomach lurched, and the space around her squeezed tighter and tighter until she thought she wouldn't be able to take another breath. She had almost begun to panic when with a little pop and a sigh like opening a can of soda, the silver light vanished.

The young couple both gasped for breath. The older woman stumbled sideways toward the kitchen counter, steadied herself with a hand, and shook her head. "Woo! I haven't done that in a while."

Romeo immediately fumbled under the driver's seat to

pull the lever and slide it back as far as it would go. He hung his head between his legs and groaned.

"Are you gonna be okay?" Greta chuckled a little, took an unsteady step forward, and gave herself another few seconds to regain her balance. "From what I think you tried to say, this isn't your first time being teleported, is it?"

"It's the first time as a hybrid werewolf," he muttered. He took a huge breath and let it out slowly. "Before that, I was simply trying not to sneeze all over everything and pass out from the magic."

"Huh. It definitely sounds like an improvement, then."

"I guess."

Lily swallowed to quell her own small amount of remaining nausea, straightened in the passenger seat, and squinted at the view through the windshield. It was some-what startling to not see bright, glittering sand and a dirt road that stretched into the distance with no apparent final destination. Now, she looked at a half-empty parking lot in the center of long, high-reaching apartment buildings that resembled crumbling concrete blocks.

"You brought us to—"

"Bucharest. Yep. You've been here before, right?" Her mother finally made her way to the Winnie's side door again and leaned back to slap a hand on the back of her daughter's chair. "Let's go dig that giant healer out of his own ditch, huh?"

"Bucharest." Romeo sat up slowly, grimaced, and pressed a hand to his stomach. "What time is it?"

"Well, there's an hour's difference from the middle of the desert, so I'd say..." The woman chuckled. "I didn't even know the time there. It's evening, which is good enough. Are you coming with us, Mr. Hybrid?"

"That's not much better than werewitch." He pushed slowly to his feet, gulped, and opened the driver-side door to slide out onto the pavement.

Lily stepped over the center console to follow him out but yanked the keys from the ignition first so she could lock the Winnie once she closed the door.

Greta came around the front of the RV and looked at the concrete buildings rising in a rectangle all around them. "It looks exactly like I remember it. And it all looks the same. Where's the building—"

"Building Five, Entrance Three." Lily gestured across the parking lot and headed toward the apartment building they needed to visit. "Come on."

"This is it," the woman muttered and stared after her daughter. "The day finally came."

"What day, Mom?" She offered the question simply to humor her mother, although she didn't turn to gauge the reaction.

Romeo stepped past Greta with a sigh, and the older witch finally moved after them across the parking lot. "The day my daughter's memory is sharper than mine."

"Don't worry. I'm not about to put you in a nursing home or anything." Lily tried to hide her smirk. "Plus, you kind of have an excuse to not remember everything."

"Oh, yes. Please remind me of my excuses."

"You were kidnapped, tortured, and forced to perform one of the most dangerous spells that would—"

The woman threw her head back and laughed sharply.

"Oh." Her daughter uttered a surprised chuckle of her own. "Yeah, that applies to us both, doesn't it? I guess my memory wins."

The block of apartments was as poorly labeled and confusing as the last time the young couple had been there, but they managed to find Entrance Three and took the rickety, squeaking, shaking elevator to the seventh floor. Romeo wrinkled his nose and grasped the handrail tightly as they jerked slowly upward in the precarious metal box. "I can't believe this still works."

"That's Romania for you." Greta shook her hands out and glanced at the floor counter above the elevator doors that definitely didn't work anymore. "It's constantly full of surprises."

"Not the good kind," he responded glumly.

"Hang in there, kid." The woman shot the young werewolf a sympathetic frown. "We'll get you tea or something."

The elevator lurched to a stop and the doors squealed open and stuck halfway before they finally creaked all the way to allow the trio into the dank, musty, poorly lit hallway. Greta moved out of the elevator like she stepped onto a stage to give the performance of a lifetime.

Only her life is the performance. I can't even imagine Mom playing music.

Lily took Romeo's hand and pulled him gently out of the elevator before the doors had a chance to clamp shut again. They followed their companion's light steps down the hall until they came to the end of it and the door to Apartment Thirty-eight on their right.

Greta flicked her hand toward the door and spread her fingers. A pale-yellow light bloomed across the wood but nothing else appeared. She turned and tilted her head at Lily, her expression a little irritated. "Did you take the wards off this door?"

"Nope. I only burned my hand trying to solve your magical puzzle. It was not my favorite surprise, by the way."

Her mother shrugged. "A little incentive to hurry up and think never hurt anyone. Well, not that much." She turned toward the door, examined it, and shook her head. "I told that man to keep things safe in here and he leaves it unprotected for any curious cat to come along and—"

"Mom, I'm fairly sure no one's gonna go through a place like this looking for anything important. And especially anyone who is isn't trying to find what he keeps in there."

"Hmm." Greta grabbed the doorknob and gave it a little twist. It was locked so she pressed her finger against the center of the handle. A bright yellow light flashed, something clicked, and she jerked the door open and stepped inside.

Romeo leaned toward Lily and muttered, "She'd make a really good burglar."

"Yeah. She's an archaeologist."

They stepped into the apartment where the older witch stood and gazed at all the cut-out news articles, drawings, black heron symbols, and connected pieces of otherwise useless scribblings that lined the walls, the couch, and every available surface of the living room. She rested her hands on her hips and scoffed. "We were so young and naïve."

"Six months ago?"

"More like eight. Darius! Get out here and explain to me what in the world you think you're doing. Because I can't make sense of it."

The living room was completely silent.

"Maybe he's not home," Romeo suggested.

"Of course he's home." The woman gave him an incredulous look. "The man never leaves. I said—"

A muffled shout came from the closed door on the other side of the tiny kitchen, followed by the squeal of a rusty handle being turned and a short, abruptly cut-off creak of an opening door. Dishes rattled on the kitchen shelves as a huge man with a wild black beard and hair to match stormed through the kitchen with a churning ball of fire in his open palm. "You picked the wrong—"

Darius stopped, gaped at the presumed-dead Greta Antony standing in his living room, and staggered against the side of the fridge. His conjured spell leapt from his hand and darted toward the far wall of the living room.

Greta stretched her hand toward the flames, snapped her fingers, and snuffed them out before they hit anything. She spread her arms and focused on the giant of a man who simply stared at her and clutched his chest. "Is that really how you wanna welcome me back?"

"You... Ha!" He lumbered forward and wrapped her in a crushing hug to lift her black boots a few inches off the ground.

"Okay." She wheezed. "That's more like it."

He set her on her feet and blinked furiously in an attempt to keep the welling tears from trickling out and into his black beard. "Greta."

"Darius." She grinned and grasped as much of his bulging arms as her much smaller hands could. "I'm glad you're happy to see me."

"I thought you were—well, at least never coming back here." The giant healer sniffed and gave her an incredulous smile, his eyes still glistening. "This is..."

"Unbelievable, I know." Greta nodded and squeezed his arms, then released him. "Slightly less unbelievable than the fact that you took my wards down."

"No. I didn't do that." He scratched his cheek through the thick beard. "They simply disappeared. A couple of days after your daughter came to—"

The man's gaze flickered toward the young couple who stood silently near the front door.

"Hi, Darius." Lily wiggled her fingers and gave him a wry smile. Romeo folded his arms and grinned.

"You did it." The healer's dark eyes widened before he smacked his hands together and roared with laughter. "Of all the impossible things, you actually did it."

"Impossible. Unpredictable. Incredibly brave. A little foolish." Greta stepped aside and watched the man almost jog across his tiny living room to pick her daughter up in the same kind of bone-breaking hug. "She's my daughter, Darius. What did you expect?"

The girl uttered a small grunt at the tightness of the man's embrace and steadied herself with a hand on his arm when he released her.

"I expected to get word that all three of you were merely numbers on the casualty list. Although I prayed every day that wouldn't happen, I expected it." Darius extended an arm toward Romeo, and when the werewolf took the healer's hand, he thought he was about to have his arm yanked off in the process. "This is fantastic."

"It's good to see you too."

He jerked the werewolf closer and thumped his huge hand on his back. Romeo winced, and Lily pressed her lips together to fight back a laugh. "We need drinks. I have a bottle of homemade spirits that still has a few rounds in it. It tastes like gasoline and sugar and goes down just as smooth."

Pointing to the kitchen, Darius wiped his eyes with the other hand and hastened to retrieve the bottle. Greta stopped him with a hand on his chest. There was no physical force involved in the gesture, which made it all the more clear that she had run the show in his apartment and he'd merely been the sidekick who'd failed to follow her all the way. "Maybe another time, huh?"

The healer frowned in confusion. "Why?"

"Because this whole crazy ride isn't over yet." She gestured toward the couch. "Why don't you sit down and we'll tell you all about it."

His mustache twitched as he studied her before his gaze flickered briefly over her companions as well. "I'm gonna get the booze first."

TEN

By the time Greta had finished telling her burly healer friend the abridged version of her journey and what she'd gone through with Lily and Romeo—and it was definitely far less detailed than Romeo's version in Mabayn—Darius had gone through two shots of the homemade liquor in an unmarked bottle. The man had sipped it without apparent distaste, which Lily didn't understand. Even she could smell the rubbing-alcohol-like fumes from where she sat on the living room floor. Beside her, the werewolf looked like the fumes alone were giving him a good buzz.

"And that's why we came here," the woman finished. "Because I still need your help."

The man must have accidentally swallowed more liquor than he intended. He scrunched his eyes shut, cleared his throat, and stiffened slightly as his face reddened beneath the black beard. "How in all this am I supposed to help you, huh?" he finally managed, his voice rasping.

"You come to speak to the Council with us. That's it."

He grunted. "You know it's never merely speaking to the Council."

"Sure. But you're the only other person this deeply involved in the whole situation who isn't either related to me or a lifelong friend of the family in one way or another." Greta winked at Romeo. "Not that it makes you any less helpful, just to be clear."

The werewolf shrugged, his arms wrapped around his knees which were pulled up to his chest. "I wasn't worried about it."

"Excellent. So you, my reclusive friend, need to come with us to share what you know. What we found together, what you found on your own, how you found yourself right in the middle of all this—"

"Now, wait a minute." Darius leaned back on the couch and frowned at her. "I didn't find myself in the middle of this. You dragged me into it."

For a few seconds, the woman looked dumbfounded. Then, she snorted. "Well, you weren't kicking and screaming, I'll tell you that much."

"No..." The healer snatched the bottle of liquor off the side table and poured a third shot. "But I wanted out, remember."

"Darius, everyone wants out when their hand's in a serpent's mouth. But you have to actually get the damn thing to let go first before you can do anything else."

"Isn't that what you did?" His narrowed eyes glittered as he studied his friend over the rim of his glass.

"Not quite. Listen, we have a long road ahead of us. Not nearly as long as the one behind us but it still requires an effort." Greta pressed her palms on her thighs. "And we don't have the time to sit back and take a break because that's merely more time these people have to regroup and find another way to get what they want. We didn't stop anything and only held it off a little longer to maybe buy ourselves more time. As long as we use it smartly."

"Then you shouldn't waste it here trying to get me to come with you."

"Mom." Lily tried not to give anything away through her expression, but Darius obviously needed far more convincing. *She hasn't said anything about the Varelos. That would get me on board in a heartbeat.* "What about—"

"I got this, Sweets. Thank you." Her mother said it calmly enough but the warning in her gaze convinced her daughter to remain silent.

She doesn't want anyone to know.

"Listen." Greta slipped the shot glass effortlessly out of Darius' fingers, downed the rest of it in one swallow, and didn't even blink. "As long as Carmichael's still out there—"

The man snatched up the liquor bottle and tried to raise that to his lips instead, but she pulled that away as deftly as she had the glass. She set it on the floor beside her boot and pointed at the healer.

"As long as he's still out there, Darius, he won't stop. He'll do whatever it takes and as many times as it takes to see his insane vision through to the end. Carmichael wants this Transference spell on a large scale and he now knows exactly what's needed to make that a reality."

The man glanced at Lily, and his bushy eyebrows drew together. "What it takes—"

"He knows Lily and I are Optatus and that he needs at least one to power his spell. Now, he also knows that whatever Optatus witch he can get his hands on needs to be the last of his or her bloodline. Do you really wanna leave some other poor Optatus in fate's hands and not do whatever's necessary to prevent the overhaul of magic as we know it? As it's supposed to be?"

Darius scowled and glanced at the liquor bottle beside her foot but made the smart move and didn't reach for it. "No Optatus in history has ever been that kind of a victim, Greta. And you know it."

"That's completely beside the point!" She jerked her head back in exasperation. "But if you want to talk victims, how about all the other magicals out there who have been or will be abducted and used to power the Transference? How about their families? Their friends? The damn magicals lined up to take their magic out of them and use it simply because they can? It doesn't even work half the time. Lily and Romeo watched a crazed mutant blow himself up because he couldn't manage to control what was never his in the first place!"

The werewolf almost cringed when her finger pointed at him, although the woman still stared at the other man. "That did actually happen," he concurred quickly.

Lily only nodded when Darius looked to her next for confirmation.

"Greta..." The healer sighed and rubbed two huge fingers repeatedly across his beard-covered chin. "I'm not even a good source of information here. The only thing I'll have to tell the Council is another echo of what they'll hear from you anyway. They'll write it off as you having convinced me and we'll be right back where we—"

"Oh, grow some balls and help me finish this!" The two old friends stared at each other for a long moment before she slapped his shoulder with the back of her hand. It wasn't a particularly friendly slap, either, but the huge man hardly seemed to feel it. "You owe me that much. And you know I don't call in a favor if I have the option to hold it over someone's head for much longer than six months."

The young couple shared a confused glance after that last statement but apparently, Greta had said exactly what her reluctant friend needed to hear.

"Fine. I'll come to the US with you, but after I say my piece with the Council, I'll come home. I wasn't made to stick around and talk politics before everything goes to hell."

"Are you kidding? You talked those Albanians out of their cursed combat boots in less than an hour." The woman pointed at him again. "And don't tell me I'm exaggerating. I timed it."

He grumbled an inaudible response and rubbed the back of his head.

"That's more like it." With a grin, she thumped him on

his broad, muscular back and stood from the couch. "Now we get to ship ourselves off to Bentley and—"

"Bentley." Darius lifted his head and frowned at absolutely nothing. "Bentley. Bentley...McClure?"

Greta glanced at him with a raised eyebrow. "You are way more involved in this than you want anyone to believe, aren't you?"

Lily drew a sharp breath. "He called you?"

"What?" Her mother's expression was one of astonishment.

Darius nodded. "A few weeks ago. He dropped all your names and told me to expect another call. I haven't heard anything since."

"Did he tell you about Gabriel?"

The healer frowned. "No."

Greta grinned at her daughter. "Look at you. Networking and setting up a support grid before you even had the proof to bring home with you."

She snorted and scrambled to her feet from her seat on the floor before she replied to her mother. "You're the proof I needed to take to the Council personally. Also, I'm kind of attached to the idea of not having the whole world thinking you're dead. But we had enough to take to the Council by the time we got through Germany."

"And it only got worse from there." Romeo stood beside her and dusted the black pants he still hadn't changed out of since the Black Heron Society had left him with a new wardrobe. "Gabriel's list of Black Heron crimes has probably doubled since we met him."

"Okay, who's Gabriel?"

"Gabriel Mercier. He's a—"

"Magical detective," the werewolf interjected and wiggled his eyebrows.

Lily nudged him gently with her elbow. "For Cadre Europa's Non-Magical Relations Department."

"You involved Cadre Europa in this." A surprised laugh burst from her mother's mouth.

"They were already involved by the time we arrived in France. They merely didn't know it yet. But Gabriel had worked on trying to find who was behind all the blatant magical attacks around Paris." She counted off on her fingers. "You know, kidnapping magicals in front of humans, threatening them with spells, murdering them in broad daylight, and leaving everything behind for non-magicals to see and freak out about."

"They're sloppy," Romeo added. "And it happened everywhere we went."

Greta looked from her daughter to the young werewolf and smirked, her expression both smug and curious. "Are there any other surprise nuggets of wisdom you'd like to spring on me?"

"Probably." The young witch shrugged. "We should probably make another stop before we go home, though."

"And where might that be?"

"Paris."

"Oh, no." Darius shook his head and stayed in his seat on the couch, leaning over his burly legs. "I don't do anything French. Except for fries and dressing."

The older woman stepped away from the couch. "Darius—"

"No, I said I'd come with you to the US, tell the Council my story, and that was it. I don't want anything to do with Cadre Europa after the last time. You can drop me off first or come back after to get me."

"It's so sad." Greta tilted her head and gave her friend a pitying frown composed mostly of sarcasm.

The healer froze and looked slowly at her. "What?"

"That you were given two incredible gifts of magic and the body of a Norseman and you're afraid of a few baguettes and berets."

Darius grunted and rolled his eyes.

"That's it." She stooped quickly to snatch up the unlabeled liquor bottle and dangled it from her hand in front of the man's face. "I'm taking your hooch."

"Greta—"

"Good luck trying to keep that buzz up on legal Romanian booze. I already know how much it takes to get you drunk. Let's go." The woman stormed toward the apartment door, jerked it open again, and disappeared down the hallway.

The man stared at Lily like he expected her to do something about the way her mother chose to deal with anyone. The young witch shrugged. "I'm not even gonna try to stop her. But I don't mind if you drink on the way. Romeo?"

"Yeah, I might even join you." When he caught Lily's incredulous look, he laughed. "I'm kidding. I like having brain cells."

With a groan of frustration, Darius pushed to his feet

again and strode through the kitchen with enough gusto to make all the dishes rattle in the shelves again.

The werewolf peered around the kitchen corner. "Is that a yes?"

"Give me a minute!"

"Huh. He seems more on edge than the last time we were here."

Lily sighed and folded her arms. "Greta Antony tends to do that to people. He'll get over it."

ELEVEN

When Lily, Romeo, and Darius—with a gray, unmarked duffel bag slung over his shoulder like a folded pair of socks—reached the parking lot, Greta stood leaned back against the Winnie's hood to wait for them. She took another swig of the healer's homegrown alcohol while Lily unlocked the vehicle, shrugged, and stepped around the RV to hold the side door open for everyone.

The young couple climbed in first, followed by the silently brooding healer. The Winnie rocked violently as he stepped into the living area. The older woman took one quick look at his duffel bag before she smirked and followed him inside. "Did you remember to pack your game face in there?"

The man had to hunch his shoulders to avoid scraping his head on the Winnie's ceiling, and he moved quickly to the couch. His massive frame made it look more like a loveseat. "I have what I need."

"Of course you do." She rubbed her hands together

and nodded at her daughter. "So where do we need to be to get this Detective Gabriel's attention?"

"Somewhere in Paris." Lily shook her head. "I think I have his card in my purse still."

"That'll help."

The young witch darted toward the front of the RV and felt under the dashboard on the passenger side to retrieve her purse.

After a few days locked in a Black Heron torture chamber, almost losing my mind, and waiting to play the best prank of my life, having a purse now seems like the least important thing in the world. She snorted and rummaged through the random, useless items she kept in there. "Got it."

The dark blue lettering of Gabriel Mercier's business card still scrolled magically across the thick paper. She watched it through an entire cycle, then moved toward her mom to hand it over. "It only has his phone number, though. No address."

"Did he hand it to you personally?" her mother asked

"Yeah, but—"

"Then this is all we need. I should be able to bring us within a mile or two without an exact location."

She raised her eyebrows. "A mile or two of?"

"Wherever the guy is right now. You know, when all this is over, Lily, I think you and I should go over a few lessons in teleporting."

"Yeah, no kidding."

"Okay. Ready?" Without waiting for a response, the

woman clapped her hands with Gabriel's card pressed between them.

"Wait, wait, wait!" Romeo stumbled toward her with his hand outstretched. "Please...keep your hands together. Only for a sec."

"Woah." Greta stepped to the side as the werewolf darted around her and into the kitchen.

He yanked open the cabinet under the sink, hauled out the trashcan, then slammed the door again and darted into the living area. His first thought was to head to the couch, but when he realized that the giant healer filled most of it, he turned toward the armchair behind the passenger seat and settled in that instead. He took a deep breath and nodded. "Okay. Do your thing."

"Hey, it gets easier the more you do it," the woman said and stepped back into place with her hands still pressed together.

"Yeah, maybe. Except I'm not really reacting to anything the way I used to—weird magic, unpredictable nausea, whatever. Go ahead."

Lily leaned forward to brush her fingers against his knee and give him a reassuring nod before she hurried into the kitchen and slid into the booth behind the small table.

"We're really making a production of this, aren't we?" Greta sounded amused.

"Mom, cast it."

The woman chuckled. "Okay, okay. Everyone relax."

Romeo snorted. "That's one of the—"

The silver light encompassed everything once more when she thrust her hands out to either side. Lily's head rocked back against the wall behind her and she wished briefly that she'd chosen the soft passenger seat instead. In the next moment, the air closed in around her, her lungs burned, and the silver light vanished.

Romeo heaved, but thankfully for all of them in such a small space, nothing emerged. The trash bag lining the can crinkled in his tight grasp. Lily folded her arms on the table and lowered her forehead slowly on top of them with a sigh. Darius fell into a fit of hacking coughs.

"Whew." Greta shook her head quickly and took a good look at the other teleported passengers around her. "Honestly, it's like none of you have been around magic before."

"It's not the—" The werewolf heaved again but thankfully produced nothing. "Magic."

"I think it's your spell," her daughter muttered, her voice both muffled and projected by the space between her folded arms.

"How many times have you done this, exactly?" The healer cleared his throat and pounded on his chest. After a few more coughs, he finally settled too.

"I've done it enough times to know that it works every time." Greta rolled her shoulders and stepped toward the couch to pick up Gabriel Mercier's business card that had fallen. "Do I need to make the three of you some kind of potion to—"

"No!" It came from Lily and Romeo at the same time. The werewolf rested his head against the armchair cushion with a sigh, and she raised her head from her arms.

Her mother looked genuinely miffed. "I had no idea you two had such strong feelings about potions."

Only yours, Mom. Melissa told us more than enough about what you used to do with them. She didn't have the heart or the stomach to say any of that out loud, though.

"What you need is an extra charm," Darius grumbled. "It would make the whole thing a little gentler."

Greta gave the man a disbelieving grin and stepped across the living area toward the steps and the Winnie's side door. "I don't do gentle. Walk it off."

"That's a hell of a way to convince someone they made the right choice in coming along for this ride." He stood, bumped his head on the ceiling, and hunched his shoulders again. The side door clicked shut behind her.

Lily slipped out of the booth and mocked her mom's last words a little louder than a whisper. "'Walk it off.' Greta Antony's sage advice for everything."

"It might be the only thing that helps right now." Romeo set the still empty trashcan down gingerly in front of the armchair and stood. His face went a little paler than its usual tan, and he swallowed thickly before he shook his head and hastened to the stairs. "And fresh air."

Once everyone had stepped out of the RV and into another parking lot only partially covered by a vehicle bridge overhead, Greta turned toward them and spread her arms. "Okay. Does anything about this look familiar?"

The werewolf gestured behind her. "Only the Eiffel Tower."

She spun and chuckled. "Thank the source for iconic landmarks. Who has a phone?"

"Ours are dead," he replied. "I checked."

"Here." Darius pulled his cell from his back pocket and offered it to her. She took it, but he held on for a second longer. "It's for a phone call, right?"

"Yes." She jerked the device away with another chuckle and held the card out so she could see it to dial Gabriel's number.

The four stood in the middle of the underpass parking lot, three of them waiting for her to call the man they were now trying to find.

"Bonjour, Monsieur Mercier." Greta flashed them all a wide grin.

Romeo leaned toward Lily and muttered, "It sounds like the DIY translator finally reached its expiration date."

"Yep." She stared at her mother, who babbled happily in French. "My guess is a few days of torture for me and being injected by someone else's magic when the Black Heron's spell backfired on you basically wiped the slate clean."

"You know, I kind of like it that we can simply be Americans in France for a second and not have to pretend to be something else."

"It might be a problem when we meet up with Gabriel, though."

The werewolf cast her a small frown. "I thought you spoke French."

"I meant for you." When she looked at him, the mock insult on his face made her smile. "We'll figure it out."

"*Merci.*" Greta ended the call with their one and only contact in the entire magical Order of Cadre Europa and tossed Darius' phone back to him. The man caught it deftly and shoved it in his pocket. "Well, he was surprisingly polite and gave me crystal-clear directions and everything. Now, we merely need to find out where we are."

The healer grunted and retrieved his phone again. "What's the address?"

"It's...wow." The woman smoothed her blonde hair away from her face and actually looked a little embarrassed. "Over six months being carted around with a blindfold on my face and never touching a piece of technology. I guess it makes sense but I'm still surprised."

"By the address?" Romeo rubbed the back of his neck and eyed the woman in concern, thinking maybe she'd lost one too many marbles in the Black Heron's High Seat after all.

"By the fact that in the twenty-first century, one can completely forget about the invention of GPS. Even an Optatus witch." That seemed to settle it—at least for her— and she stepped toward Darius to repeat the address and look over the top of his beefy forearm as he typed it into his phone.

The werewolf bumped his shoulder into Lily's and nodded at her mother. "Does she seem a little—"

"Don't." The young witch slipped her arm through his and lowered her voice too. "I don't think either of us will ever know the whole story behind what she went through. And technically, since Mabayn doesn't really count, she's only been out of the High Seat for, like, an hour and a half. Let's give her a little more time."

"Sure. Yeah."

"If it keeps getting worse, we'll say something about it. Okay?"

He nodded and placed a kiss on top of her blonde head. "Got it."

"All right, kids." Greta patted Darius' huge back and grinned at them. She pointed toward the stairs leading out of the parking lot toward another pedestrian walkway. "We're headed this way. I know this is the City of Love and everything but try not to fall too far behind."

"Oh, boy." Lily slipped her hand into Romeo's and bit her lip through a smile. "I have a feeling she has more bad jokes about us up her sleeve."

"She always has." They headed after the other two. Lily's mom talked animatedly but in a hushed tone to the massive healer who looked like he belonged with a den of bears instead of walking through the middle of Paris at night. "Only now, they're actually kinda funny."

She shot him a playful frown. "Seriously?"

"Yeah. 'Cause it actually applies to us this time."

The young witch snorted and gazed at the lights that glittered along the boulevards and over the water, beckoning them to experience Paris in the way none of them had the time to enjoy right now. "Huh. Lily and Romeo all grown up, right?"

"Right."

"It's weird that sometimes, I still feel more like the adult with her, though. Even after everything we did to get her out of that stupid castle."

Romeo shrugged. "She has her moments."

TWELVE

"This is it." Greta pointed to the frosted glass pane in the door in front of them and the black lettering across the top. "It's amazing that he didn't even mention the time."

Lily raised her eyebrows. "He definitely looked like the kinda guy who'd rather work around the clock, even if it meant going without sleep."

"And he looked like he needed sleep when we first met him," Romeo added.

"Well, he'd better not be sleeping now." The older woman straightened her shoulders and raised her fist for a light, polite rap on the frosted glass. It rattled under her knuckles and she drew her hand back to wait.

"*Entrez-vous.*"

She turned to look over her shoulder at her daughter in mock surprise, then opened the door and pushed it open slowly. "Monsieur Mercier. I hope you still have a little time in your day for a short conversation."

The man who stood behind the long desk in front of the office window nodded slowly and watched the giant duck through the doorway, followed by two magicals he most definitely recognized. Gabriel's mouth twitched into a tired smile, and he stepped around his desk. "English is fine if that suits you all."

"Oh." Greta looked quickly at Lily, then gave the man a comical shrug. "How did you know we'd be happy with English?"

"Most people in Europe are if they only speak two languages. But beyond that, it was your accent over the phone and just now that gave you away."

"My—I don't think so." She pursed her lips and tried to wipe the smile off her face. "I know the accent's not perfect but I do know my French is."

"Yes." The man leaned against the edge of his desk and folded his arms. "You do seem to be fluent. Those two sealed the deal."

He nodded at the young couple, who glanced quickly at each other before they stepped farther inside the office. "I'm sure you didn't hear us speaking English the last time we saw you," Romeo said.

"No. That's not what I heard. But I don't think you were really speaking French. Would you close the door, if you please?"

"Yeah." He pulled the office door gently behind him.

Gabriel pushed himself from his desk, went to Lily, and extended his hand. "It is good to see you again, Lily."

She shook his hand and nodded. "You too. Thanks for sticking around so we could see you in person."

"Yes. Romeo." The French detective nodded at the werewolf, who raised his hand in greeting before he shoved them both into the front pockets of his black slacks. Finally, the man turned toward Greta. "And you would be..."

"Greta Antony. Pleasure to meet you." She pumped his hand with unbridled enthusiasm. "And this is Darius Balsur."

"Hello." Once Gabriel had greeted everyone, he folded his arms again and eyed them with silent, slightly unnerving poise.

He's waiting for us to explain why we came back and located him. And probably why he had a call from my mom instead of me, too.

Greta drew a sharp breath. "You know, I had no idea Cadre Europa had founded a Non-Magical Relations Department."

"Ah. Yes. It is fairly new. I helped build the department close to a decade ago now."

"It seems like it was well-timed."

"Indeed."

Another round of silence permeated the office, and Lily finally had to jump in with both feet. "Gabriel, I gave your number to a friend of ours in the US. Have you had a call from—"

"Yes, I have already spoken to your friend Mr. McClure. We've been in regular contact over the last few days."

"Is that right?" Her mother stepped to the side so she could look at everyone at the same time with a wry smile bordering on a grimace. "It sounds like the only person who hasn't talked to Bentley yet is me."

"Do you want my phone?" Darius asked blandly.

"No, thanks. We'll make that a surprise."

He inclined his head toward her and looked like he wanted to tune her out but was beholden by the ritual of politeness to not ignore her completely. After a moment, he returned his gaze to her daughter. "Tell me. Did you send me that stone on purpose or was it simply a lucky stroke of fate?"

Lily's mouth dropped open and it took her a few more seconds than she would have liked to come up with a response. "You have the stone?"

"*Oui*. Well, I did."

"Please don't tell me you tossed it into the Seine, Monsieur Mercier." Greta pressed her hands together and raised them until her fingers touched the underside of her chin. "I know it was probably a confusing surprise to have that little secret dropped anonymously on your doorstep—"

"Right there on my carpet, actually." The detective nodded at the middle of his office. "And believe me, Mrs. Antony, there is very little that surprises me after the last few months."

"Ms. Antony." Greta corrected, the corners of her mouth drawn into a tight, tense smile.

"I beg your pardon?"

"Not Mrs. It's a formality, really, but I rather prefer to be exactly what I am and nothing else."

"Of course." He once again acknowledged her with a small nod. "My apologies."

What's going on with her? Lily studied her mom and tried to keep a blank expression. "So what did you do with it?"

"Honestly, I wasn't planning on doing anything with it. But Mr. McClure happened to call me not five minutes after I found it waiting for me in my office. He couldn't explain the stone, of course, but he did share with me what I imagine very few people are privy to at this point. That included where the two of you were headed, Lily, and how we might all be able to help each other."

"That is definitely high up there on our priority list." Greta nodded. "Right next to retrieving that stone again and taking it with us for a particularly important meeting with the Council of Magic."

Gabriel's eyes grew wide. "You've scheduled a meeting?"

"Not yet. We were hoping to have everything else lined up before then." Lily's mom sounded a little impatient. "Right now, I'm more concerned with making sure that stone is somewhere safe and still accessible to us."

"Hmm." The magical detective frowned at the stained carpet of his office and nodded slowly. "It is secure. For now." He swallowed and tugged at the hem of his jacket sleeves one at a time. "I cannot say with any certainty how long that item can be contained, even under the best security. There's too much magic in it. It is...incredibly volatile."

"We know." Greta smoothed her hands down the sides of the tan leggings she'd taken from Mabayn and finally seemed to have slid into her usual calm, collected, diplomatic self. "The original spell that gathered so much unstable magic in one place was targeted within an onyx pillar about two feet high. Onyx is one of the best stabilizing elements for—"

"Yes, I know its properties, Ms. Antony. And I am quite aware of the fact that the glowing stone now holding that same magic is, in fact, not onyx."

"So then you know how much time we don't have," Lily interjected. "At the very least, let us take it off your hands and out of the city. It might give you a little more peace of mind knowing it's all the way on the other side of the Atlantic."

Gabriel and Greta both turned to look at the young witch with matching expressions of surprise.

She frowned at them in return. "Unless I'm missing something."

The detective cleared his throat. "Not at all. I would enjoy nothing more than to simply pass it into your hands and be done with it. But at this point, there is a certain...uh, protocol we need to follow."

Greta clicked her tongue against her teeth and tried to smile. "You brought it to Cadre Europa, didn't you?"

The last time Lily had met the detective, she'd thought he was particularly skilled at hiding any emotion whatsoever beneath the mask of sheer exhaustion. Now, she was convinced of it.

"I have a duty to my order and my country to uphold the laws of both, Ms. Antony. You cannot fault me for doing the best I could with what few choices I was offered."

"And I don't. It was a very good choice. Let's start the process of getting it back now, shall we?"

Gabriel studied the woman for a few more seconds, then turned to pick up a black messenger bag from behind his desk. He nodded at her and the others before he moved quickly to his office door. "Come with me."

"Thank you, Monsieur Mercier."

The man opened the door and gestured for everyone to step out into the hallway first. "If you please, Ms. Antony. Call me Gabriel."

Greta was the last out of his office, and she grinned as she stepped past him into the hall. "Then I expect you to drop the Ms. Antony in return."

"Agreed." The French detective locked the door to his office, cast a quick, simple security ward over it, and stepped briskly past his guests to lead them down the hall.

There she is. The Greta Antony who could charm a cobra out of its fangs.

Lily shared a skeptical glance with Romeo and behind them, Darius exhaled a massive sigh of disappointment.

"Great. Now we're taking a detour for a ream of paper-work. This is why I didn't want to come to France."

The young witch couldn't come up with anything to say to that, so she let the disgruntled healer have his moment unchallenged.

THIRTEEN

N_one of them could have predicted that the shortest route from Gabriel Mercier's office to Cadre Europa headquarters was actually via the Paris Métro. They moved quickly through the underground station and casually passed the commuters that still milled around at this hour, none of whom paid the group any attention at all.

Romeo lowered his head toward Lily and muttered, "If he tells us to walk through the wall, I say we skip the Harry Potter tricks and find a different way to get that stone."

She snorted. "We won't have to walk through an actual wall in the Métro. I think."

Gabriel turned down a narrow corridor off the main platform and removed a heavy keyring with at least two dozen keys from his messenger bag. He took his time to search calmly through all the options before he found the one he wanted, then unlocked one of the doors labeled *Employés Seulement*.

"My guess would be that's for employees," the were-wolf whispered.

"Yeah, of Europe's magical Order." Lily grinned at him and followed her mom while their guide yet again held the door open for everyone else first. Romeo remained close behind her, but Darius seemed to have a little trouble squeezing his huge frame through the narrow doorway. The detective glanced around the platform, seemingly unaffected by how much time it took the healer to move through, but they all made it inside without much of a delay.

The second the man shut the door again behind him with a sharp click, the lights in the small storage room turned off and left them in complete darkness.

"Well, this is fun." Greta sounded like she really meant it.

Romeo gazed around in the dark and let himself shift enough into his wolf form that he could mostly see. "Hey, if you need someone to turn the lights on, tell me where to find the switch."

"One moment, if you please." Gabriel didn't move from where he stood in front of the door, and Romeo looked over his shoulder at the detective.

"You do know werewolves can see in the dark, ri—oh, jeez!"

The lights returned in a brilliant flash of bright white and instead of the awfully close, cramped space of the supply closet, they now stood at the end of a long, wide hallway. The polished marble floors reflected the blinding glare overhead, and from either side of the corridor, more lights glowed from within recessed archways.

"All the way to the end, if you please." Their guide motioned them forward and waited until he could follow at a safe distance again.

"Wow." Greta peered into the recessed archways, which all held closed, unmarked doors. "This order's really stepped it up a notch."

"We've had some recent renovations, yes. Nothing too fancy."

"Ha."

Lily glanced hastily over her shoulder and finally saw a subdued but very real smile on the detective's face.

They passed at least two dozen doors on either side before they reached a long, wide brown desk set against the far wall. The woman seated behind it looked up from the magazine she was reading and adjusted her horn-rimmed glasses with a polite smile. *"Bienvenue dans le complexe principal du Cadre Europa—"*

Gabriel cut her off with something swift and casually polite in French as he stepped between the Antony witches and approached the desk. He said something about bringing his guests, and the receptionist grinned.

"Ah. Oui, Monsieur Mercier." She gestured toward their right and smiled sweetly at all of Gabriel's apparent guests.

"Merci. This way." The detective didn't stop to make sure they were following. At the far corner of the back wall, a black door shimmered into focus where it hadn't previously existed—or, at least, it hadn't been visible at all.

The man opened the door, pushed it into the room beyond, and stepped aside to let everyone through. "Quickly, yes?"

The whole process was as smooth and effortless as they could have expected, but Lily didn't miss the two separate glances their guide darted toward the entrance at the other end of the hall and the brief smile he gave the receptionist between them. *Either we're really not supposed to be here, or he's worried about someone else seeing us.*

Gabriel closed the door behind him and gestured to the large conference table with obviously expensive black leather executive chairs at each of the twelve places around it. "Here we are. Feel free to sit. I will only be a moment. Does anyone care for a drink? A...you call it a snack, correct?"

Romeo and Darius pulled out chairs at opposite ends of the table. The werewolf shrugged. "Actually, I—"

The Frenchman's fingers flicked toward the right-hand wall as he passed to reveal a minibar with a wicker basket of assorted snacks on top. "Complimentary. Excuse me."

The man hurried across the conference room, where another door materialized out of nowhere a second before he grasped the handle and pulled it open. When he closed it and behind him the other side, the door vanished too.

"Look at that." The werewolf stood again from where he'd half lowered into the chair and walked around the table toward the minibar. "Does anyone want anything?"

"Water, if there's any in there," Darius muttered, his hands resting in his lap as he studied the blank wall on the other side of the conference room.

Lily looked at her mom and wanted to raise the topic of

Gabriel's well-hidden but still discernible discomfort in bringing them there but Greta peered over the table and tried to see what was laid out in the wicker basket. When she reached her mother's side, she folded her arms and watched Romeo as he squatted in front of the minibar's fridge and searched through the drinks.

"Mom—"

"I know, Sweets. I saw it too." The woman didn't look at her, but she inclined her head slightly in acknowledgment.

I can't simply come right out and ask if we have something to be worried about. We're inside the headquarters of Europe's magical order. There's no way they're not watching us and listening to everything we say. Instead, she settled on a less direct way to ask essentially the same question. "Is that something we need to pay special attention to?"

"I don't know. We'll simply have to wait and see how it all plays out."

Yeah. That means pay attention but don't do anything about it. Yet.

"Okay."

"Here you go, man." Romeo turned in his crouch and offered Darius an extra-large bottle of water. "I swear the back of this mini fridge goes on forever. They probably keep all the real expensive stuff way back where no one can reach it."

The healer snorted and took the bottle. "Thanks."

"Yep. Greta?"

"If there's a Perrier, I'll take one," she replied. "If not, whatever beer you can reach will be fine."

"Lil?"

"Yeah, the same for me. Thanks." Lily decided to follow her mother's lead on this one, although she fully understood what she was doing. *Go for the polite option first but don't refuse a beer if that's all they have. If I were watching a group of foreign magicals waiting for a meeting with the top of my order, all of them drinking water would make it look like they were suspicious enough to not want to relax. And then, I'd be suspicious of them.*

"It looks like they're fresh out of Perrier. But there is something called a chou...a shoola—"

"Oh, stop butchering the French language and bring it here." Greta waved him toward her and pulled out the chair beside the head of the table. "And bring the whole basket too. We can dump it out and spread everything around."

Romeo chuckled. "Sure."

He closed the fridge with two beer bottles in one hand and a third tucked under his arm, then stood and snagged the wicker basket of packaged goods. That went in the center of the table before he left a beer in front of the older woman and took the other two around the table to sit beside Lily.

"Thanks." She took the offered beer and rolled the executive chair a little closer to the table.

"Thank Cadre Europa, huh?" With a grin, he patted his pockets before he realized they weren't technically his.

Then, he shrugged, grasped the bottle cap, and popped it off with his hand.

She cleared her throat and tried not to laugh. "These aren't twist-offs, are they?"

The werewolf took her beer, opened it in the same way, and tipped it toward her with a wink. "Nope. I have useful skills too, remember?"

The young witch took her beer and lifted it to her mouth for a long but very slow draught. *I can at least make it look like I'm drinking more.*

Romeo extended a hand across the table. "Greta, do you want some help with—"

The woman flicked her finger at her bottle cap. It popped and hissed before it toppled onto the table and wobbled a little before it finally settled into silence.

The werewolf puffed out an exaggerated sigh. "Yeah, I've seen that one before."

"Thanks anyway." She raised her beer toward him in a mock toast and laughed softly before she took a seemingly long drink with very much the same intention as her daughter.

"I guess I'll be the one to sort this mess out." Darius dragged the basket of snacks toward him and rifled through the selection. "Macaroons. I hate macaroons."

"Here." Greta snatched up a smaller package and tossed it onto the table in front of him. "Take the chocolate chip cookies and give it a rest, huh? We're in France and we'll be in France longer than you're comfortable with so you need to get over it."

The healer's beard and mustache twitched when he

sniffed and picked the cookies up. "Do you think it would send up a red flag if I went back to the RV and got the drink I actually want right now?"

Romeo choked on his beer.

The older woman smirked but didn't look at her friend. She took the package of macaroons, slid the basket across the table toward her daughter, and took another sip of French beer. "Drink your water, Darius."

FOURTEEN

"See? Merely one more reason why I didn't want to be here." Darius dusted cookie crumbs from his beard and spilled them over his lap, the conference table, and the floor. "The French don't have the same definition of 'this won't take long' as we do."

"You have to let this go." Greta nursed her beer and popped the last of what she thought was a protein bar into her mouth. "Do you want me to get you a beer? Will that help you to chill out a little?"

"I'm chill." The healer swept his huge arm across the table and scattered the crumbs on the surface onto the floor with the others. He pulled his cell from his pocket, scowled at the screen, and put it back. "I simply don't appreciate being made to wait in a room with doors we can't open for almost two hours. How long does it have to take these people?"

"As long as they need." The woman leaned back in the leather executive chair, spun slowly from side to side, and tipped her bottle toward the young couple across the table. "You two didn't have somewhere else to be today, did you?"

Lily ripped off another piece of fruit leather and popped it into her mouth. "Very funny."

Romeo took another sip of his second beer, glanced around Cadre Europa's conference room, and nodded. "Do you know what they need in here?"

"That list is bound to be incredibly long," Greta quipped.

"Think about it. They have the secret headquarters inside the Paris Métro. They have a magically appearing hallway and doors that are there and aren't there. Plus the convenient minibar and snacks, obviously."

"It's a very nice touch."

"Right, but it doesn't all work together when they have to shove their visitors in a room and make them wait for who knows how long. It messes up the flow."

Leaning slightly away from him, Lily gave him a playful frown. "Messes up the flow? What, did you pick up corporate feng shui and forget to tell me about it?"

"Naw, Lil. This is literally coming to me right now. Listen."

Both Antony witches chuckled and shook their heads.

The werewolf spread his hands across the table like he unrolled a floorplan. "These guys need their own dimension. Somewhere they can pop into whenever they have something important to discuss that's gonna take a while. Except, of course, that dimension gives them all the time they need and it only takes a few minutes out here."

Lily glanced at her mom and pressed her lips together. Greta's smile had faded a little. *Yeah, I didn't think openly talking about our two days in another dimension is a good idea here either.*

The young witch placed her palm on the table beside his open hands and hoped he'd get the hint. "Uh...Romeo?"

"It's a great idea, though, right?"

The older woman shook her head slightly, but he didn't seem to notice. Darius, on the other hand, kept himself busy opening another package from the assortment of snacks.

"I'm serious. That would solve all our problems. Give Cadre Europa some kinda key into Ma—"

"Wow." Greta slapped her hands on the table and stood. "Well I, for one, get thirstier and thirstier the longer I sit here without any news from anyone."

With wide eyes, she nodded at the young couple, then spun to jerk open the minifridge's door and rummage in there with an unnecessarily loud clinking of glass bottles.

The werewolf scratched the back of his head and frowned at the table. "Did I say something?"

Lily leaned toward him and whispered, "We'll talk about it—"

The door through which the detective had disappeared burst open with a loud click, although it made no sound whatsoever when it struck the wall and bounced back.

"Please excuse us for keeping you waiting for so long," Gabriel said. He walked quickly into the conference room and spared only a quick glance at Greta who crouched in front of the minibar. "Thank you for your patience with this...red tape, yes?"

Darius scowled at the man and the five other people in corporate suits and jackets that entered behind him. "Red tape for almost two hours?"

"We have protocols." That was all Gabriel would say on the matter before he gestured toward the conference table. The others behind him fanned out silently and took seats on either side of Romeo and Lily but politely left Greta's chair untouched. The detective circled the table and drew out the chair at the end closest to where his guests had entered, effectively putting the Antony witches, Romeo, and Darius between himself and the gathering of Cadre Europa's representatives.

"There it is." Greta snatched another bottle of water out of the expanding minifridge, rose smoothly to her feet, and studied the almost completely full table. "Does anyone else want something while I'm here?"

With only polite headshakes and a few hands raised to decline in response, she nodded and brought her unnecessary water bottle to the table. She slid into the executive chair beside Darius and hastily swiped aside the last few cookie crumbs the giant healer had missed.

"Shall we begin?" Gabriel asked.

A weary-looking witch in his late sixties with long, gray, thinning hair pulled into a ponytail gestured toward the detective with a nod. "The floor is yours, Gabriel."

"Excellent."

Lily studied the Cadre Europa magicals—three men and two women, all of them at least a decade older than her mother. The woman with short, spiked black hair and earrings dangling to her shoulders—both bearing the symbol of Cadre Europa's Order at the bottom of thin silver chains—was clearly the youngest. She also appeared the least pleased to be there out of all of them.

"Before we begin, I want to state for the record that this gathering is being fully supervised and recorded for Cadre Europa as a governing body to use in the future in any way it sees fit. Do all parties give their consent to proceed?"

Of course, everyone around the table nodded. *We didn't wait here for almost two hours to stonewall now for anonymity.*

"Good," Gabriel continued. "Note that all parties have given consent. Now, I want to thank everyone present for gracing this meeting with their time and attention. From what I know of the situation, we are here to discuss an incredibly vital and rather time-sensitive state of affairs, brought to me through Miss Lily Antony, Ms. Greta Antony, Mr. Romeo..."

"Oh. Stephens." The werewolf nodded.

"Stephens. Thank you. And Mr. Darius Balsur. I have also been in contact with a final outside party, Mr. Bentley McClure in the United States, who reached out to me a little over a week ago on Miss Antony's behalf. In the time between Mr. Bentley's first phone call and this meeting, I have received more crucial information that may change the circumstances around Cadre Europa's possession of a certain volatile artifact."

"The stone," Greta cut in.

"Yes. The stone."

"Are you aware, Ms. Antony, of the particular nature of this stone?" The aged fairy in a silver-and-violet pinstriped suit didn't immediately make it clear which Antony he addressing. His accent was thick and somewhat ponderous. When he turned his violet gaze to Greta, Lily deferred to her mom on that question.

"Am I aware?" the older witch smiled politely and looked at the tabletop.

Lily was the only magical in this room who understood the true nature of that expression. *She was already getting antsy before. Now, she's insulted.*

"Of course I'm aware of its nature. My daughter and I are the ones who sent that stone to Mr. Mercier in the first place."

The Cadre Europa officials reacted to that with a range of surprised glances as they shifted in their chairs and looked hastily at one another. At least two inhaled sharply.

"Then I assume you can tell us what's inside the stone," the fairy added.

Greta pressed her lips together and studied her interviewers. "I thought we were already on the same page, here —to talk about moving forward."

"Ms. Antony. Please." Gabriel extended a hand toward the center of the table and looked like he was walking the fine line between confidence and extreme nervousness. "Your answers are for our records and absolutely necessary."

Lily's mom closed her eyes, exhaled a long sigh, and

turned again to address the fairy. "Until only a few hours ago, that stone was nothing more than the personal talisman of a man who expected to have far more power and influence right now than he actually does. To stop him from succeeding in his attempt to successfully cast a large-scale Transference spell on at least two dozen receiving magicals—"

"I'm sorry." The youngest Cadre Europa witch with the spiked hair leaned forward and stared at her. "Did you say Transference spell?"

"Large-scale. Yes."

"That's impossible." The man with the ponytail shook his head and his sallow cheeks wobbled. "There's no viable way to cast such a spell—"

"Oh, yes, there is." Greta raised an eyebrow, then glanced at each of the other officials before she chuckled humorlessly. "If the magical who wanted to cast it got their hands on an artifact specifically created to do exactly that. And an Optatus witch or two."

More grumbled dissent rose from the order officials, and she leaned back in her chair with a restrained but incredulous smile. After a moment, she looked at Gabriel. "Do none of these people know who I am?"

"I'm sorry?"

"You should be." She placed her hands on the table again and leaned forward. "I'm usually not the one to start pointing fingers, but it's obvious France's magical community has lived under a rock for the last seven years." She glanced at the ceiling. "Or under the Métro."

"I beg your pardon, Ms. Antony." The fairy scowled at

her. "Cadre Europa is one of the world's most prestigious and oldest—"

"Yeah, I can see that."

The detective tapped the table but no one heard him. "Ms. Antony, please try to—"

"You people need someone up top who knows how to read the news on whatever device is available to keep up with the times." She waggled her finger sternly at the startled officials at the table. "None of you have any idea what you're dealing with."

"I will not sit here and be insulted by a common witch who cannot so much as provide us with viable evidence. This information is unbelievable at best and mere fantasy at its worst. She has no way to substantiate such outlandish claims." The fairy in the silver and violet suit stood abruptly and pressed his fingertips onto the table. His executive chair rolled silently back behind him.

"Common?" Greta didn't blink this time but stared hard at the fairy and his unseemly outburst. "I'm a common witch, hmm?"

"You've had your fun wasting all our time, Ms. Antony. Goodbye."

"Okay, you hollow-boned dinosaur." She slid a clenched fist over the table and slowly opened her fingers. A swirl of black energy flickered in the tiny opening.

Lily leapt from her chair and smacked both hands on the table. "It does exist."

The entire conference room fell into absolute silence. Beside her, a wide-eyed Romeo bowed his head and rubbed a knuckle over his lips.

FIFTEEN

The old fairy scoffed. "It is a brave attempt, girl, but I've heard enough." He turned toward the door that hadn't yet appeared in the wall.

"The Transference artifact exists," Lily said and raised her voice enough to make sure she caught his attention. "We know of at least two."

"Then bring those in and we might choose to listen." He pointed at Greta. "You may leave your mother behind when you return."

"One moment, Altrath." The other woman among the Cadre Europa officials—her age-whitened hair pulled into a tight, neat bun at the back of her head—raised a finger and turned her head toward the blustering fairy, although she didn't take her eyes off Lily. "I am interested in hearing what young...ah. Your name one more time, if you please."

"Lily."

"Lily. Stay until she has finished saying her part."

When the angry official didn't move or make any reply, the woman added, "Consider that an order."

She lowered her finger toward the empty chair, which had rolled almost all the way toward the wall. A pale purple light flashed at her fingertip, and it rolled smoothly toward the table and stopped with enough room for Altrath to seat himself. He did—quickly and silently—and scowled his obvious displeasure.

"Please continue, Lily."

The young witch nodded and glanced at her mom. Greta leaned back in her chair with her arms folded, but the intensity of her gaze on her daughter, the tiny nod, and the barest flicker of a smile betrayed her true intentions. *She made herself unreliable to these people deliberately. She wanted me to tell them what we're facing.*

It didn't make sense in the moment, but nothing ever did with Greta Antony. Instead of searching for reasons, she pushed all that aside and took a deep breath. "Two Transference artifacts, as far as we know, have been uncovered. The first was found seven years ago and donated to the Smithsonian by Margaret Antony."

She pointed at her mother, and all eyes turned toward the woman Altrath had dubbed the common witch. Greta's shrug made it look like she couldn't care less, although her companions all knew better. The fairy looked like he might actually puke.

"I don't know how the second Transference artifact was found, but three of us in this room saw it with our own eyes only a few hours ago. A man named Carmichael Cantus used it for the Transference spell cast together with a seriously dangerous group of dark magicals who call themselves the Black Heron society."

"Oh, *c'est ridicule*." Altrath had slipped into French for his muttered outburst, but no one needed to understand his words to know that he thought the whole thing was a load of bull.

"Let her speak," the witch with white hair snapped and her gaze remained fixed on the young Optatus witch.

Lily swallowed and thought about how she'd phrase the rest of it. "Greta, Romeo, and I were there when Carmichael tried to cast this spell. My mother wasn't exaggerating. This was a large-scale spell, and once that man masters it, he'll not stop with only his society members. He's trying to make it available to anyone, anywhere, who's willing to pay whatever he asks to be on the receiving end of the Transference."

"Where does the stone come in?" the man with the ponytail asked and stroked his hairless, wrinkled chin with agitated motions.

"We interrupted the spell. I suppose the simple version is that we rerouted it into that stone and turned it into a vessel."

"A vessel for what?" The white-haired witch's voice was calm and even-toned but incredibly quiet.

"For stolen magic," her mother replied. "That's putting it bluntly, but there's no other way to describe it when we're dealing with something like this."

"Stolen. Hm." The fairy glared at her. "Even if that were true, there is still no available spell—in any form of existing magic as I understand them—that would effect such a Transference. There is no way to get this so-called stolen magic into whoever wishes to receive it."

Greta opened her mouth to refute that, but her daughter beat her to it.

"With all due respect, Monsieur Altrath," Lily said, "but if that's what you believe, you clearly don't understand everything about existing magic."

The fairy blustered and turned his attention to the young witch who stood calmly and apparently unmoved by his aggression. His face reddened visibly, which only made his violet eyes darken that much more. Beside him, the white-haired woman who clearly pulled rank here—at least over Altrath, if no one else—chuckled softly. That only made the insult worse for the fairy.

"These are very large claims," the witch with black spiked hair added. "Especially coming from a young, inexperienced witch such as yourself. After all that has been said in the last few minutes, I cannot help but entertain the possibility of your mother having indoctrinated you with these wild fantasies."

Lily bit down on her lower lip and took a deep breath as her nostrils flared. *These people really don't want to believe what's happening, exactly like most of the others we tried to help. Except now, we need their help.*

Greta cleared her throat. "I'll have you know that this young, inexperienced witch tracked the Black Heron Society through North America, half of Europe, and into Africa to find me and Carmichael and interrupt that Transference spell, all at incredible cost to herself. I would still be chained by my wrists instead of seated here if it weren't for her, despite her inexperience. My daughter is solely responsible for both my freedom and Cadre Europa's opportunity to heed this warning."

"Not exactly." The girl glanced at the werewolf beside her. "Romeo was there with me for all of it, and there would be a few dozen magicals on the loose somewhere with every kind of magic running through them if he hadn't helped us interrupt the Transference."

He stared at the table and smirked as he shook his head slowly.

"Carmichael will most definitely send the magical world into chaos." Her mother nodded at the order officials, her previous irritation replaced by the respect everyone had expected of her from the beginning. "Unless your council agrees to give us what we absolutely need."

"And that is?"

"The stone."

The only other official who hadn't yet spoken hummed in thought, then tapped a few slightly longer than appropriate fingernails on the table. "I would like the answers to two separate questions if you please."

"If we have those answers, Monsieur, we'll give them." Lily nodded and waited for the witch to ask for what he wanted.

"I do not believe you were allowed an opportunity to elaborate on your clear position that Monsieur Altrath does not fully understand existing magic." He spoke slowly and thoughtfully, his blue eyes focused on her as if they were the only two people in the room. While all the other officials had some type of discerning feature, he merely looked like another ordinary senior citizen she might have found seated outside a café in the middle of the afternoon —including the newsboy cap. "So first, Miss Antony, I would like to hear if you have any proof of what we may be hesitant to believe."

"Proof that the magic can actually be transferred into someone else?"

"Yes."

Lily didn't look away from the silent intensity of the official's blue-eyed gaze as she lowered an open hand slowly toward Romeo. "He's seated right here next to me."

The werewolf looked quickly at her, then at the table again, and leaned back in his chair.

Greta scanned the faces around the conference table and finally allowed herself to smile now that her daughter had revealed the only real leverage they had—at least until they convinced Cadre Europa to hand back their greater leverage to take to the Council of Magic's door.

"Thank you, Mademoiselle Antony." The white-haired witch nodded at Romeo. "Monsieur Stephens. The room is yours if you please."

In the silence that followed, Lily lowered herself into her chair and gave her friend a reassuring smile.

He looked like he wanted to bolt out of the room. It made sense, given that he was now the first werewolf in remembered magical history who'd both been accepted into an order's headquarters and invited to speak freely in front of everyone.

The young witch gave his wrist a little squeeze and

scooted the chair closer to the table. "You got this," she whispered. "Think of it as a practice run for the Council."

"Was that supposed to make me feel better?"

"Romeo." Greta nodded at him when he looked at her. "Go ahead."

"Right." He chewed the inside of his cheek, sighed, and pushed to his feet. "So...I'm not gonna pretend that everyone doesn't already know what I am."

The fairy muttered something else in French but was abruptly silenced when the white-haired witch snapped her fingers.

"Our apologies, monsieur," the witch with spiked black hair added. "Do continue."

"And I haven't pretended to be anything else." His shoulders rose toward his ears in discomfort before he smoothed his hands down the sides of his pants and straightened his posture. "I'm not pretending now, either. But I am...something else."

Lily caught the questioning glance Gabriel Mercier gave her mother. Greta returned his gaze and winked.

The witch with the spiked hair leaned back in her chair, her earrings dangling wildly on either side of her neck, and tapped two fingers against her lips. "What might that be, please?"

"Well, uh...I'm not sure there's a name for it yet." Romeo exhaled a sharp breath to steady himself and raised his open palm in front of his chest. For a few seconds, it looked like nothing would happen, but a small, faint white light appeared in the center of his hand. It grew slowly and took almost a full minute before the illumination orb he'd summoned had reached its full size. When it did, he lifted it carefully and released it. His spell reacted to the tension in the conference room and his own frayed nerves and didn't quite echo his gentle gesture.

Instead, the light orb rocketed to the ceiling, ricocheted with a small pop, and careened across the table until it stopped on the far corner of the room. It quivered there with a low, buzzing hum.

Romeo cleared his throat. "I'm...uh, still working out a few kinks."

Every official of Cadre Europa had turned in their leather chairs to stare at the illumination orb a werewolf should never have been able to conjure in the first place. A thick, staccato choking sound issued from the fairy Altrath's throat before the old witch in the newsboy cap started to laugh.

It was low at first but quickly built into a thunderous roar of amusement. The witch spun in his chair and continued to laugh, holding his belly with both hands. The other officials slowly followed his lead to turn toward the table. The only one who didn't look amused or impressed or both was the fairy.

"Indeed!" The blue-eyed witch laughed again. "This is a very good display, monsieur wolf. One cannot pretend that."

Romeo chuckled breathlessly and sat again. "Not even a little."

"And you are able to do this because of the Transference?" The man with the ponytail asked.

"Yep."

"How did you manage to do this?"

Lily shook her head. "It was done to him. By Carmichael's people."

"Yeah, I didn't really have a choice."

"If you did have a choice, Monsieur Stephens," the spikey-haired witch said, "would you choose this for yourself a second time?"

"Uh..." He glanced at Lily but she didn't have any answers for him this time. "I really haven't thought about it. So I don't know. Sorry."

"Well, either way, you seem to have come to terms with it fairly well," the white-haired witch added and leaned back in her chair again. "Is this the danger of a large-scale Transference spell you want us to help you stop?"

"No." Mother and daughter said it at the same time, and the officials found it a little difficult to decide which of the Antony witches they wanted to look at next.

"The problem isn't the actual Transference spell." Lily gestured toward Romeo again. "Besides the fact that these people use it on anyone who happens to be in the wrong place at the wrong time and without their consent. Romeo didn't get to choose but he does get to decide how he wants to use the magic he has now moving forward."

"The problem," Greta added, "is the Black Heron's methods for removing that magic from some and transferring it to others—also without the victims' consent."

"Victims?" The fairy Altrath blinked furiously.

"That's exactly what they are," she said. "And I promise you that the kind of magicals who will be on the receiving end of Carmichael's Transference are not nearly as competent or conscientious as Romeo."

The werewolf tried to hide his smile and failed. "Hey, thanks."

The woman ignored him and reached out toward Gabriel seated beside her at the head of the table. The man glanced at her hand but didn't do or say anything else. "I'm sure you've all heard the reports coming in from your top detective with Non-Magical Relations."

The officials' expression darkened at that, and the only one of them who didn't avert their gaze in fear, discomfort, or disapproval was the witch in the newsboy cap.

"I have shared everything I could find with my order's ranking officials, yes." Gabriel stared at Greta for a few seconds, then inclined his head toward the leaders of Cadre Europa. "And I defer to their decision on the matter."

Another uncomfortable silence filled the air. Romeo's hand brushed against Lily's under the table and she slid her fingers between his with a little squeeze.

The witch in the newsboy cap took another deep breath and folded his hands on the table. "My second question, Mademoiselle Antony, is perhaps not so easy to answer with actions rather than words."

She nodded and waited.

"Exactly how much magic is inside that stone as we speak?"

The young witch uttered a chuckle of disbelief and gazed at the ceiling. *How am I supposed to answer some-*

thing like that? She licked her lips and gave herself a few more seconds. "Well, I didn't get the chance to measure it."

The old man's mouth twitched in amusement, but his blue eyes bored into hers.

"But let me put it this way. That stone contains the magic stolen from hundreds of different magicals across the world over the last six months, at the very least. And that's a dangerously conservative estimate. But if we hadn't interrupted the Transference, it would have been enough magic to make two dozen members of the Black Heron Society as close to unstoppable as anyone can become. Not only that, it took two Optatus witches to divert it from them into the stone."

The Order officials all stared at her with wide eyes and not even Altrath the fairy had anything to say in argument. The blue-eyed witch inclined his head toward her, making it look very much like a bow, and spread his arms decisively. "Then it is best we remove the artifact from our vaults before it brings everything crashing down around our heads, no?"

She couldn't tell whether he was talking about a literal explosion within the Cadre Europa headquarters under the Parisian Métro system or the chaos Carmichael would unleash on the magical world if he ever managed to succeed with his demented scheme. Either way, there was no mistaking that the man might as well have told her she now had Europe's entire magical order as an ally.

SIXTEEN

"Claude, *vous ne pouvez pas être sérieux à ce sujet—*"

"We are still in the presence of guests, Altrath." The blue-eyed witch—apparently named Claude—gestured toward the Antony witches, the werewolf, and the still completely silent giant of a healer seated at the conference table. "In English, if you will."

The fairy's eye twitched as he stared at the apparent leader among all five officials. When he repeated his sentence, the words came out in a slow, barely restrained growling tone. "You cannot be serious about handing that artifact over to these...these..."

"Americans?" Greta suggested.

"Common witches?" Lily added.

Across the table, Darius snorted.

Claude gave each of the Antony witches a nod of acknowledgment. "Hmm. I am sure the two of you are only one of those things, no?"

He pushed himself up from his chair with surprising

agility and clasped his hands behind his back. The other four order officials followed suit, and Claude turned toward the space in the wall where the door still hadn't reappeared.

"Come with us, if you please. You must have many other places to be and conversations to have. Much like this one, if I am not mistaken."

"Thank you." Lily released Romeo's hand and everyone else who'd come to speak with the leaders of Cadre Europa pushed from their chairs as well, including Gabriel Mercier.

It seemed a well-established habit for the French detective to stand at the ready while everyone else entered or exited before him. Finally, he tapped his knuckle on the conference table and stepped around the chairs toward the opposite side of the room.

The door materialized in the second before Claude's hand reached the doorknob and he opened it swiftly and silently before he stepped into the next room. No one in the group said a word until Lily and Romeo reached the door last, with only Gabriel behind them.

The young witch leaned toward her werewolf companion and whispered, "Where did you find the time to practice that illumination spell?"

"I didn't," he muttered through a smirk. "But I had hours watching an Optatus witch teach it to her nine-year-old apprentice in the mountains of Chiapas."

She choked back a laugh and pressed her fist against her lips before she stepped through the doorway. The group's footsteps echoed in every direction within the massive room on the other side. The floor was a checkered pattern of cream and white marble with huge stone pillars interspersed every few yards to rise toward a vaulted ceiling that was almost too high above them to see. Hundreds of low doors, cabinets, shelves, and recessed niches lined the walls of the room on either side, although for how far, she couldn't say. She couldn't see the other side of the room, either.

Claude turned sharply to the right and stopped at one of the massively tall pillars. In front of it rested an old wooden trunk that looked like it had already been rotting by the time a Cadre Europa member had found it and brought it in. The old witch waited for everyone else to gather around, then flicked his fingers toward the lock. A pale-blue light burst within the lock, followed by a click and hollow thump as the trunk's lid popped open a few inches on old, bent hinges.

Even with only two inches of space beneath the lid, the glowing, pulsing red light emanating from inside the trunk was unmistakable. Lily lowered her head to try to get a better view. *They filled that to the brim with stacked wards.*

When the leader nodded, the witch with spiked black hair and her fellow official with the long gray ponytail stepped forward on either side of the trunk. Together, they pulled the lid up and over until it dropped back against the pillar with an echoed thump. Red light blossomed from within and cast the same hues over the glistening, checkered marble floors.

Romeo released a silent huff of amusement and shook his head.

"What?" Lily whispered.

"If we opened that trunk a few days ago, I'd either have to stuff my face with wolfsbane or be laid out flat on the floor by now."

"Yeah, it's definitely a ton of magic."

"Way more than that, Lil. I might not be allergic to magic anymore, but I can still smell it." His eyes were wide, reflecting the deep red glow of the vast quantity of magic that filled the trunk.

So many wards simply to keep a tiny stone secured. And they wouldn't be anywhere near enough if it decided to quit playing nice.

The two witches extended both hands toward the open trunk and chanted a spell together in French. Silver and red light illuminated at their fingertips and streamed in undulating ribbons toward the glowing wards. Lily hadn't seen wards unraveled quite like that before, and she had to admit it was impressive.

On the other side of her mother, Gabriel glanced at Darius' huge, bearded face—the healer stood at least a full foot taller than the French detective—and narrowed his eyes. "You were very quiet during our meeting, Mr. Balsur. I am curious as to why you came with us at all."

In response, the man nodded at the open trunk and the French witches working to release it from their heightened magical security wards. "I'm here in case someone does something stupid with that rock and I have to clean up a few messes."

The detective shook his head. "I can assure you this will not happen. Honestly, I am surprised that anyone would feel the need to bring their own hired muscle. Tell me, does your job require you to actually be...physical with these so-called messes, or is it purely for the purpose of intimidation?"

The bearded witch grunted and his face settled into a scowl.

"Neither."

"I don't understand."

On the other side of Gabriel, Greta leaned toward him with a conspiratorial grin and muttered, "He is one of the best healers I've ever known."

For the first time, the detective didn't manage to hide his surprise. "Truly?"

She raised an eyebrow and nodded slowly.

Darius finally turned away from the trunk to look at both his friend and the Frenchman. "Mostly, I'm here because she took my hooch."

"Your what?"

The woman mimed drinking out of a bottle before she turned her smile toward the trunk. Gabriel stared blankly at the floor a few feet in front of him and couldn't quite decide how to put all those pieces together.

Finally, the last of the red wards inside the rotting wooden chest fizzled away and vanished entirely. The room somehow seemed much darker and colder without the protective glow of so many security wards, but from where she stood, Lily saw nothing but an empty space.

Claude stepped forward and stooped to reach inside. The group held a collective breath until he straightened again and turned toward her. In both hands, he held a neon-pink fanny pack with a stripe of neon-green around it in the center.

Greta laughed before she could stop herself, then clamped a hand over her mouth.

"Uh..." Lily stared at the item being offered to her like a highly prized totem and tilted her head in confusion. "What is that?"

Gabriel put a fist to his mouth and cleared his throat. "It was the only thing I had on such short notice after your friend Mr. McClure called me."

"Are you sure you wanna get rid of that?" Romeo asked and tried not to laugh.

The detective nodded brusquely. "I haven't worn it in years. It is not a problem."

"But you have worn it."

Lily glanced at Claude's bright blue eyes, ignored the poorly restrained snickers from both Romeo and her mom, and smiled. "Thank you."

"We will all thank you when this is finished." He set it carefully into her outstretched hands.

The minute the full weight of it settled in her palms, she sucked in a quick breath and held it. It might have been wrapped in one of the more ridiculous fashion accessories from the nineties, but that didn't alter the thrumming pulse that emanated from unfathomable amounts of magic inside that single fist-sized stone.

Romeo peered over her shoulder grinned at the black straps dangling over the sides of her hands. "Is it in there?"

"Oh, yeah. This is it."

"I do not recommend trying to touch that with your bare hands," Gabriel added with a wary nod.

"Did you try to touch it?" Greta asked.

He frowned at her and looked a little insulted. "Absolutely not."

"Good." Lily released a long, careful breath and stared at the incongruous packaging that hid such a volatile and dangerous artifact. "I don't think you'd be standing here right now if you had."

"Lily." Claude studied her with that same inscrutable intensity in his blue eyes. "We agree that the crimes of this Black Heron Society must be put to rest. It is too much within Paris and now, I think, everywhere else."

"I'm glad you understand."

"Yes. Know that you have the full support of Cadre Europa in your endeavors. But I must remind you that we cannot involve ourselves or our members any more than this meeting with you today."

Her mother heaved an exasperated sigh behind her.

"Unless you successfully convince the Council of Magic that more...drastic measures need to be taken," the man added.

"Well, that was already the plan," Lily said quickly.

"Good." He glanced a little fearfully at the neon bag. "Our order has made multiple attempts over the last two years to reach out to the Council. We wished to bring their attention to the abductions and murders of our people in Paris and across France, especially since Détective Mercier came to us with his more recent updates. But for some reason, the Council does not seem interested in listening.

Not to us, at any rate. If you can gain their full support, you will also have Cadre Europa's resources at your disposal and we will help you end this."

"Thank you." She nodded and gazed at each of the five order officials who watched her and the volatile vessel of magic in her hands intently. "For your time and for meeting with us, and for..." She raised the fanny pack a little higher. "This. You'll hear from us again soon."

"I have no doubt." With a slightly tense smile, Claude nodded at her, then glanced at Gabriel. "Détective Mercier, would you be so kind as to show our friends the way out?"

"Of course." He inclined his head toward the order officials and indicated for the others to follow him across the expanse of Cadre Europa's vault which, no doubt, was full of highly dangerous magical items.

"How you doin', Sweets?" Greta sidled up to her daughter as their footsteps echoed across the marble floors.

"I'm not sure yet." Lily stared at the pink bag and the stone inside vibrated like an egg about to hatch.

"Are you set on carrying that, or..."

The young witch shot her mother an incredulous glance, then laughed dryly. "You look way too excited about this, Mom."

"There's no such thing."

"Well, don't let me stop you. Here." She handed it over and instantly felt lighter and less on edge.

"Fantastic." Greta grinned at it, then unfastened the buckle and strapped it around her waist. When she finished, she rested her hands on her hips and sauntered forward, her walk a few moves short of modeling it down a runway.

"Yeah, that's a great look for you." Lily closed her eyes but had to open them quickly so she didn't run into Darius in front of her.

Greta chuckled. "You think so?"

"For sure." Romeo nodded with a frown of mock seriousness. "You might even start a new fashion trend with equestrian riders, you know? Boots. Leggings. Weird, flowy...blouse? A neon fanny pack's gonna be a hit."

Lily elbowed him in the ribs and he flinched jokingly with a grin.

"Naw." The woman rubbed her daughter's back a few times before she put her hands on her hips again. Only then did the girl realize that it might be the only way her mother could walk without her hands actually touching the nylon and the stone inside it. "I've never been one to follow fashion trends, let alone start one. I'm perfectly happy being the only witch packing a deadly magical vessel in one of these babies. The only common witch."

A round of subdued laughter echoed from the group of friends as they followed Gabriel toward yet another door in the huge room. The detective started to turn, either to see exactly why they were being so loud or to admonish them for it, then changed his mind and merely shook his head and reached for the doorknob.

But now Cadre Europa knows they had two Optatus witches sitting down for a little chat in their conference room. We didn't even have to prove what we were once I said it. The Council of Magic definitely won't be this easy.

SEVENTEEN

The conversation died after that, and Gabriel Mercier led them out of Cadre Europa headquarters, into the underground Métro station, and up to the street again in the heart of Paris. The sky was still completely dark, the stars overheard overpowered by all the glittering lights of the city around them.

He stopped, turned toward them, and dusted his hands off. "Well. Would anyone care to join me for café? A good cognac for you, Monsieur Balsur, if you like. Huh?"

Darius actually smiled at the man, and that seemed to loosen the tightness that defined the detective's body.

"That does sound like the perfect way to end this day." Greta glanced at the city lights and took a deep breath. "But unfortunately for us, the day's not over yet. We still have work to do and we need to get this out of Paris." She gestured to the fanny pack. "Thank you, Gabriel."

The French detective looked genuinely surprised when she thrust a hand out in front of him with a grin.

"Ah...yes." He took her hand and shook it once, then quickly let go with a brief, seemingly apathetic glance at the pink bag. "My pleasure, Greta."

"It was good to see you again." Lily offered Gabriel her hand too, and the man's thin-lipped smile looked a little more genuine.

"And you. I admit, Lily, your methods confuse me more often than not, but ever since we met, I've appreciated what you are trying to do."

"Right back atcha."

The detective released her hand, then nodded at Romeo. "Monsieur Stephens. Healer Balsur."

"Thanks, Gabriel." Romeo shook the man's hand, followed by Darius very clearly trying to be extra gentle with the detective's hand in his.

Gabriel turned away from them and took a few steps toward the street. Then, he stopped and turned halfway. "Oh. And Lily, I must ask you to please not send me any other unstable magical surprises without a phone call first, if you would. My office can hardly hold itself together as it is."

She couldn't help but laugh a little. "Got it."

"Yes." The man studied them all again for a short moment before he turned and stepped off the sidewalk onto the street to quickly and effortlessly navigate through the sparse Parisian traffic with his hands in the pockets of his slacks.

"He's exactly like I thought." Greta squinted after him. "A very polite man. He could use a little night on the town to loosen him up now and then but who doesn't, huh? Come on. Back to your house on wheels, kids."

She clapped briskly and immediately returned her hands to her hips to avoid the bag as she led them back across Paris toward where they'd parked the Winnie via teleportation.

"Did you hear that, Lil?" Romeo swung his hip into hers with his hands in his pockets now too.

"What?"

"Our house."

Lily looked at him and bit her lip with a playful frown. He merely grinned. "Yeah, okay. It doesn't sound all that bad."

"Ha. Nope. Not too bad at all." The werewolf's smile faded a little when he looked at Darius' broad back in front of them. "It'll be much better when we have the place to ourselves again. How long to do you think your mom and Darius are gonna want to hang around?"

"I have no idea. But I'm fairly sure we're headed to Charleston now anyway. Do you and your dad still have that guest room at your house?"

Romeo's mouth dropped open and he took a sharp, confused breath before he closed it again. "Yeah..."

"Cool. If we want the Winnie to ourselves again, you'll probably have to give up your bedroom, too."

"You know, Lil, that's a sacrifice I'm willing to make."

She grinned. "Yeah, I thought so."

Once all four of them had piled into the Winnie again —which now felt way more than a little cramped—Greta set her to-go cup of coffee and baguette sandwich wrapped in brown paper on the kitchen counter. The group had stopped at a corner café that was still open as they decided to get something before they left Paris. She turned a few times and studied the cabinets built high on the walls.

"Okay. Please tell me that with all these updates you made to Bentley's RV, you didn't forget to add some kinda secret drawer or hidden panel or something."

Lily pretended ignorance because she had a feeling her mom was trying to very quickly mask her discomfort with the magic-injected stone hanging from her hips. "Why would we do that?"

"Lily, don't play games with me right now. I feel like I've walked with a jackhammer in this fanny pack, and I'm ready to call it a night as a vessel pack animal. Okay?"

There it is.

"All right. Chill out." She crossed the living area and shooed her mother across the kitchen toward the back before she knelt beside the table. "I have a good place to hide that right here."

It took her a little more effort than she wanted to half-pull, half-spin the giant red clay pot out from under the table once she'd manhandled it free of the depression in the floor. The leaves and stalks of their apparently immortal wolfsbane plant rustled violently as she pulled it across the kitchen. Purple flowers studded the whole plant and not a single one of them looked like it needed water or sunlight or even slightly like it had been alive for a normal floral lifespan and was ready to die and start over.

"Nice plant," Greta muttered.

"Thanks." She grunted and finally dragged the huge

pot out of the way. That done, she crawled under the table and set to work to slip her fingers in the narrow groove beside the removable panel at the base of the booth.

"We got it from a kid witch in Chiapas," Romeo added. "A witch who literally creates life with her magic. She...uh, grew it for us, I guess. It always has flowers on it that apparently never die and don't actually need anyone to keep them alive."

"Well, that was very thoughtful of her." The older woman leaned against the kitchen counter in front of the sink and raised an eyebrow at him. "Is there any particular reason she gave you highly poisonous wolfsbane?"

"Mom, we saw wolfsbane first when we met Melissa. If she knew what it does for werewolves, there's no way you don't already know too. So you can stop pretending to be surprised." Lily set the wooden panel aside and rearranged the remaining brown purses she and Romeo had collected from all Greta's clues over the last four months. One of them had opened somewhere along the way, and she stacked the scattered coins one on top of the other with a repeated clink so she could put them back where they belonged.

"Oh, fine. Spoil all the fun." Her mother chuckled and grinned at Romeo. "So, you know all about the wonders of wolfsbane then, huh?"

"Yep." He settled into the armchair behind the passenger seat and leaned his forearms on his thighs. Darius dropped onto the couch again. "I'm reasonably sure I would've been completely useless without it."

"That's not true." Lily finished stacking the gold coins

and dropped them all into the open purse. She pulled the drawstring tight again and stuffed it against the side of the opening with all the others. "You weren't useless before Melissa gave you that little baggie of her wolfsbane for the road."

"Yeah, barely."

The young witch laughed. "Okay, admittedly, things were much easier when I didn't have to babysit a magic-drunk werewolf every time we ended up with a group of magicals and a ton of spells flying around. Which happened often, actually, now that I think about it."

"Fair enough."

Darius slurped his own to-go cup of Parisian coffee and smacked his lips, still staring at what little he could see of the open cubby beneath the kitchen table. "Are those gold coins?"

"What? Oh." Lily crawled backward from under the table and sat back on her heels. "Yep. Thanks for that, Mom, by the way. They really came in handy for all kinds of different things."

"Yeah, not as much as you might think, though." Romeo scrunched his nose and folded his arms. "Who knew how hard it actually is to try buying regular stuff with gold?"

"Ah. That's the trick. You simply have to know where to go and who to barter with." Greta winked at him. "It looks like you did okay, though. I'm glad it helped."

"It definitely did." She held her hand out toward her mom. "I never thought I'd say this but hand the fanny pack over."

The woman snorted. "You got it."

She moved quickly to unfasten the buckle, then lowered the neon-pink accessory with a strap in each hand and that was how Lily took it from her. "I'm sure this'll be safe enough down here. It's not like RV's get broken into and robbed, generally, but whoever was in here while we were in Libya didn't find the hidey-hole. So that's a—"

"What?" Romeo jerked forward in the armchair.

"What?"

"You said someone was in here."

She paused with the bag dangling in front of her, then shrugged. "Yeah, but they didn't take anything so it's fine."

"Not really, Lil. That's like saying, 'Well, I didn't end up cooking those steaks we bought last night, so I guess I didn't buy them.'"

"It's always some kinda meat with you, isn't it?"

Greta chuckled. "And has been for as long as we've known him."

"Okay, those jokes would be funny if we weren't talking about someone breaking into the Winnie—wait." The werewolf frowned. "How do you know someone was in here if they didn't take anything?"

"The wardrobe was open. So was that box with the lily carved into the lid, which was also on the bed and not on the shelf." She ducked and scooted under the table again, held the fanny pack at arm's length, and tried not to bang it on the pole attached to the table's center.

"In the bedroom." Romeo ran a hand through his curls. "That's even worse—like in a creepy way now."

"Relax. It was probably a random society member who

showed up late to the party after I destroyed the Varelos. Lucky for them, 'cause it probably saved their life." Lily set her precious burden gingerly inside the cubby and took extra care to nestle it within the mostly full purses of gold coins to keep it from sliding around. Finally, she refitted the panel until it clicked into place, wiggled it to test it, and crawled out from under the table again. "So like I said, it's not a big deal. And the stone should be safe in there, at least for a little while. I don't know how much longer it has before it—"

"Explodes?" He stared at her with wide eyes.

"Or something."

"Right." He slumped against the back of the armchair and pointed at the kitchen table. "Until we decide what to do with that, no one sits in the far booth."

Darius shook his head. "I didn't plan on trying to squeeze myself in there anyway."

"Good." The werewolf nodded vigorously at the healer, then realized he was probably overreacting a little and dropped his head back against the top of the armchair. "Excellent."

"Lily, when exactly did you find the open wardrobe and that wooden box on your bed?" Greta asked.

The young witch turned toward her mother, her expression one of exasperation. "Really? I promise nothing important went missing. It's fine."

"What about anything unimportant?" The woman narrowed her eyes and searched her daughter's face.

"Not even something unimportant, Mom. I checked

and I can tell when something's not where it's supposed to be. You taught me how, remember?"

"Yes. Still..."

Lily sighed. "When we dropped out of Mabayn and I stepped into the bedroom to change my clothes, okay? That's when I noticed someone had gone through our stuff."

Greta opened her mouth to impart some other words of wisdom, but her daughter cut her off.

"I already thought about the fact that it could've been Carmichael, even before we realized the Varelos pieces were missing. But he didn't take anything and he didn't leave anything behind, either. I checked with a revealing spell. So yes, before you ask, I'm completely sure."

Her mom leaned back against the kitchen counter and raised an eyebrow. "I'm impressed, Sweets. It sounds like you thought the whole thing through."

Lily laughed. "Mom, I tracked you across the world, faked my way through insanity-by-torture, and helped you interrupt a Transference spell before we destroyed an entire fortress in the middle of the desert. Covering all my bases after someone broke into the Winnie, whoever it was, doesn't even come close."

"Oh, you're incredible at covering all your bases when there's much at stake," the woman replied. "Under some kind of immediate threat. But seeing the bigger picture all the way when everything's smooth sailing for a little while—"

"You're impressed because I can think clearly when

there's nothing wrong." She frowned and allowed herself a dry, mirthless chuckle of disbelief.

"No, I'm impressed by how far you've come without me in the last six months."

"Wow." She stared at her mother and wanted nothing more than to get out of the crowded Winnie and take a walk to cool her head. But they were in Paris and they needed to be somewhere else. "Thanks for having so much faith in me."

"Lily, you know that's not how I meant it. I always have faith in you. We wouldn't be here otherwise."

"It's fine, Mom." With a nod, she turned and headed toward the bedroom in the back instead of following the urge to leave.

"Honey, I'm still learning who you are after everything that's happened over so much time. That's all—"

"We can talk about this later." Lily reached the open bedroom door and paused long enough to add, "Let me know when you're about to teleport us to Charleston so I don't fall off the bed or anything." Without waiting for a response, she stepped inside and slid the bedroom door calmly and quietly shut behind her without turning.

She went to the bed, sat on the mattress, and flung herself onto her back with a sigh. *I forgot what it's like to be in the same room with her all day, every day. And now it's in a tiny RV that definitely isn't big enough for three people, let alone four.*

Thoroughly irritated, she closed her eyes and brushed her hair away from her forehead. *It's only for a little longer. You found her and you got her out, and that's all that matters. That and finishing this whole mess with Carmichael so I can have my personal space back.*

Out in the living area, Greta stared at the closed bedroom door.

"She'll cool off in a while," Romeo ventured with a shrug.

"I know." The witch turned to face him and smiled. "And I can't fault her for any of that. Things are a little off for all of us right now."

Darius sipped his coffee and stared at her over the rim of the plastic lid.

Greta pointed at him. "Don't give me that look, Darius. You're the only person I know who can say whatever they want without uttering a word."

The healer didn't say or do anything else but drink his to-go Parisian coffee and watch her.

With a small, dismissive laugh, she shook her head and put her hands on her hips. She looked at the giant potted wolfsbane in the middle of the kitchen and gestured toward it. "Do you want me to put this under the table for you?"

Romeo frowned. "No, that's okay. It's not like I need it anymore, so I thought I'd toss it out anyway or give it to someone who could actually use it."

"Oh, definitely don't do that." She waved dismissively and bent to push the heavy pot toward the kitchen table. "You're gonna need these gloriously deadly purple flowers for our little meeting with the Council. Whenever that turns out to be."

"Uh...nope. Hybrid werewolf with someone else's magic, remember?"

The Optatus witch chuckled and lowered the pot gently into the depression before she stood and dusted her hands off. "I wasn't talking about you using them, Romeo."

The young werewolf winced a little and sent her a sidelong glance. "Greta, please tell me you're not planning on poisoning a council member if things don't go our way. Or more than one council member."

She looked at him in surprise. "Of course not. The thought never even crossed my mind. But I like the way you think."

EIGHTEEN

In a crumbling neighborhood in Kingston, Jamaica, Carmichael opened the passenger door and stepped out of the Honda CRV one of his members here had donated for his use. After all the time he'd spent focused on completing the circle with both Greta and Lily Antony's blood for his Transference spell and the trouble the rebel contingent of his own Black Heron Society members had stirred up without orders or direction, he'd quickly realized the unintended usefulness of these rebel mutants. None of them had turned against him, per se, nor had they had word of the short, brutal battle outside the warded walls of the High Seat—or that their leader had ordered the deaths of over a dozen of his own followers.

They weren't really my followers when they fought each other to take Lily for their own magical gain first, were they?

Either way, the low-level members who'd known of his plan with the Transference spell and that he'd waited for Lily Antony to complete the circle still fully believed that he acted in their best interest. All it had taken was another massive text sent to those members scattered across the globe who remained truly loyal to him and the cause.

Change of plans for now. We will embrace the unstable faction among our members until we are no longer in need of additional support. Expect a gathering in Kingston in forty-eight hours.

The rebellious mutant members had offered him whatever he requested without any hesitation. This was, he knew, with the expectation that they would be rewarded, even if it was with the slightest crumbs left from his successful Transference spell still yet to come. They would not, of course, but he was careful not to dispel their assumptions.

The driver's door of the Honda opened and Ingrid stepped out onto the street. Her door shut with a soft click, and he waited until she stepped onto the sidewalk beside him.

"That was Devara," the necromancer muttered. "She's gathered over a dozen of her own to meet with the others tonight."

"Good. Then we'll have ourselves a little rally."

"Honestly, Carmichael, I don't trust any of them." She jerked the hem of the dark-maroon blouse a warlock-witch hybrid who'd happened to be her own size—with a few inches to spare—had lent her. The navy-blue pencil skirt was rather too business casual for her liking, but she'd found a pair of knee-high boots with stiletto heels in the same maroon color, and the outfit somehow managed to look like it wasn't cobbled together from three different closets. "Seeing what they've done to themselves with a few botched spells is enough. You know I'll follow you to the end of this as I always have. But I'd be doing you a disservice if I didn't say what's on my mind."

Carmichael brushed the sleeves of his smoking jacket and stared at the duplex in front of them on the other side of the gravel drive. "Then say it."

The necromancer nodded. "I don't think they'll be able to handle themselves after the Transference. If it were up to me, when it's finished, I wouldn't give them anything."

The man cast his only remaining necromancer—now at the top of his most loyal followers who still remained—a sidelong glance from his one good eye. "You've been with me for a long time, Ingrid. I'm inclined to think that's because you and I have always been of the same ideology with the same cautionary outlook."

She smirked. "I'm glad you agree."

"We'll use our less-competent members to achieve what the Transference requires. When it's finished, you'll be happy to know I don't plan to give them anything at all." He smiled and raised an eyebrow at his necromancer. "Since it's not up to you."

She grinned. "Well, then. Don't let me stop you."

"Never." He turned his attention to the duplex and smoothed his already slicked-back hair. Ingrid remained beside him but a few paces back. *It's always nice when the others know their place.*

The five-foot-tall chain-link fence at the end of the gravel drive clinked and squealed when he raised the latch and pushed the gate open. Dry brown grass grew haphazardly across the unkempt front yard, and while the garden bed in front of the porch was studded with pink, white, and yellow flowers, they bloomed on tall, wild crops of invasive weeds. Half the gutter had come loose from the front of the house and now hung lopsided and twisted from the edge of the roof. The second poorly built wooden step to the cement block of a porch wobbled dangerously beneath his shoe, but he corrected his balance and continued to the top.

The screen door in front of the solid front door had two giant slashes through the screen itself and the corner of one tear dangled toward the porch. The woman joined him on the stoop and gazed at the precarious gutter. "It looks like the augur could use a maintenance crew."

"Or she's already seen a reason not to bother with any of it." Carmichael pulled the screen door open and rapped gently on the solid wood behind it. A few chips of dull, dirty-white paint flaked away beneath his knuckles.

"Yes. I'm sure she has many more important ways to spend her time and energy." The necromancer's upper lip twitched toward her nose in distaste.

"You've made your opinion of augurs quite clear, Ingrid. But now would be the time to keep those opinions to yourself until we're finished." The Black Heron's leader stared ahead at the front door, but he could feel the necromancer's bottled tension as she closed her mouth and resigned herself to silence. *Maybe I've made her feel too comfortable. It doesn't matter. She won't question me again after this.*

When no one came to open the door, he rapped again

on the peeling wood. His knock was interrupted by the squeak of the doorknob twisting sharply before the door jerked away from his hand. The young woman on the other side of it—she couldn't have been much older than seventeen or eighteen—peered cautiously around the edge and squinted against the late-afternoon light.

She studied the two relatively well-dressed magicals on the front stoop for a moment before she raised her chin in a slightly challenging gesture. "What do you want?"

"I'm here to see Amoy," Carmichael replied. "I've been told this was a good time."

The girl pressed her lips together and studied Ingrid critically. "What does she want?"

"To bear witness." He nodded to reassure her. "That's all."

"Right. Come on, then." The girl pulled the door all the way and held it open for her two guests.

The acrid scent of mildew, citrus, and frankincense assaulted them as soon as they stepped into the duplex's dark, dusty living room. The young woman closed the front door again, sniffed, and stepped forward toward the kitchen in the back. "Down the hall. Last door on the left."

He gazed around the living room, which held more half-opened boxes than furniture. A sitcom played on the twenty-five-inch TV in front of the drawn living room curtains, the volume turned down so low it was almost inaudible. Water dripped every two seconds from what he assumed was the tap at the kitchen sink. A cat mewled and rubbed against his pant leg.

"Thank you." The man moved quickly toward the

hallway on his right and ignored the short, angry yowl of the feline robbed so quickly of its new scratching post. Ingrid followed closely behind him, and the girl slumped onto the crooked couch in the living room to watch her show.

The first door on the right obviously led to the teenager's bedroom—as evidenced by the unmade bed, jeans, t-shirts, and underwear flung everywhere, and a few pictures of the girl herself with friends. He didn't bother to glance at the bathroom on his left, which he didn't intend to use anyway, and the last door on the right was closed. He turned to the left and a thickening wall of gray-blue smoke that drifted slowly through the open doorway. *There's the frankincense to cover it all. She must burn it twenty-four-seven.*

With a quick nod, he stepped through the entrance. Something thick and cold brushed against his head, which immediately made him duck. He looked up quickly and grimaced at the thick, brown, hairy-looking vines that dangled from the ceiling, which was completely invisible beyond the haze of smoke that had gathered above him. Something crunched beneath his next step, and he lifted his shoe to find the tiny skeleton of a newt or gecko crushed against the floor. The bones of two other creatures lay scattered against the wall to his right.

Nothing ever changes with these augurs. She simply traded a cave in the sixteenth century for an outdated duplex in the twenty-first.

From within the smokey haze came the slurp and gulp

of someone drinking, the ping and scrape of metal striking metal, and a single low, dry cough.

"Hello, Oliver." The augur's voice was like sandpaper on tree bark, although the words were loud enough and perfectly clear.

Carmichael paused and straightened where he stood. He took another slow step in the direction of the voice. "I'm sorry. I think you're mistaken."

"We both know that's not true."

He took a deep breath. "My name is Carmichael Cantus."

A low, wheezing chuckle followed. "If you say so."

As he moved farther into the room, he glanced briefly over his shoulder toward where he expected to see Ingrid. Instead, the smoke had filled the space between them. The necromancer remained silent but he heard the slow, soft click of her stiletto boots across the hardwood floor behind him.

"Tell me, then, Carmichael. What brings you to an augur's doorstep?"

He slid one foot slowly in front of the other now, trying to still be discrete in his probing through the smoke. *The last thing I need is to fall onto a ritual knife.* "I expected you to already know why I'm here."

"Oh, I do. Yes. But you've already proven yourself so skilled at spinning tales. I thought I'd give you another opportunity to entertain me with your half-cocked fantasies."

She's testing me. But she won't find any fault lines. Not today. Carmichael stopped and drew his shoulders back as he watched the thick smoke swirl around the room with walls he couldn't see. "No fantasies. I have the Varelos in my possession—"

"Split in two, dead and dull and useless." This time, the owner of the voice was much closer.

"Yes."

The wheezing cackle rose again. "And you want me to help you put those pieces together again for a great and glorious resolution—to finally fulfill everything you've worked so hard to achieve."

That's rather simplistic. He raised his chin. "Yes."

"Yes, something like that." A muted, whispering clap of aged hands echoed and the smoke immediately in front of him scattered toward either side of the room.

Behind the cleared smoke sat a wizened old crone in a stained-gray terrycloth robe. The woman all but disappeared within the material draped around her body, the effect only enhanced by at least five different scarves she'd wound around her head. They might have once been bright and colorful but had now all washed out to the same stained, muted gray as the robe. The woman's face was the same color gray as her odd choice of clothing, and milky, yellowed eyes stared blindly at him. The smell of mildew was ten times stronger.

"Not what you expected, eh?" The augur tittered from where she sat on the bedroom floor, of all places, lounging upon strategically stacked pillows. "I can feel you staring at me, son. Sit."

It was more command than invitation, and Carmichael obeyed without hesitation. He breathed through his mouth instead of his nose and lowered himself to his knees in front of the short breakfast tray designed to deliver breakfast in bed—not on the floor. He sat back on his heels and waited for her to speak. Instead, all he received was a wide, toothless black hole of a grin. He thought he saw something red inside the woman's mouth but had no interest in double-checking.

Amoy merely tittered again on her pillows.

He decided to force the conversation forward instead of waiting. "Is that something you can do?"

"Oh, no." The augur tipped her head back and studied something above their heads with blind eyes. "I have no interest in taking on that role. You will be the one to breathe new life into the Varelos."

"So it is possible." His one good eye glinted in the bedroom light muted by so much smoke and dank, aged fumes.

"Anything is possible. As long as one is willing to pay the price of that possibility." Amoy extended a frail hand crippled by arthritis. Her upturned palm remained incredibly steady over the breakfast tray between them.

Carmichael removed the new switchblade from the inside pocket of his smoking jacket. All his ceremonial tools had been lost to him in the fall of the High Seat, so he'd been forced to purchase a few extra things on his way there. *Only the purpose matters and this blade is equally as sharp.*

The augur gave him another toothless, drool-covered grin when he flicked the switchblade open. He pressed the edge into his palm and made a quick, precise slice. The sharp, hissing inhale came not from him but the augur herself as he raised his bleeding hand over the old crone's open palm and squeezed his fist. Blood dripped quickly into Amoy's hand, and he counted each of them. Only five —no more and no less—before he lowered his fist into his lap.

The augur stared him with sightless eyes, still grinning, and waved her palm over the breakfast tray. "And..."

Carmichael pressed his lips together but didn't argue. *Augurs and their disgusting payments.*

He leaned over the crone's open hand and spat into the small pool of his own blood already gathered there. The second he finished, Amoy retracted her gnarled hand and brought it to her mouth to lick his payment like a starving dog lapping at someone else's spilled trash. He fought not to let his disgust show.

"Ah, yes." The augur cackled, her mouth smeared with blood and foam. "Yes! I have exactly what you need."

"Then tell me."

"You are so impatient. Are you not curious as to what reviving the Varelos will cost you?"

He pressed his lips together in irritation. "I already paid you."

"You did." Amoy's head bobbed up and down over the folds of the stained robe. "But the Varelos requires payment as well. A sacrifice is always necessary for this kind of work, especially when it involves something with that much power in one person's hand."

"I have no problem with sacrifices," Carmichael

replied. "And I haven't come this far to be warned away from the cost. Whatever the cost, augur, I will pay it."

She uttered another wheezing laugh. "Of course you will. There is always a fine line between certainty and stupidity."

The crone reached slowly toward a tarnished silver jewelry box nestled within her pile of pillows. The lid creaked when it opened, and she drew out two items before she set them each on the breakfast tray. A short, thick bone clacked against the wooden tray and beside it, she spread a strip of aged and yellowed parchment. It was completely blank until she pressed one gnarled fingertip to the paper. A dull, dirty-brown light blossomed beneath her skin and only a few lines of rust-colored script appeared. She leaned back against the pillows and her hands vanished again within the soiled bathrobe. "A runic element and a spell to do what you so desperately want."

"Thank you." He snatched the bone and the parchment and shoved them into the inside pocket of his smoking jacket. When they were secure, he nodded brusquely. "Until next time."

The augur wheezed another laugh. "If you say so."

He pushed himself off his knees, stood, and turned toward Ingrid with a curt nod.

"Only do this when you are fully prepared to finish what you started, Oliver," the crone said behind him. "And know that once you reanimate the Varelos, you will never be able to use it again."

Carmichael blinked and forced himself to reply calmly. "My name is—"

"It does not matter who you pretend to be or which name you think sounds prettiest," the augur retorted. "It will matter even less once you bring the life back into that ancient artifact. Now get out."

The leader of the Black Heron Society nodded at the crone once more, then turned quickly on his heel to leave the room. He caught glimpses of Ingrid's maroon blouse through the smoke, which now thickened around them once more. In moments, they were out in the hall and moved swiftly through the dimly lit, stifling duplex toward the exit.

The teenager in the living room didn't even look up from the TV as Ingrid opened the front door and held it for him to step through. He walked swiftly outside, across the narrow cement stoop, and down the rotting wooden planks toward the gravel drive and the CRV parked on the other side of the fence.

By the time his necromancer reached the car, he was already in the passenger seat. Ingrid slipped behind the wheel, started the engine, and paused to look at her boss. "Where are we going now?"

"To meet with the others." He pressed his hand against the small weight of the bone and spell parchment in his jacket pocket. "It's time to show them we're serious about finishing this."

She eyed his jacket, then glanced briefly into the back seat at the two halves of the Varelos' copper rod nestled on the upholstery. "Do you have everything you need?"

"Now, yes. We have to plan this right, Ingrid. That old

bottom-feeder deals in riddles and half-truths but she's not as hard to interpret as she likes to think."

The woman nodded. "You can only use that spell and the Varelos once."

Carmichael gave her a sidelong glance and the corner of his mouth twitched. "So we're still on the same page, Ingrid. It's a good thing you pulled yourself out from under all that rubble, huh?"

Ingrid snorted and shifted into drive. "Probably."

"Let's go." He leaned his head against the headrest and stared through the windshield as his second in command drove them out of the neighborhood. *If I had anyone else with me, I'd tell them to keep their mouth shut about the augur. But I got lucky with Ingrid.*

The leader of the Black Heron Society—or what was left of it, at any rate—was sure his luck was about to change completely. All his plans would come to fruition thanks to a dark augur's spell and the most powerful magical weapon in history resting in the back seat.

NINETEEN

The bedroom door slid open, and Romeo stepped into the bedroom before he pulled it shut again. Lily sat up on the bed to see his cautious smile. "Hey, Lil. I—"

"Get ready, kids. We're heading out in five!" Greta's voice drifted toward them from the Winnie's living area.

He shook his head. "Huh. It's a good thing I didn't come here to tell you that."

She sighed heavily and brushed her hair away from her face as he came to sit next to her on the comforter. "I'm sorry about...that. I guess I simply forgot what it's like to be around her all the time without any breaks."

"Yeah, months of driving around the world in an RV with your favorite person tends to do that." He caught her hand and laced their fingers together. "I still live with my dad too, remember? And it's definitely not all bad jokes and beers and good times every single day."

The image the words conjured made the young witch laugh. "I honestly can't picture your dad being nearly as—"

A blinding silver light burst through the walls toward them and blocked out everything else. All the air squeezed out of her lungs, and for a few seconds, she couldn't even feel Romeo's hand in hers. When the light blinked out with a little pop, she gasped in breathlessness and relief.

Romeo slid off the edge of the bed and landed with a thud on the floor. His hand tugged out of hers and with a groan, he curled his knees to his chest and rested his head against the mattress.

"She said, 'leaving in five,'" Lily protested and still tried to catch her breath. "That implies minutes, not seconds. I'm sure that's universal."

"Who does that?" The werewolf groaned again.

"Are you okay?" She closed her eyes to try to settle her own small bout of nausea and fumbled for his hand. When she located it, she squeezed it and he returned the gesture almost immediately.

"Yeah, I'm good. I guess she wasn't wrong when she said it gets easier the more we make the jump."

Lily opened her eyes and frowned at him. "Don't tell her that."

Together, they stood from the bed and stepped out of the bedroom. She had to support his weight a little until they made it through the sliding door into the narrow hallway. He managed to steady himself with a hand on either wall until he could walk without swaying.

In the center of the living area, Greta turned toward them with a grin but it faded when she saw the young couple clearly. "Wow. I didn't think it was possible for either of you to look worse every time I teleport us some-where. I guess I was wrong."

"It's only the lack of warning, Mom," she muttered.

"I did warn you."

Romeo swallowed thickly. "'Leaving in five' usually means five minutes, not seconds."

Still seated on the couch, Darius shifted his weight and cleared his throat.

Greta turned toward the massive healer and pointed. "Don't say anything. And get up, why don'tcha? This is our last stop before we drive around in this thing. I hope."

"You hope?" The werewolf squinted against the early-afternoon sun that streamed through the RV's windshield.

"I'm kidding." The woman waved a dismissive hand and brushed past them both toward the Winnie's side door. "Obviously."

"Obviously. Where are we this time?"

"Can't you smell it?"

Still completely disoriented, the couple exchanged a confused glance.

"Come on, kids. We're home." Greta grinned and opened the side door, then thought better of it and shut it again. "Actually, I probably shouldn't step outside right now. That's a fairly incredible feat for a dead woman."

"Right." Lily exhaled a slow breath, moved toward the door, and placed a gentle hand on her mom's shoulder for a few seconds before she walked down the two stairs. "What do you need us to do?"

"Bring him inside and we can all have a little chat together, okay?" She winked at her daughter and Lily and

Romeo stepped out into the hot humidity of a September morning in Charleston, South Carolina.

"Who are we bringing in?" he muttered. The side door clicked shut behind him.

She was about to shrug and say they'd find out when they got there but she looked at the long, neatly kept row house on King Street painted a pastel mint-green. Despite her head still spinning a little from so many teleportations in under twelve hours, she couldn't help but smile.

"Bentley."

"Oh. Yeah, that's a good first stop."

They walked quickly up the cement walkway toward the front door on the long porch, and the door opened almost before she had finished knocking. Bentley McClure stared at them with wide eyes behind his black-and-silver-rimmed designer glasses. The man's mouth opened and closed soundlessly, and the young witch gave him a reassuring smile. "Hi, Bentley."

"Well, I'll be..." His gaze darted around his front driveway and the not-so-busy side street where he lived. "Come inside, both of you. Come in."

"We kinda prefer the fresh air, actually," the werewolf hedged, his hands shoved into his pockets.

"And we have a few things to show you first." She motioned for her mom's long-time friend to step out onto his front porch.

For a few seconds, the man looked at them both like they'd each grown an extra arm or another pair of eyes. Then, he stumbled forward and fell against her to wrap her in a tight embrace. "I had no idea you'd be back so soon."

"Neither did we." The young witch laughed and hugged him in return. "We had a little help making the return trip much faster than the route we took on the way out."

"I'll say." With a surprised, confused chuckle, Bentley released her, studied her intently, then nodded at her companion. "It's good to see you too, son."

"You too." Romeo shook the accountant's hand and gestured toward the Winnie parked at the curb. "You'll definitely wanna see this."

"My God." The man stepped forward off the porch and gaped at the RV with a few charred dents and dings along the side. In all fairness, most of the upgrades the young couple had made were completely unnoticeable from the outside. "Lily, when I gave you this RV, it was under the assumption that it was exactly that. A gift. After everything you two have been through, you're worried about bringing the Winnebago to my front door?"

"Not quite." She looped her arm through his—he wore a loose, short-sleeved t-shirt and a pair of light-blue Bermuda shorts—and steered him down the walkway toward the street. "We can answer all your questions once you see this, okay?"

"Sure."

They stopped and waited for Romeo to pull the side door open. She finally remembered that not everyone she knew had been through the same time warp as she had—who knew how many days locked away in a torture cell, two days in Mabayn and maybe an hour and a half in this world, and then three of Greta's rusty teleportation spells. "What day is it?"

"What..." Bentley frowned at her. "It's Saturday."

"Good."

"Why?"

Lily shrugged. "I wanted to make sure I didn't have to worry about you being at home and not at your office."

The werewolf shook his head and held the door open. "We have the worst jetlag ever."

When the accountant gave her a confused, slightly disturbed frown, she simply gestured for him to enter the Winnie. "We'll explain that later too."

Even after only a few minutes under Charleston's hot, bright sun, the Winnie's living area seemed much darker. *All the better to surprise him, I guess. If Mom jumps out and shouts, 'Surprise,' he's gonna have a heart attack.*

Fortunately, Greta was perfectly aware of how important it was to be gentle, especially with an old friend who really had no idea what he was walking into. Bentley stared, his mouth agape, at the new bamboo flooring instead of carpet. His gaze settled on Darius' rather large pair of boots in front of the couch. The healer gave the newcomer a slow nod to which he responded politely. Finally, the man looked around and saw Greta Antony standing beside the booth of the kitchen table. "No..."

She grinned. "Oh, yes."

"You—" He whirled to gape at Lily, then couldn't make up his mind about which Antony witch required more of his attention. "She was right."

"If you're talking about Lily, then yes. Of course she

was." With a playful shrug, Greta laughed. "Otherwise, I can't confirm or deny who you're—"

"Ha! You were right!" This time, the man whipped toward Lily and spread his arms wide. "I'll tell you right now, Lily, the next time you come to me with something no one else believes, I'll be behind you one-hundred-percent."

The young witch fisted her hands on her hips. "I thought you already were."

"Well...you can't fault me for having my doubts, however small they were." He turned to Greta and laughed again.

"You didn't believe her, huh?" The woman narrowed her eyes. "I thought I knew how to choose my friends better than that."

"I believed her enough to send her on her way with my RV and my blessing." The two old friends stared at each other so intently that Lily started to wonder what had gone wrong and how she'd missed it.

She tried to think of some way to make it right when her mother laughed and crossed the Winnie's living area with open arms. "You did exactly what needed to be done."

Bentley's spine cracked a little under the strength of her embrace, but he laughed along with her. They pulled apart, and the man quickly adjusted his crooked glasses and blinked back tears and surprise and disbelief. He held her by the shoulders and sniffed. "You can't possibly know how good it is to see you here right now, Margaret."

"Well, you're using my full name so it must be high up there."

"Ha." He released her and took a few steps back before he cleared his throat. Then, he smoothed the front of his t-shirt—which made him look much more unsure of himself than when he did it in a suit—and turned to Lily again. "You did it. Both of you. You actually found her and brought her back."

"I told you we would." Her cheeks already ached from grinning. It was impossible not to when she stood there and watched this reunion. "And we couldn't have asked for a better person to have on our side. I'm really glad you actually called the numbers I gave you."

"Of course, Lily." He sniffed and dabbed the corners of his crinkling eyes with his fingertips. "What else would I have done after everything you told me? Speaking of phone calls, is there a reason you didn't let me know you were already on your way home? I would have been more prepared...and less..." He shrugged.

"Speechless?" Greta nodded. "We had to make a few stops first. And let's say the first few were far more unpredictable than even I'm comfortable with."

Still seated on the couch, Darius snorted. "I assume that was before you came to badger me out of my own apartment."

Bentley took a startled step, having completely forgotten the giant man who virtually took up the entire couch. "I'm sorry. You...oh. You must be Darius."

"It's good to meet you face to face, Mr. McClure."

"No, no. Don't get up. I imagine you're much more comfortable where you are than standing under this roof." He leaned forward to shake the healer's hand and the two men shared a brief chuckle at Darius' expense. The accountant rubbed his palms against the sides of his Bermuda shorts and his gaze drifted around the returned friends. "I simply... I don't know what to say."

"You'll have to think of something," Greta replied. Her smile faded a little and her gaze intensified. "And I hope a few days is enough notice for you to be far more prepared because we still need your help."

The man's dark eyebrows drew together. "With—oh. Yes, of course. I can pull a few strings. Trust me, it won't be hard to reverse your death certificate now that you're here in the flesh. Because you're obviously not dead—"

"No, Bentley. Bringing me back from the dead needs to hold off a little longer. It's still not safe to make that announcement to the whole world yet."

He stared at her in obvious confusion. "And why's that?"

"We got her out," Lily added, "but the Black Heron isn't gonna stop their insane plans with the Transference spell until we stop Carmichael from getting back on his feet again."

Her mom's friend mouthed the name of the Black Heron's leader, then sent Greta a wary look.

"Yeah, I know." She shrugged. "Carmichael."

"This is..." Bentley rubbed a hand over his dark hair—receding a little at the temples—and shook his head. "Of course I'll help you. Whatever you need. But I'm not sure how much I can offer when it comes to stopping dark magic—"

"Oh, we'll handle that part. Don't worry." Lily's

mother rested a hand on the man's shoulder and nodded. "We need your powers of persuasion and impeccable timing."

He waited with a slightly wary expression, and when she remained silent, he gestured impatiently. "Just say it already."

Greta gave him a tight-lipped smile that was neither reassuring nor entirely amused. "We need you to set up a meeting with the Council."

"Well, that certainly won't be hard. I imagine they'll be more than happy to meet with Margaret Antony come back from the dead after six months."

"Yeah…" She wrinkled her nose and shook her head regretfully. "Without telling them I'm alive and back in the States."

"And why the hell not?" The question burst out of him as a sharp, startled shout.

Lily rubbed her fingers over her mouth, watching for the signal from either of them that meant she needed to step in and diffuse things herself. But instead of retaliating to the not entirely unwarranted outburst, her mother simply sighed and spread her arms in a gesture that expressed patience at the fact that she had to explain herself.

"Because, Bentley, if we want even the slightest chance of getting the Council on our side—of getting them to listen—we need to catch them with their pants down."

Romeo choked on a laugh and rubbed the back of his neck while he smirked at the floor.

The woman ignored him. "You know that the only way

to bring them down off their high horse is to hit them where it hurts. Right in their ignorance."

Licking his lips, Bentley thrust both hands into the pockets of his shorts and raised an eyebrow. "Oh, I remember."

TWENTY

Greta gave Bentley the short version of their story and brief instructions for setting up their meeting with the Council of Magic, including the terms of keeping her return from the dead a secret for a little longer. Half an hour later, after saying their goodbyes and sending a slightly baffled but determined man into his house, the travelers headed off once more. This time, they avoided the rough transportation spells and Romeo got behind the wheel to drive them across Charleston.

"Do you really think he can make it happen?" Lily asked as she twisted in the passenger seat to glance at her mom in the armchair behind her.

"Of course he can make it happen, Sweets. He's Bentley McClure." The woman chuckled. "He may seem like a head-down pencil-pusher and he's missing the pocket protector, but that man has more influence up his sleeve than most people I know. He's merely incredibly conservative about when to actually bring out the big guns and use them."

The werewolf tightened his hands on the steering wheel as he eased the Winnie around a wide turn onto Highway 17. "He used to work for the Council specifically, didn't he?"

After a moment of complete astonishment, she uttered a sharp laugh of surprise. "How in the world did you find out something like that?"

"He told me the first time I met him." He shrugged. "That he spent a good deal of his time tracking werewolves before you changed his mind about us."

The woman leaned back in the armchair and crossed one leg over the other. "I'm actually impressed."

He snorted. "Hey, thanks a lot."

"Lily, my love, you and this werewolf with magic are better matched than I would have guessed."

Despite feeling obliged to move the subject away from their relationship, Lily still couldn't resist a grin. She glanced at him and noticed him hiding a smirk too. "Come on, Mom."

"Well, it's true. You know, I really hoped you'd choose to bring someone along with you when you finally decided to start following all my clues, Sweets. You couldn't have picked a better person."

Romeo looked at Lily for a second and winked. "Yeah, we already knew that too."

Greta laughed and brushed her hair away from her face. "Yes. Bentley used to work for the Council. As an independent contractor, if I remember, and he was very good at what he did. He quit after he met your dad, Romeo, and put all his attention into his work as an accountant and financial advisor. So in a way, you might also say he turned over a new leaf for you. For both of you."

"Man." He shook his head and tried to process all that without completely tuning out the traffic on 17. "An ex-werewolf-bounty-hunter who gave Lily an RV is the one guy with enough pull to get us into a meeting with the Council."

"Bounty hunter? That's a little simplistic. Bentley was a Council-appointed Sentinel."

"Oh, yeah?" He glanced quickly over his shoulder but realized he couldn't stare at her the way he wanted to and focus on driving at the same time. "How are they different?"

Lily went ahead and stared for him. She turned to watch her mom trying to come up with a good explanation that didn't paint her long-time friend in a completely unflattering light.

Greta scrunched her nose and looked for her answers in the Winnie's ceiling. "The name, I guess. That would be the only difference. So well-played, Mr. Stephens."

"Yeah, I've learned a thing or two in the last seven years since you saw me last." He uttered a wry chuckle. "It doesn't mean I hold anything against the guy. He didn't even flinch when Lily and I sat down with him at that fancy restaurant—"

"Fancy restaurant, huh?"

Lily turned toward her mom again and muttered, "McCrady's."

"Oh, good choice."

"And he was honest from the beginning about what he used to do," Romeo finished. "My dad remembered meeting him, and Bentley obviously did everything Lily asked him to when she made a few calls from the road."

"That's how they got you on board, isn't it?" Greta pointed at Darius.

The healer folded his arms on the couch and tilted his chin at her. "Bentley called me and filled in the missing pieces. You're the one who took my hooch."

"And look how much fun you're having." Laughing again, the woman gestured enthusiastically and leaned back in the armchair. "When this is all over, Darius, I will take you to any bar in this city and foot all your drinks for the whole night. You have my word."

For a few seconds, the bearded giant studied her with glistening eyes. Then, he shrugged. "It's as good a start as any, I guess."

"Yeah, I thought so."

The Winnie fell silent for the next five minutes while Romeo navigated the RV across town and toward Ashley Avenue. When they reached the neighborhood, Greta slid out of the armchair and crept forward in a crouch. With a hand on the back of each front seat, she peered through the windshield at the houses that lined the street, the oaks that spread their branches over rooftops, and the not quite autumn colors bursting in well-tended flowerbeds. "Wow."

Lily joined her in studying the street she'd grown up on. "It's a little weird, right?"

"We moved only twenty minutes away and I haven't

been back here in seven years." Her mother shook her head slowly, her eyes wide above a small, nostalgic smile. "Talk about a blast from the past."

"Yeah, well, the past is much more recent for me," the werewolf muttered. "I still haven't officially moved out yet."

"Is that right?" Greta grinned at his profile. "You know, I'm sure we've all thought about it on our own over the last few hours or so, but it wouldn't hurt to make sure we're all operating under the same assumptions, here."

Lily rubbed her forehead. "Please don't tell me you're bringing up bad news this last-minute."

"Not bad news at all, Sweets. I only want to be doubly sure we're going about this the right way. The Julian Stephens I know isn't easily surprised, worried, or over-whelmed by very much at all. So, Romeo, how much has that changed in the last few years?"

"Not much." The Winnie drew up to the curb in front of the house he shared with his dad and he pulled the gearshift into park. "He was laid back the last time I called him. Which, okay, was admittedly much longer ago than it should have been. He, uh...he thinks Lily and I went for an extended road trip slash camping tour across the country."

"Camping." The woman stared at the young werewolf and pursed her lips, unable to decide whether or not she wanted to laugh at that. "That's the story you went with, huh?"

"It's believable." Lily shrugged. "Mostly."

"For the two of you to reunite again after so long and take a four-month road trip down memory lane together?

Sure. What I want to know is why neither of you told him the truth."

"Mom, Julian thought you were dead like everyone else did."

"So did Bentley, and you changed his mind pretty darn quick."

The girl sighed. "Bentley's not a werewolf."

"Without a pack," Romeo added.

"Right. And after whatever Black Heron idiot tried to murder me downtown the day I stopped here to ask for Romeo's help..." The young witch puffed a sigh. "I wasn't about to bring Julian into the equation and unload my problems onto him."

"We decided it was the best thing to not let anyone know what we were doing unless we totally had to. Bentley agreed with that too."

"Huh." Greta gazed from her daughter to the young werewolf she'd known for most of his life. "Well, I guess now's as good a time as any to fill the man in on everything that's happened in those months. Including the fact that neither of you ever really believed I was dead."

"Man." Romeo unbuckled his seatbelt and ran a hand through his dark curls with a sigh. "We really did come full circle, didn't we?"

"That simply means you're getting the job done right." The woman winked at him, pushed to her feet, and motioned toward the door. "I'd like to get out of this Adventuremobile for the rest of the day if that's all right with you."

Lily unbuckled her seatbelt and stood to face her mom.

"I'd have no problem with it, except for the fact that we can't let anyone see you yet. Especially not here outside Romeo's house."

"Come on, Sweets. Don't tell me you haven't already come up with a solution for that insignificant setback."

The young witch bit back a laugh. "Nope. I definitely won't tell you that. I have it covered."

"That's my girl." Greta fluffed out the loose white blouse tucked into her tight riding leggings, shrugged, and put her hands on her hips. "I'm ready when you are."

"Great." Lily turned to look through the windshield at the quiet, mostly empty street of the neighborhood she grew up in. "The coast looks clear to me."

"You're going with the purple bubble again, aren't you?" Romeo stood too and followed her toward the Winnie's side door.

Her mother snorted. "Is that what you call it now?"

"That's what I call it," he told her cheekily.

"Well, let me tell you something, Mr. Hybrid-Wolf Stephens." Her mother actually shot him the guns with both hands, and Lily closed her eyes to make it that much easier to ignore. "You may not have paid much attention to the names of spells and the mechanics of how they're cast —although I will say that illumination orb with Cadre Europa was unexpectedly impressive for only having magic a few days."

"Uh...thanks."

"But the point is you don't really have an excuse not to pay attention anymore. Got it? That purple bubble is on the list of things you now have the ability to learn and perform. It's time to change your thinking." She pointed to the side of her head and slowly nodded, her eyes wide.

"Okay..." Romeo glanced uncertainly at Lily, but she was already lifting the handle of the Winnie's side door. "Thanks for the advice."

"Anytime. Now go learn something and let me know when I can step out of this box on wheels without anyone seeing me."

The couple stepped quickly out of the RV and shut the side door behind them. That was when Lily finally couldn't contain herself any longer, and a sharp laugh burst from her mouth before she covered it quickly with both hands.

"Wow." The werewolf scratched the back of his head and uttered a low, confused chuckle.

"You had your first taste of Magic 101, Greta Antony style."

"I think I'm starting to understand what you meant every time you said your mom's training was a little unorthodox."

"Hey, that's nothing. Wait. If she gets another chance to crawl under your skin and lecture you about spellwork and your responsibility with it, she will. I promise." She caught his arm and gave it a reassuring squeeze. "But you're also a werewolf and you're not her kid. So count yourself lucky."

"Huh. Right." He smirked at her and stepped away from the Winnie with a sweeping gesture toward his dad's front yard. "Are you sure I can't get my training from someone I already know I vibe with a little better?"

"Are you seriously asking me to be your magical teacher right now?"

"Well, it kinda makes sense." He froze and his gaze darted away quickly before it returned to his companion's face. "Doesn't it?"

Unable to resist the temptation, she took a few more seconds to respond for effect. "Yeah, I'll think about it."

She clapped and summoned the illusion dome she'd used so many times on their trip around the world to keep everyone else from seeing exactly what she and Romeo were up to. When she drew her palms apart, the thin veil of violet film stretched between them. It spread around them and curved over both the Winnie and Julian Stephens' house. When the spell finished and the dome of violet light settled with a shimmer, the young witch nodded. "And now, all anyone's gonna see is a giant RV parked inconspicuously at the curb."

"It's not like it hasn't happened before."

Lily opened the side door where her mom already stood at the edge of the top step. "Let's go give Julian the surprise of a lifetime."

Greta chuckled and Darius stood from the couch, hunched his shoulders, and ducked his head to keep from scraping it on the roof of the RV. The woman leapt down the two stairs and onto the sidewalk. "This is new."

"What is?"

"I don't know what to expect. The man's about to think he's seen a ghost and I'm not entirely sure what that's gonna look like."

"Here's my take." Romeo gestured expansively as all

four of them moved up the cement walkway toward the Stephens' ranch-style house. "There's either gonna be a ton of yelling and pacing, or we'll get complete silence and not much else."

Greta turned toward him and quirked an eyebrow. "So which one are we hoping for?"

"Honestly? I have no idea."

TWENTY-ONE

R omeo opted to simply retrieve the key from under the front mat on the porch and unlocked the door to let them all inside. It would have been more than a little weird to knock on his own front door despite the fact that he had brought two new guests with him this time—one who was, for all intents and purposes, supposed to be dead.

He slipped the key into the pocket of his Black-Heron-issue slacks and shook his head. "I seriously need to change."

With a shrug to hide his nervousness, he pushed the front door wide and led them all into the short entryway of the house he grew up in with his dad.

"Hey, Dad," he called to eliminate any possibility of confusion. Not that Julian wouldn't be able to smell his own son. "Guess who?"

"Romeo!" His father's joyful shout came from the kitchen on their right. When the young couple stepped through the entryway, they found the man seated at the long dining room table, a pile of bills and other mail laid out in front of him. He stood abruptly from his chair and opened his arms, his eyes wide behind his tiny pair of CVS reading glasses. "Lily! Y'all are home."

"Yeah, we thought we'd come surprise you instead of calling first," she said. Before the man could say anything else, she and Romeo moved aside.

Greta stepped forward out of the short hallway, folded her arms, and leaned sideways on the wall that separated the entryway from the dining room. "How you doin', Julian?"

The middle-aged werewolf froze when he saw her and the smile faded rapidly from his lips. After a long moment of silence, he whipped the reading glasses off and held them at his side over the table as he narrowed his eyes like he didn't believe what he actually saw in his own house.

"I know what you're thinking." The woman tossed her hands into the air and eyed the ceiling. "How the hell did this, happen, right?"

The reading glasses fell onto the bills on the table, and Julian strode briskly toward the woman, his expression unreadable.

"It's okay to be angry. If I were in your shoes, I probably would be too. But I would like an opportunity to expl—"

The minute he reached her, he caught Greta's face with one hand, jerked her toward him with the other, and laid a long, fierce kiss on the woman he thought he'd never see again.

Lily and Romeo leaned away from the surprising

scene, wide-eyed and almost as speechless as the woman herself. "This was definitely not on my list of possible reactions," the werewolf muttered.

"Tell me about it." She felt like her eyes were about to pop out of her head. "This is awkward."

Finally, her mother regained her faculties and pushed the man away from her with a laugh.

"Well. You sure know how to one-up a girl's entrance."

Julian stepped back, his hands raised in surrender as he studied her intently. His mouth opened and closed in silence before he found his voice again. "Of all the... Well, I'll be damned. It's really you."

"You didn't need to kiss me to figure that one out." Greta grinned at him and patted his cheek. "It's good to see you too. You know I love you, Julian. But that's the first and last time that will ever happen."

"Yeah, I know. Sorry, I... I don't know why I did that."

"Shock and a weird reversal of grief make people do all kinds of crazy things. I promise I won't hold it against you."

A surprised laugh burst out of him before she pulled him in for a tight hug that was platonic and definitely lacking in more kisses.

"I can't believe this." He pulled away to trail his gaze over her face, then wrapped her in another crushing embrace a la Julian Stephens.

"Well, you'd better." Greta pulled away from him again, grinned, and squeezed his forearms. "I'm standing in your dining room."

"That's the most obvious part about this whole thing, woman." The man laughed and turned toward the young couple, who'd both gotten over their shock enough to not still look like they were about to crawl out of their skin. "Y'all weren't really out there campin' in the boonies for the last few months, were ya?"

Romeo stuck his hands in his pockets and raised his eyebrows. "There was...some camping in there."

"There definitely was," Lily added quickly. "But no. Not for the entire time."

"Then where in the heck were y'all?"

She shrugged. "Everywhere, really."

"Now don't be holdin' out on me, darlin'.'" Julian shook a finger at her and stepped away from her mother to pull her in for a hug too. She coughed a little at the crushing pressure around her lungs. "The cat's outta the bag, now. Define everywhere."

The young witch took a deep breath and smoothed her hair away from her face. "Literally everywhere, Julian. Canada, Mexico, Europe. Libya."

"What the—where'd you leave that giant RV?"

"We took it with us," Romeo said.

"All the way to..." The man shook his head vigorously, ran his hand through his short hair with a remnant of curls like his son's, and continued that movement down the side of his face. Then, he gestured toward Greta again. "And where'd you find her?"

"In Libya." The older woman folded her arms again. "That was the end of the line for the most part. Except not really, because we're still not done."

Julian nodded slowly as the shock and disbelief finally caught up with him. He almost looked like he might fall to the floor at any second, but he managed to pull himself together enough to look at Romeo. When he embraced his son, they obviously didn't need words to express how they felt. But the man tensed in that hug, pulled away slightly, and searched the younger man's green eyes flecked with gold. His brow furrowed. "Somethin's different."

"Yeah." Romeo chewed on the inside of his cheek.

His dad took a quick sniff and turned his head slightly away. "What happened to you?"

"It's kind of a long story."

"Which we have time to sit and tell, at least tonight," Greta interjected. "As long as you don't mind having a few guests for the night."

"You better not be pullin' my leg." Julian stepped away from Romeo and took a deep breath. "Of course we got room for y'all. Greta, you know by now that you and Lily always have a place here. No matter what. Even if one of y'all's been dead for the last six months."

He gave an incredulous laugh and seemed to startle himself out of his next thought.

"It's not only us." The woman turned halfway to nod at Darius who stood silently in the entryway.

Julian blinked at the huge, black-bearded healer and chuckled. "You been standin' there the whole time?"

"Yep." He stepped forward and extended a hand toward the slightly overwhelmed werewolf. "Darius Balsur."

"Pleasure." They shook, then Julian huffed another unsure laugh and couldn't decide which unlikely person he wanted to look at the longest. "I hope it goes without saying that all y'all are more than welcome to stay as long as you like. Hopefully long enough to tell me what in the blue blazes y'all got yourselves up to in the last few months. I'll fix us something to eat."

"I think we can handle that," Lily said with a grin.

Romeo slipped his arm around her shoulders and pulled her closer against him. "We'll stick around for the next few days. I thought Darius could take my room for the next night or two."

His father's mouth twitched into a knowing smirk. "Uh-huh. Give the guest room to Greta while you two head on out to that giant rig parked in front of the house. Is that it?"

"Basically, yeah."

"Sure. Sure. That'd be fine." The man rubbed his head again and spun in a slow half-circle, obviously trying to think of what to do next. "Y'all hungry? I got some crab dip in the fridge. I can pull out one of them tomato pies I keep in the freezer. Or sandwiches. I got fixin's for sandwiches. Y'all let me know."

"If you're making it, Julian, I don't care what it is." Greta clapped a hand on the man's back and walked with him toward the kitchen. "As long as you think you can keep your head in the cooking game and listen to the craziest story you've ever heard at the same time."

"Oh, come on, Gret. Don't tell me you've lost faith in my ability to multitask."

"Never."

With a soft chuckle, Darius stepped past the young couple to head after their parents toward the kitchen.

Romeo tilted his head and watched the hulking man move through his house. "I only hope dad's old chairs can hold up under all that healer."

"Those chairs made it through all your uncles until your dad got them." Lily looked at him and wrapped her arm around tighter around his waist. "I'm sure they can handle a little more."

"Yeah, fair enough."

"Hey, are you okay?"

He stared at nothing for a moment, almost like he hadn't heard her, then finally met her gaze and shrugged. "I think so. You heard what he said, right?"

"Yeah. We have to tell him about your magic. You know that, don't you?"

"I know. But I have no idea how he's gonna react to that."

Lily chuckled and moved with him after the others. "Well, it probably won't be a giant kiss."

"God, I hope not. Maybe that's what's bothering me."

"What?"

"The thought of my dad and your mom." He was obviously joking when he gave an exaggerated shudder, but she'd had the same thought. "You don't think that was ever a thing for them, do you?"

"You mean like the two of them...together?" He nodded, and she watched her mom laugh as she leaned against the kitchen counter. Julian muttered something and grinned as he opened the fridge and reached into it. "You know, I don't think I actually wanna entertain that thought at all."

"Right?"

"Okay, she basically shot him down after that weird welcome home he gave her."

Romeo nodded. "Yeah, I definitely caught that too."

"So we can pretend it never happened."

"Exactly like they're doing."

"Yep." She raised her eyebrows when her mother turned toward her and gestured dramatically, still laughing at something else Julian had said while he set whatever he was so excited to make them for lunch out on the counter.

Mom and Romeo's dad. That would be way too weird. We definitely don't need any more weird right now.

TWENTY-TWO

Julian ended up supplying a little of everything—crab dip with chips, tomato pie out of the oven, and ingredients for sandwiches left out for everyone to make their own. He'd even taken the time to fry sliced pickles and stuck them in the center of the dining room table next to a huge bowl of ranch dressing. They had to take their lunch out of the kitchen, given that five people wouldn't fit around the table, especially not with a man as big as Darius joining them. Lily actually preferred the extra space in the dining room once their host had cleared all his bills and stuck them with his reading glasses on the other side of the kitchen.

Sitting at the kitchen table would feel way too much like we're kids again. Only the four of us, and we're about as far from that as we can get right now.

Lunch was excellent, exactly like everything Julian Stephens prepared for people he enjoyed feeding. The conversation was light, superficial, and full of shared glances between the four magicals who'd teleported from Romania to France to Charleston only a few hours before. No one wanted to break the lighthearted reunion, despite the weight of what Greta's return from the dead really meant for all of them. But eventually, Julian was the one who finally cut through all the niceties to get right down to it.

"So." The man took a long sip of his homemade sweet tea, sighed heavily, and glanced at each of them around the table. "Y'all still have some serious explaining to do."

"Yes, we do." Greta popped another pickle chip into her mouth and leaned back in her chair. "Lily, why don't you go ahead and fill him in on everything there is to know?"

"Uh...I don't mind if either of you wanna tell the story instead." She sighed heavily and offered a weak smile. "I'm actually really feeling the instant time change, especially after all this food."

"That's an even better reason for you to tell our tale." Her mom wrinkled her nose and nodded at Julian. "This'll keep anyone awake."

Romeo leaned toward her and muttered, "It is kinda your turn."

"My turn, huh? I didn't know we were keeping score of who gets to tell the story of our grand adventure." She laughed. "Okay, I guess it's fair."

"That's it. Fair." Her mother winked at her. "You'd better make the rest of us sound good, Sweets."

She rolled her eyes playfully and took a long drink of

her own sweet tea. *Plenty of sugar and a decent amount of caffeine. I hope it helps.* "Yeah, I'll try."

It took her about an hour and a half to cover all the points of her and Romeo's adventure across the world, plus finally finding Greta, manipulating their way into Carmichael's good graces, and tearing down the Transference spell before their little stint in the alternate dimension of Mabayn. Julian asked a few questions occasionally but mostly listened intently with wide eyes. Romeo and Greta interjected here and there to add the details they each felt were particularly important to share, and she finally finished the remainder of what really was an unbelievable tale.

"So now we're merely waiting to hear from Bentley, and when we do, we'll get everything ready for our meeting with the Council of Magic."

Julian stared at her for a few seconds, then shook his head. "Unbelievable."

"I told you," Greta muttered with a coy smile.

"I'm as serious as a heart attack. If you weren't sittin' right here in front of me, I'd have one hell of a time swallowing anything you told me."

"Yeah, that's exactly what we expect from the Council, too." Lily gestured toward her mother with an open hand. "Which is why we have to keep Mom hidden until that meeting. They can't know she's actually here until we're ready to show them everything and ask for their help."

The older woman leaned toward him. "Which, if they have any brains whatsoever, they won't hesitate to give. Because we intend to show them exactly what they'll be dealing with if they don't take a stand in this against what's left of the Black Heron. Against Carmichael, at the very least."

"Greta's the strongest proof we have that something needs to change," Romeo added.

Lily wrinkled her nose and shook her head. "Not exactly."

Julian glanced from one of the four magicals sitting at his table to the next, his expression enraptured and a little skeptical at the same time. "Is there somethin' y'all forgot to mention?"

"Not really. We simply haven't quite expanded on it yet." Greta nodded toward Romeo. "Your son's the other half of the evidence we'll bring to the Council."

"Evidence. Huh." The werewolf stuck his elbow on the table and rubbed his chin. "You know, I think I'd actually feel better about the whole thing if y'all told me he was goin' in there to defend himself for some tiny magical misdemeanor than tryin' to convince the whole Council that everything y'all are sayin' is true."

Romeo snorted. "Thanks a lot, Dad."

"Oh, you know what I mean, son. That Council of Magic ain't gonna take lightly to a werewolf steppin' in and tryin' to tell them what needs fixin'."

"They will if that werewolf's a living representation of what Carmichael's trying to do en masse with his Transference spell." Greta raised an eyebrow at her friend and inclined her head toward him so he was forced to look at her. "They'll have to listen when they see that everything I warned them about years ago is actually happening right now, right under their noses. It's hard to keep a tight hold on one's convictions when a dead woman shows up in the flesh with a whole group of people there to back up her claims."

Julian squinted at her. "It doesn't mean I have to like it."

"It sure doesn't. But I'd really like to have your support in this."

"Can we back this up for a second?" Darius asked. He unfolded his arms enough to tug at the bottom of this thick, wiry black beard. "Define 'a whole group of people.'"

"Yeah..." Romeo nodded at the massive healer with a curious frown. "I actually wondered the same thing. You said you had a whole group of people to back up your claims, but I'm not sure the three of us qualify as a whole group. You coming back from the dead or not."

Greta glanced quickly at the young werewolf, and her smile seemed strained and a little too forced. "You two really know how to hit the nail on the head, don't you?"

Lily leaned back in her chair and folded her hands in her lap. She turned an expectant look on her mother. "Mom? This would be the part where you tell us what else you've planned that we don't know about."

"Oh, I wouldn't say I've planned anything..." The woman closed her eyes and she uttered a dry laugh. "It's more like working my way up to a plan."

"Margaret." Julian gave her that stern, open-ended look that both Lily and Romeo had come to learn meant abso-lutely whatever the man wanted it to mean, depending on the circumstances. "I'm gonna side with them on this one. So spit it out already."

Greta sighed and gestured toward the young couple. "Okay, fine. This shouldn't come as any surprise to you two. Obviously, more support is better than no support. I thought we'd hit two Council items with one werewolf stone and knock them out of the park all at once."

"See, I know that makes sense in her head." Julian pointed at her but frowned at Lily and Romeo. "Does it make sense to either of y'all?"

His son shook his head. "Not like this is unusual or anything, but no. I have no idea what she actually said."

"Oh, you two are so alike, it might be giving me a headache." As Greta rubbed her temples, the Stephens' dining room fell completely silent. It took her a few seconds to realize the conversation had stopped completely and she paused, removed her hands, and glanced at the others. "What?"

A short laugh bubbled up her old friend's throat but he cut it off with a cough and forced his face into an unconvincing semblance of seriousness. "You don't get to hold that stance, Greta. Not when you're sittin' at my table with the twenty-two-year-old version of yourself right next to you."

Romeo snorted and the infectious humor spread to Darius beside him. The two couldn't hold back their laughter and finally, Julian too was unable to contain himself. While the men were almost incoherent in their amusement, Greta turned slowly toward her daughter and gestured toward everyone else in general. "What's wrong with them?"

Lily bit her lip and her smile tugged at the corners of her mouth despite how hard she tried to keep it under control. "He's not wrong."

"About you and me?" Her mother scoffed. "Please, Lily. We're not nearly as alike as everyone thinks—"

Julian barked out another laugh and leaned forward over the table.

The woman gave him a startled frown. "Do you need a minute?"

"Mom." She waited for her mother to turn toward her and spread her arms in exasperation. "You might be the only person sitting here who doesn't get it. Every single person I've met in the last few months who already knew you would agree with me on that."

Romeo ran a hand through his hair, still chuckling. "You have no idea how true that is. The first line out of their mouths was always, 'You look so much like your mother,' or, 'You're exactly like Greta.'"

Lily pressed her lips together and fought back more laughter. "It was annoying, actually. But they're not wrong. I might even go so far as to say that I'm proud of it."

"Well." Greta gave her a closed-lipped smile and inclined her head. "That's awfully sweet of you."

Julian stopped laughing, reached out toward her, and shook his hand in the air to get her attention. "It might be sweet for y'all. But trust me, Greta. You're not the only one with a headache."

Darius threw his head back and released a rolling laugh. The mere sound of the massive healer finally losing the rest of his discomfort at being whisked halfway across the world to stand behind them when they faced the Council broke down the remainder of Lily's resolve. The young witch joined the rest of them, and Greta finally had to give in.

"All right, already. You've made your point." She grinned at her daughter and nodded. "But I think it's the other way around, honestly. Sure, Lily and I might have some similarities—"

"The apple doesn't fall far," Julian cut in with another chuckle.

"But if anyone's proud of anything, it's me. Because my daughter's done more and gone farther than I ever will."

She met her mom's gaze and knew she was being absolutely serious. "Thanks, Mom."

The woman simply winked.

Julian let out a long, chuckling sigh and wiped at the corners of his eyes. "I tell y'all what. I've spent a long time almost forgettin' how to laugh like that. Then Lily comes back a few months ago and has me in stitches with a walk down memory lane."

"Oh, yeah?"

Romeo nodded. "The raccoon Lily thought was a bear."

"That was a good one, wasn't it?"

Lily pointed at her mom first, then at him. "Don't."

Julian burst into laughter again and Greta chuckled with him. This time, he took control of himself far more quickly and simply shook his head.

"And now you're back too. A part of me always hoped you would be, even after…" The other laughter around the table died at the man's unexpected emotional swing from one end of the spectrum to the other. He sniffed and smiled at his friend. "All I'm sayin' is it's good to have you back at my table."

"It's good to be back. As crazy as our story might seem, Julian, I'm also really glad to hear that you stand behind what we're doing. Because we need your help too."

"My help?" He laughed again, this time in surprise, and made no effort to hide his confusion. "How in the world is a wolf like me supposed to help the four of y'all go up against somethin' as big as the Council?"

"Well, come with us, for one." Greta took a long, deep breath before she placed her palms flat on the surface of the dining room table. "And bring a few other werewolves with you."

That statement did, in fact, leave Julian Stephens completely speechless.

"What?" Lily glanced quickly at Romeo, who looked as bewildered as she felt.

He frowned and leaned toward Greta. "Yeah. What?"

TWENTY-THREE

"You seriously didn't consider this?" Greta gave the young couple a blank stare. "Either one of you?"

"Not really," Romeo replied. "You want us to show up to this meeting with a handful of pack-less wolves and that's what's gonna make them take us seriously?"

"Huh. I really expected you to connect the dots."

Lily glanced from her mom to him, then it clicked into place. She caught his arm. "Romeo."

He turned his head toward her but still couldn't take his wide eyes off her mother.

"The wolfsbane."

"Yeah, I know, Lil. I was gonna—oh." He finally turned to look at her and everything dawned on him too. "Oh. You said I'd need to save those flowers for later."

The woman raised her hands when the werewolf pointed at her. "And now you've found the right use for them. Although we don't necessarily have to take poison off the table right now—"

"No. No poison." Lily frowned at her. "That's more likely to land us in some kind of magic-dampening prison than anything else."

Greta shrugged and nodded toward Romeo. "It was his idea."

"What? It wasn't—" He huffed in disbelief and shook his head firmly. "She told me to hang onto the wolfsbane. I thought she wanted to keep it 'cause it's, you know...it's actually poisonous."

"Okay, well, we'll take that option off the table." She closed her eyes and shook her head. "It wasn't even an option, to begin with."

"All right, now I feel like the one speakin' a different language over here." Julian scratched his head, drained the rest of his sweet tea, and almost slammed the glass down on the table. "What are y'all goin' on about?"

"Dad, Greta's right." Romeo leaned forward and held his gaze. "We would make some big waves if you brought some of your guys with us to this meeting."

"Son, those people aren't gonna let a group of wolves waltz in there. You know that."

"If you come in with Bentley McClure," Greta added, "I promise you, the Council won't turn any of you away."

"Oh, yeah? How does that even work?"

"He used to work for the Council," Lily said. "They owe him a few favors at this point."

"That sharp-lookin' accountant?" When everyone nodded, the older werewolf frowned and rubbed his jaw. "Why would I need to show up there at this meeting with a handful of wolves, huh? That's not exactly a smart move."

"Actually, it would really help." Romeo paused to gather his thoughts and tapped his fingers on the tabletop. "I'm essentially the outlier here, Dad. Only one wolf who happened to have someone else's magic blasted into him. So what, right?"

"Well, yeah. It's a little strange—"

"But if you bring in a few others who all stand behind us and want the same thing—for the Black Heron to keep their hands off everyone else's magic—the Council has to listen. Because the Black Heron will start taking magic from many more wolves if no one stops them. They've already done it, so it's not like we're safe simply because we don't have the same kind of magic."

Julian blinked at his son for a few seconds, then leaned back in his chair and shook his head. "You want to bring in a group of wolves to prove that we're upstanding citizens like everyone else."

"Because you are," Lily added.

"Do you want us to get down on our knees too and beg the Council to help you?"

Greta waved dismissively. "Don't be so dramatic."

"I'm being realistic." He gazed at each of them in turn, his frown unchanging. "It's a fine dream to have, sure. Hell, I'd love to have some recognition that lightens the load off all our backs. I've spent a lifetime keepin' to myself with my head down because I know what the rest of the world thinks of us. I never pretended otherwise."

"So what's the problem?" the woman asked.

"Come on, Greta. You know how this works. If I bring a handful of my buddies into that meeting, we'll end up proving them right. None of those wolves will be able to control themselves in a room filled with that much magic. They're good guys and they're strong, but someone's gonna do one kinda spell or another, and then it's game over for all of us who came to be on your side." He nodded at his son. "Except maybe you."

"Yeah, but you've missed a very important piece, Dad." Romeo gestured toward the front of the house and the Winnie parked at the curb. "We can make sure that doesn't happen."

"With an RV?" Julian clicked his tongue. "I wasn't born with half a brain, son."

"What? No, I know." He chuckled wryly. "You also weren't born knowing about wolfsbane."

His dad's eyes narrowed. "That's what y'all were talking about, huh? I heard wolfsbane and poison in the same sentence, though."

"It's only poisonous to virtually everyone else," Lily interjected when she felt the need to jump in before either of the Stephenses got a little too passionate about the completely different points they each tried to make. "Except werewolves."

"Okay, now see, this is where none of y'all seem to be hearin' yourselves." Julian raised both hands and set them to one side of the table in front of him, then the other. "You got wolf, and you got bane. Now I don't have a dictionary on me, but I'm very sure one of those words is a synonym for curse."

"Dad, I'm serious—"

"Look it up if you want. G'head. I'll wait." The older werewolf folded his arms and nodded curtly.

Lily eyed them both with a little apprehension. *If we were kids, this is the part where he'd yell at Romeo to mind his elders and send him out of the house. And then comes the part where I'd try to fix it.* She stood from the table.

"Where are you goin'?" Julian asked.

"To get the one thing that'll literally change your life, Julian. Since this is apparently the one thing out of everything we've told you that you still can't wrap your head around, I can see you need something a little more concrete."

The man frowned at her.

"Lily." Greta slid her hand gently around her daughter's wrist. "Wait a second."

"We have to show him—"

"And we will. Sit down for a few more minutes, Sweets. And when Julian feels a little more comfortable with what we have to say and a little less skeptical of the whole thing, you can bring the entire pot into this house, okay?"

"Not if it's poison, you won't."

The woman ignored Julian's angry mutter and nodded at Lily, who finally swallowed her frustration and lowered herself slowly into the chair again. When she settled, her mother turned toward the older werewolf and raised her hands in a placating gesture. "You have every right to be cynical, Julian. Anyone who promises a solution to the one thing that casts werewolves in a negative light is probably trying to run circles around you."

The man snorted. "Including you?"

"Don't ask stupid questions when you already know the answer." She leaned forward and tapped her finger against the table. "You know I would never lie to you. And you also know I wouldn't step inside this house and ask you to do something that goes against all your instincts if I didn't actually need your help."

He nodded after a moment and raised an eyebrow for her to continue.

"I've known about wolfsbane for years and I'll be the first to admit that it was entirely wrong of me to keep this kind of information from you for so long. To keep it from both of you." She nodded at Romeo, who widened his eyes and looked like she'd pointed the barrel of a gun at him instead. "But I knew it was an issue of your pride, which is why I kept my mouth shut. This, though, is an issue of life and death. Quite literally. For more people than we can imagine if Carmichael has his way with that Transference spell. And it's definitely much more than a meeting between us and the Council.

"We need to show them this isn't only about Carmichael either or the Black Heron Society. That it's about the magical community everywhere who are legitimately and rightfully afraid of and outraged by the idea that someone without any regard for the natural order of things will have the ability to walk up to them and take the magic out of them. Out of you or your son. Out of your friends. Your employees. We need you to bring in as many wolves as you can to help us show the Council that we can all be united in this because it will affect every single one of us if we don't stop it before it begins."

The dining room fell silent again and all eyes turned to Julian as he mulled over what she had said and decided whether or not to take her seriously. "You know, if you wanted to practice your Council speech on me, you could've simply said so."

Darius snorted and shoveled a handful of fried pickle chips into his mouth.

Greta stared at Romeo's dad a little longer, then puffed out a dry laugh. "Yeah, that did sound good, didn't it?"

"You should've written it down." He ran his hand through his hair. "All right. So assuming I want to be involved in this any more than I already am, what exactly does this mystical wolfsbane do?"

The couple exchanged a quick, relieved glance before the young werewolf gestured toward himself. "It gets rid of the allergy, Dad."

"The what now?"

"The...all the crazy stuff that happens when we're around too much magic."

Julian stared at his son, his expression one of quiet scrutiny. "It doesn't really apply to you, though, does it? Now that you have someone else's magic runnin' around inside you. Or whatever."

"Right," Lily said. "But before that happened, Romeo had wolfsbane on him all the time."

"I practically lived on the stuff and carried around a little baggie of it with me everywhere." He shrugged.

" 'Cause we were running into insane amounts of magic basically everywhere."

"You..." His father stared blankly at them both. "You've actually used the stuff?"

"Yeah, for months."

She fought back a laugh. "He could always handle himself but it definitely made things easier after Mexico."

Romeo snorted. "Thank you, Melissa Bore."

"Huh." Julian stared at the table for a while longer, then smacked it with a hand and nodded. "Y'all shoulda led with that. Let's see what the darn stuff can actually do, yeah?"

The chair screeched across the hardwood floor behind him as the man stood abruptly from the table. It made Lily jump but Romeo merely sighed and shook his head.

Greta laughed. "Like an old man trapped in a younger body."

"Oh, sure. Except for my body's startin' to catch up to me." The man snickered. "I may be set in some of my ways, Greta, but I tell you what. If my boy says he has a magical weed that can make me act like a normal person with my head screwed on straight around a group of magicals throwin' a spell party, sign me up. Wait. Do I have to smoke the thing or—"

"Definitely not." With wide eyes, his son shook his head vehemently. "It's a flower, Dad. And you eat it."

"Even better."

Lily stood from the table and set her hand on Romeo's shoulder. "Do you wanna come help me bring in that giant pot of flowers that's gonna change your dad's life?"

"I thought you'd never ask." He pushed his chair out and turned quickly toward the entryway and the front door. "We'll be right back."

"I'll be here waitin' for y'all." Before they reached the front door, she heard him ask her mom, "Now tell me why it's called wolfsbane, huh?"

I don't care what she comes up with to answer that question as long as he's open to helping us. That's all that matters.

TWENTY-FOUR

Eight hours later, Lily and Romeo finally had enough of an excuse to call it a night and head out to the Winnie alone. Greta and Darius would take the guest room and Romeo's bedroom, respectively, and both young magicals were more than ready to get out of the same room as their parents. Especially after the way the rest of the day had turned out.

"I wonder how much longer they're gonna keep this up." He stared at the muted lights in a variety of colors that flashed through the partly open curtains of the Winnie's bedroom window.

She snuggled closer to him, her head on his chest as they lay together on the bed. "It could all night. Honestly, that wouldn't surprise me even a little. I'm merely glad I put up that illusion dome earlier."

"Do those things have a shelf life or do they simply hang around indefinitely?"

She laughed and draped her arm over his waist.

"When you carried the wolfsbane inside, I stopped to reinforce the spell. It'll be there until I take it down."

"Good. The last thing we need right now is for the whole neighborhood to see your mom's spells exploding in the living room while my dad jumps around like a lunatic because he's not getting high off her magic."

Tipping her head back so she could look at him, Lily managed to frown and laugh at the same time. "It's kinda the exact opposite of what feeding your dad wolfsbane was supposed to do, huh?"

He snorted. "Yep. I haven't seen him that giddy about something since...man. Probably since the first time you guys came camping with us."

"Oh, no. Really?" It made them laugh a little. "No one should have to wait...what? Fifteen years for that kinda happiness."

"Well, it seems like Greta Antony plus wolfsbane equals a very happy, non-allergic Julian Stephens."

"He can keep it together at the Council meeting, though, right?" Lily brushed the few strands of blonde hair away from her face.

"He'd better. We should make sure that whichever guys he ends up bringing with him get to try the little purple flowers out first too. I don't think a group of grown werewolves running around in awe of themselves is gonna do us any favors. Whenever we get to that meeting, that is."

She laughed. "You know, I would have said I find that incredibly hard to imagine, but I literally spent hours watching your dad do exactly that. It's not really an image I want in my head for the rest of the night."

"Yeah, you and me both."

They lay there on the bed in silence for a few more minutes, the darkness inside the bedroom punctuated by the flashing lights of Greta's spells bursting through the living room windows and shining into the Winnie. A few minutes later, the flashing stopped, and she released a huge sigh. "Finally."

"Hey, was that what it was like when you had that giant golden tractor beam or whatever keeping you up all the time in Libya?"

She burst out laughing.

"What?" Romeo's clueless grin made her laugh even harder. "Why's that funny?"

"It's not even close. My mom's spells are like a night-light compared to the light that connected me to a tree in the middle of the desert."

"Nightlight. Huh. We don't need one of those in here, do we? 'Cause I actually like it when it's completely dark."

Lily pressed her cheek against his chest again and shook her head. "You're not making any sense."

"Maybe it's 'cause I feel like I haven't slept in a week."

"Join the club."

They had no sooner started to drift off into much-needed sleep after so many teleportation spells through so many time zones in only a few hours when her phone rang. She jerked awake and for a moment, couldn't identify where the sound was coming from. Finally, she saw her phone buzzing on the little shelf built into the wall beside her bed, exactly where she'd left it after plugging it in to charge for the first time since before they reached the Black Heron's High Seat.

"Wow."

Romeo's snore cut off abruptly, and he startled awake when she crawled away from him toward her phone. "What? What's going on?"

"I forgot what my phone sounded like when it's ringing," she mumbled, still half-asleep despite not having actually fallen completely asleep. *And maybe I understand a little better now how Mom could've forgotten about GPS being a thing.*

Lily snatched the device off the shelf, unplugged it, and stared at the name lit up in the center of her screen. It was Bentley. She took the call. "Bentley, hi. Is everything okay?"

"Is everything..." The man cleared his throat. "Yes, Lily. Everything's fine. Are you okay?"

"Yeah. Sorry." She leaned back against the headboard and rubbed her face. "I didn't expect a call from you this late. That's all."

He chuckled. "I didn't know you considered just shy of nine o'clock at night to be all that late."

"Jetlag."

"Of course. I would have called your mother but her cell phone was disconnected months ago. This number, at least, I know still works."

"And again, I still plan to pay you back for fronting me the phone bill while I was out in the middle of nowhere. You can't get out of it that easily, now that you..." Her head dropped toward her chest and her cell phone slipped away from her ear. His voice brought her back to reality.

"Are you sure you're okay?"

She shook her head. "Yep. But I haven't slept a full night in...oh, I don't know. Probably a week. Or more. But I'm good. I'm listening."

"Okay, well, I won't keep you too long. I wanted to pass along the message that I just got off the phone with Beatrice Calvin, secretary to Councilmember Brast. Our meeting's scheduled for seven-thirty tomorrow night, Lily."

That news immediately yanked her out of her exhausted haze. "Wow. Really? That fast?"

"That fast. They're expecting you, Romeo, Mr. Balsur, and myself. Although I did arrange for the doors to be kept open should anyone else wish to make an appearance and argue their case to the Council with us."

Lily nodded. "Yeah, I'm sure we'll fill a few extra seats in that meeting. Thank you, Bentley."

"Of course. Is there anything else I can take care of on my end before then?"

"Uh..." She rubbed her eyes, sniffed, and tried to focus her vision on the bedspread. "Nothing I can think of right now. But I'll let my mom know and if anything comes up, we'll call you."

"All right. I'm available whenever you need me. Get some sleep, Lily."

"Yep. I'm tryin' to get on it."

"I won't keep you, then. Good night."

"'Night." She ended the call and stared at her backlit

phone until Romeo rolled toward her again and flopped a hand on her thigh.

"Bentley, huh?"

"Yeah. He has that meeting set up for us. Seven-thirty tomorrow night."

He grunted, half-asleep again and fading toward full unconsciousness. "That'll be fun."

With an exhausted little chuckle, she rolled her eyes and set an alarm for herself with a note about the Council meeting in less than twenty-four hours. *I don't know if I'll even remember this conversation in the morning.*

She slid down onto the comforter again beside Romeo and couldn't stay awake long enough to put her phone back on the shelf.

At the same time in Kingston, Carmichael sat out on the back porch of the house one of his members—a werewolf, necromancer, and partial warlock hybrid whose magically enhanced skin had taken on a glow like bioluminescent algae—had lent him for as long as he wished to stay. He had almost finished the last of the gin and tonic no one but Ingrid had the ability to mix with any amount of respect for cocktails in general when his cell phone rang.

It was new, of course, purchased on their trek to this house in Kingston but full of all his old contacts. This particular number hadn't been saved in either of his phones, but it didn't matter. No one but his society members had his new number anyway.

He accepted the call and lifted the phone to his ear. "Yes?"

Beside him, Ingrid sat in the second lawn chair and stretched her legs out in front of her. She didn't have to hear the other end of the conversation to know he was getting some useful information dressed up as good news. The necromancer could feel his excitement hanging in the air between them.

"Really? How long ago? Excellent. No, we'll handle it. Personally." The man ended the call and slid the new device into his back pocket before he swirled the ice in his almost empty drink. With a flourish, he upended the glass, tipped the contents into his mouth, and crunched on the ice.

"It sounds like someone found something." His companion folded her arms and watched the twinkling lights of the city over their host's backyard fence.

"Something quite useful, yes." He set the glass on the cement patio, then draped his arms over the armrests and leaned against the chair with a sigh. "It looks like our time-line's moving up a little sooner than I thought. We'll head out tomorrow afternoon. Get hold of those who are ready to stand with us. I think I'll stake my claim and clear two Optatus witches out of the way at the same time."

The necromancer closed her eyes and took in a deep breath of the warm night air. "How convenient."

"Quite."

TWENTY-FIVE

Lily had set her alarm for 11:00 am the next morning. At the time, she'd thought sleeping almost fourteen hours all the way through would have been the easiest thing in the world after how little sleep she'd had in the last seven to ten days. She woke at 7:00 am instead, all on her own because apparently, ten hours was more than enough.

And, of course, Romeo was already up at that point too and waited for her in the Winnie's kitchen with a fresh cup of coffee and waffles.

"Wow. What's the occasion?" She rubbed her eyes as she shuffled out into the kitchen.

"Oh, you know. We're not out in the middle of nowhere. We got your mom away from the Black Heron. No one's chasing us...for now. And my dad's fridge is on the other side of the yard, basically. It makes a kitchen raid super easy."

"Very nice." She accepted the still-steaming cup of

coffee carefully and turned to slide into the booth closest to the bedroom.

"Not that one." He paused with his hand stretched toward her, then cleared his throat. "Magically unstable rock in a fanny pack down there, remember?"

She stared dumbly at the booth, then took a few steps back. "Oh, yeah. That."

Instead, she simply leaned back against the kitchen counter for the first few sips of her coffee. When he handed her a plate of waffles, she had no problem digging in while standing beside the fridge. *Normal has never felt or tasted so good. Enjoy it while you can, Lily.*

As she took the last bite of waffle, he whisked the plate out of her hands and started washing it in the sink. "Hey, so I had a weird dream last night."

"Oh, yeah?" She finished chewing and ran her fork under the faucet.

Romeo dried the plate, took her fork, and jiggled it in the air. "Yeah. That Bentley called you and said we had a meeting with the Council tonight."

"Oh!" Lily gulped the rest of her coffee, realized the mug didn't belong to the Winnie, and shrugged as she took it with her toward the side door. "That wasn't a dream. Thanks for the reminder."

"Okay..." Stacking both their plates and snatching up his own coffee mug, he followed her outside into late-September air, which was still ridiculously hot and muggy for not even 8:00 am yet. "So that's real, then. Council meeting tonight."

"Yep. Seven-thirty." She turned and gave him a reassuring smile before she reached the front porch. "Don't worry.
That's still more than enough time for us to get everything
together and get everyone on the same page. Or whoever's
gonna show up with us in the end. Do you think your dad's
gonna be able to convince a few of his friends to tag along?"

"Uh...maybe." He frowned. "We really passed out hard
last night, huh? I could've sworn that was a dream."

"It was definitely not a dream." She opened the front
door and stepped inside to walk backward as she talked. "I
even set an alarm on my phone to make sure I wouldn't
forget about it. But I didn't sleep as long as I wanted to, so
—woah."

She turned quickly to find Julian frying a massive
amount of bacon on the stove while Greta stood beside
him, whisking a huge mixing bowl full of eggs. On the
counter in front of her was a grocery receipt from the
Harris Teeter and an open carton that held eighteen eggs—
completely empty.

"Good morning," she said cheerfully and continued to
whisk briskly.

"It's good to see y'all got some decent shuteye," Julian
added. He stuck one hand on his hip and flipped slice after
slice of bacon on the pan that was big enough to cover two
burners.

The couple froze just inside the kitchen, and Romeo
lowered their breakfast dishes slowly into the sink. "Did
we miss something?"

"Nope. Everything should be ready in about ten

minutes. Fifteen tops, depending on how fast Greta can move with those eggs."

"Oh, I can be fast." She whisked even faster with a competitive glint in her eye.

Lily gave both parents a sheepish look. "We already ate breakfast."

Romeo nodded slowly, totally confused. "Yeah, and even if we hadn't, you guys are making way too much for only the five of us. I know I can definitely eat and I'm sure Darius doesn't have any problem putting away a good meal, either. But this is enough for, like—"

"An extra three or four mouths?" his father interrupted and continued to flip the bacon. The grease hissed and spat in the pan. "That's the idea."

"And they'll be here at any minute," Greta added.

"Mom." Lily stepped back away from the whisked eggs and the sizzling bacon. "Who did you invite?"

"Julian invited them. I'm merely helping with the eggs. Oh, and he put biscuits in the oven."

"Who?" The couple exchanged a confused glance.

"Y'all wanted to bring some extra werewolves into the mix, right? Well, I got us some extra werewolves." Julian jerked away from the pan as one of the bacon strips jumped a little and sent a spray of hot grease across the stove. "Hey, someone grab me one of them mason jars outta the cupboard."

Romeo jumped toward the pantry and retrieved exactly what his dad asked for. When he handed it over, the man slid the entire massive frying pan off the stove and poured the excess grease into the mason jar. He placed the jar on the counter and simply continued to cook like he did this every single morning for no other reason than because he liked it.

"It's good to see you guys getting a head start on things," Lily said. "Uh...Mom, I had a call from Bentley last night. He has our meeting scheduled—"

"For seven-thirty tonight. Yes, I know." Greta glanced at her daughter and gave her another wink. "But thanks for being so on top of things, Sweets."

She drew a sharp breath. "How do you already know?"

"Bentley called Darius about half an hour ago. He has the man's number and it sounded like he didn't think you'd remember your conversation with him from last night. Bentley McClure is nothing if not thorough and prepared for almost every possibility."

Romeo fought back a laugh as he leaned toward Lily and muttered, "See? Thinking the whole thing was a dream isn't that far out of the question."

He did laugh when she elbowed him in the ribs. A loud knock came from the side door on the other side of the kitchen.

Julian startled and glanced nervously over his shoulder. "Someone get the door, please."

"Yeah." His son hurried to the side door, which they hardly ever used, and leapt out of the way as Darius stooped through the doorway with a long, white plastic event table slung under his arm.

"You guys should probably think about cleaning your shed out. It's almost impossible to get to anything in there without stepping on something else." The bearded healer nodded at Romeo pressed up against the kitchen wall. "Thanks for gettin' the door."

"No problem." He scratched the back of his head and watched the large man move through the kitchen with the long fold-up table trailing a few feet behind him.

"All right. Where do you want this?"

"I think right up next to the dining room table should be fine." Greta glanced at Julian and the bacon. "How much longer until you finish those?"

"I dunno. Another minute? Feel free to start scrambling eggs whenever you're ready."

"Oh, no. If I'm gonna make these all at once, I need the whole stove. Oh, Darius, go ahead and put the wolfsbane on the table. It's gonna be a conversation piece anyway so we might as well make it a centerpiece too."

"And part of breakfast." Julian barked out a laugh. "It wouldn't even taste that bad with everything. It'd make a good staple for every werewolf who wants to keep his nose clean with or without magic flying all around him."

Romeo joined Lily at the entryway between the kitchen and dining room. "They're acting really weird."

She tried to laugh it off but it came out as more of a groan. "That's literally the only thought I've had in the last five minutes. Were they this weird when we were kids?"

"You know, part of me thinks that's a yes." Tilting his head as if in thought, the young werewolf scrunched his nose at their parents and folded his arms. "And then the other part of me doesn't really wanna know."

"So we should probably let happy Greta and sparky Julian do their own thing for now. Maybe it's only nerves about tonight. And, apparently, getting to share some wolfsbane with your dad's friends."

"Sure, we can go with that."

The doorbell rang, and both young magicals startled and whirled to face the door. Lily had a handful of crackling red sparks held out beside her before she even realized what she'd done.

"Ha! I can smell your magic, Lily, and it didn't even make my nose twitch." Julian laughed again and hoisted the huge pan of bacon off the stove. "It's all yours, darlin'."

"Thank you." Greta snatched an egg pan out of the cabinet under the counter and got to work.

"Hey. What's gotten into y'all?" The older werewolf jerked a finger toward the front door. "One of y'all better find your manners quick and open that door."

Lily killed her attack spell and shook her hand out as she looked at her friend. "It's probably better if you get it. Just in case they're not expecting a witch on the other side of the door."

"Yeah, good point." He headed toward the front door and she took a hesitant step after him.

With a little squeak, she jumped back in time to avoid Darius as he strode down the hallway from the back of the house with the huge pot of undying wolfsbane in his arms.

"Coming through," he muttered.

"Thanks for the warning." She watched him set the pot on the wooden dining room table—definitely the better choice to hold something so heavy—and shook her head. *This place feels like a zoo. And we're about to have three or four more werewolves join the party. Awesome.*

Romeo jerked the front door open, and a chorus of voices greeted him from the front porch.

"Romeo!"

"Hey, bud. It's been a while."

"You...smell different kid. What'd you get into?"

Smiling and nodding, he simply stood aside and held the door open for three of his dad's friends and muttered, "We'll get to that part eventually."

He closed the door and met her gaze with a shrug.

"Maxwell. Chris. Donnie." Julian clapped loudly and spread his arms in welcome. "It's good to see y'all."

"Comin' over this early on a Sunday mornin', Jay, we expected the place to smell as good as it does."

Their host grinned and laughed, shook hands with his werewolf friends, and introduced Greta to them. Lily sidled toward Romeo and couldn't quite bring herself to look away from the oddly high energy that suffused the kitchen. "Are you ready for this?"

"I don't know how to answer that, Lil. We're about to break open everything they thought they knew about...everything."

"Well, we got your dad on board. And they actually came, so that's a start."

"Yeah." He scratched the back of his head in obvious nervousness. "We'll see how far it goes. It's a little weird to see everyone so smiley, right?"

She nodded and tugged on his hand as she headed toward the dining room table. "A little. I guess we should simply let 'em keep smiling while they can, huh?"

"Yeah. I guess we should." They stopped at the table

but didn't pull their chairs out yet. Julian and his friends moved quickly around the kitchen to gather plates, silverware, and cups while Greta finished the eggs. "We'll see what happens when they hear what the wolfsbane's for."

"If your dad's this thrilled about it, I don't think we'll have a problem."

TWENTY-SIX

Greta, Darius, Julian, and his three friends cut through the impressive heaps of eggs, bacon, and biscuits in under half an hour. With all the plates cleared and the pitcher of orange juice completely empty, the lively conversation died down enough for everyone at the table to feel the serious business ahead of them.

Julian cleared his throat. "So, fellas. I'm glad to have y'all here for a Sunday breakfast."

"You never disappoint, Jay." The gray-haired werewolf named Maxwell leaned back in his chair and drained the rest of his coffee. "I only wish you pulled out all the stops more often, you know? It's been a while."

Beside him, Donnie—who happened to be about an inch shorter than Lily—released a massive belch. "Oh. 'Scuse me."

Greta chuckled. "I'm actually gonna go ahead and take that as a compliment. And you're welcome."

The friends had a good laugh at her quip, and Donnie shook his finger in her direction. "I like this one, Jay."

"Yeah, how long have y'all known each other again?" Chris—his skin a darker tan than even Romeo's although the man was completely bald—pushed the sleeves of his shirt up and propped both elbows on the table as he demolished the last piece of bacon.

"Oh. Well..." Julian glanced at Lily and wrinkled his nose. "A hot minute."

"A really long time." Greta laced her fingers together and lowered her folded hands onto the table. "Which, I'm sure you've noticed, is how he does so well with three witches in his house."

"Uh-huh." Maxwell sniffed and glanced around the table. "But this guy doesn't look like he's from around here."

Darius shrugged. "I'm only here to look pretty."

That brought another round of laughter, and Julian finally raised his hands to gesture for everyone to settle. "All right. So now for the real reason I asked y'all to stop by this morning."

Chris feigned insult with wide eyes and leaned far forward over the table. "You mean you didn't really want a group of old guys eatin' up all your food?"

"Well, that was definitely up there on my list." He shook his head and smiled as he stood from his chair and leaned across the table to pick a handful of the bright purple flowers blooming in the large red pot. "But we have something a little more important than me playing breakfast host of the year, all right?"

The other three werewolves stared at the flowers he placed in front of each one of them. Donnie lowered his head and took a few deep sniffs. "What's this now?"

He sat again. "That right there—"

"Is something you boys aren't gonna want to live without after today." Greta nodded and smiled at them. Either she was completely unaware of her friend's slight discomfort with her taking over or she simply chose to ignore him. "We'll tell you what it is after you see what it does."

Maxwell picked his wolfsbane flower up by the stem and dangled it in front of his face. "What does it do?"

"You gotta eat it," Julian said with a shrug. "I know, I know. It sounds like a buncha hooey, but I'm serious, now. Y'all eat those pretty little purple flowers and we'll let y'all in on something real big."

The other werewolves around the table eyed each other without even trying to hide their skepticism, but they obviously trusted Julian Stephens enough to do what he said without asking any more questions. For now, at any rate.

"All right." Donnie sucked purple petals out of his teeth. "I probably shoulda asked this before I stuffed this into my face. It ain't gonna turn us inside out like those magic mushrooms back in high school, is it?"

Lily's mouth dropped open, followed by a surprised laugh that escaped before she could stop it. Romeo almost choked on the last of his orange juice, and Darius uttered a long, low chuckle. Greta sopped up the bacon grease on her plate with another biscuit and smirked at her long-time friend.

Julian huffed out a dumfounded laugh, then shook his head. "Nope. And I'd managed to forget about that whole night, so thanks for bringing it up decades after the fact, brother."

Donnie shrugged. "Hey, that was the night I learned to ask before I eat."

Maxwell slapped him on the shoulder. "Except you didn't do that this time."

While everyone else gave Donnie a hard time for his obvious lapse in logic, Lily leaned toward Romeo and knocked her hand against his shoulder to get his attention. With a snort, he pulled his gaze away from his dad's friends and met her gaze. "What's up?"

"You remember that deal we made in New Mexico after the art museum?"

He bit his lip and wrinkled his nose at her. "That we'd focus on finding your mom first, and after that, we'd talk about fighting for werewolf equality. That deal?"

She rolled her eyes but couldn't completely wipe the smile off her face. "You make it sound like a soap opera, but yeah. That deal."

"That's not something I could forget very easily, Lil."

"Right." She glanced across the table at the other werewolves who'd taken their first dose of wolfsbane as Julian explained what the purple flower actually did. "It looks like we're doing more than simply talking about it now, huh?"

Romeo took a deep breath and nodded. "Yeah. It looks like we're rolling it all up into one giant meeting with the Council. We convince them to help us stop Carmichael, plus an extra helping of battling the system for werewolves everywhere."

"So the deal's on, then. I wanted to make sure you know."

"Yeah, Lil. I definitely know."

She leaned farther toward him and bumped her shoulder against his. "And I didn't even have to remind you."

"Come on, now, Jay." Chris shook his head and leaned back in his chair. "You're some kinda thickheaded if you think we're gonna buy that explanation."

"Hey, fellas. Would I lie to y'all?"

The three friends glanced at each other with tilted heads and barely contained smiles. Maxwell nodded. "If you thought you could get a good laugh out of it, then yeah."

"Well, I ain't lyin'." He pointed at the other werewolves. "And now's the part where I prove it. Okay, not me personally."

"Oh, boy," Romeo muttered. "Here it comes."

His dad gazed at him for a few seconds, which convinced the young hybrid werewolf that he'd be put on the spot to cast a spell for show. Before he could respond, the man made his mind up and took things in a completely different direction.

"Greta. Go on and show these boys that I ain't blowin' smoke, will ya?"

Her tight-lipped smile was almost feral as she stood slowly from the table and nodded at him. "Gladly."

She snapped her fingers and a spray of multi-colored sparks erupted from her hand and arced over the table without leaving so much as a charred speck on the wood. The werewolves all lurched away from her magic in trepidation.

"Aw, now that's not nice." Maxwell turned his head away from the sparks and refused to look at them. "I don't wanna step on any toes here, but you oughtta know what's gonna happen with that and a room full of wolves."

"Oh, I know." Her smile widened, and she raised both hands to conjure two massive illumination orbs in her palms. "And I'm waiting for someone to figure it out."

Donnie sniffed and wiggled his nose like he expected it to twitch before an attack of sneezing. And if it weren't for the wolfsbane, that definitely would have happened. The man paused, sent a totally baffled frown at his host, then slapped Chris' shoulder with the back of his hand. "Do you feel that, man?"

Chris swallowed. "Nope."

"Exactly." They turned to look at each other, then began to giggle like a couple of boys about to play a prank on their teacher.

"What the heck got into y'all?" Maxwell folded his arms and glared at them. "We get invited to breakfast followed by some weird purple flower for desert and now, we're sittin' here with this witch flashing her spells in our faces. No offense, ma'am."

"None taken. And drop the ma'am part, all right? It's Greta."

"Okay. Well, I don't know why these idiots think this is so funny. 'Cause any second now, we're about to be hit with a—" Finally, the purpose of the wolfsbane petals struck Maxwell with full force too. He sniffed the air, looked at her again with wide eyes, then turned slowly toward Julian. "No..."

"Yeah, man." Julian grinned. "I stayed up half the night trying to find the point where it wears off. Something like six hours is what I figure."

"Are you serious?" With a startled chuckle, Maxwell rubbed a hand down the side of his face and couldn't settle on the best way to react. "Man, this...this changes everything."

"Uh-huh."

He turned toward the others. "Y'all puttin' two and two together right now?"

Donnie spread his arms and scoffed. "What do you think, man? I feel better'n I did after fillin' up on breakfast."

Chris merely shook his head and gazed at Greta, who ended her spells and lowered her hands. "Huh. Ain't that somethin'."

"It sure is." The woman sat in her chair and let the werewolves have a few more seconds of awe and amazement before she got right down to the core of things. "And now that you know what this plant can do, we have a really big favor to ask of all three of you."

Donnie laughed. "I'd stand up right now and dance the Macarena if that's what you said you wanted."

Romeo snorted. "Please don't."

"Ha! You and your dad took some of this magic flower too before we got here, didn't y'all?"

He played it off well enough and simply shrugged. "Something like that."

Lily didn't miss the look Julian shot his son in that moment. For a split second, the man looked terrified of what he might have told his friends instead. *That's something else we're gonna have to deal with but after meeting with the Council. They'll find out about Romeo's magic tonight, anyway.*

They spent the rest of the morning explaining to the visiting werewolves as much as they had to in order to get their point across. All three of the pack-less werewolves wholeheartedly agreed, without hesitation or any more questions, to come with them to speak to the Council of Magic later that night.

"Y'all opened up a whole new can o' worms now," Chris said, laced his fingers, and bent them back until his knuckles cracked. "Of course we're coming with you. This is big."

"Bigger'n big." Maxwell nodded and clapped Julian on the back. "I can't thank you enough for this, brother."

"That's fine." He glanced across the living room where they'd moved their little gathering and nodded at his son. "I think if Romeo has his way after this, every pack and every rogue wolf out there on his own are gonna get themselves a handful of these little purple flowers."

"Yeah, man." Donnie nodded and raised a fist at Romeo. " 'Bout time things started to change a little around here."

The young werewolf nodded.

"So, now that you boys know everything you need to know about this little purple flower and how all of you can help us help...well, everyone else," Greta said. "I think the best way to spend the rest of the afternoon at this point is to get you ready for the kinda magic you'll hang out around once we have our meeting with the Council."

"Get us ready?" Maxwell glanced at her and frowned.

"Yeah. Think of it like...practicing to take the witness stand in a court trial." She grinned and headed toward the hallway.

"It's nothing like a court trial," Lily muttered.

Romeo leaned toward her. "Only if the witness has an allergic reaction to being questioned on the stand."

The older woman clapped and turned quickly. "Darius."

"Yeah." Yet again, the healer had positioned himself on the couch, this time in the living room.

"Go ahead and get these werewolves ready for some serious Council magic, huh? We only have about five hours 'til we need to start heading out, so we gotta make 'em worth it. Oh, and don't go easy on any of them, all right?" She winked and disappeared behind the living room, heading toward the bathroom at the end of the hall.

The healer didn't need any more coaxing than that. His wiry black beard twitched as he rubbed his hand together and extended his palms toward Julian and his friends gathered in the living room. "I have to admit, I've always wondered how something like this might turn out."

"Bring it on, man." Chris gestured enthusiastically at the large man. "Show us what we're in for."

"Probably not much now that you took a giant magical Benadryl," Darius muttered. "But okay."

The huge bearded man put on some kind of light show for the werewolves—who were probably enjoying magic for the first time in their lives simply because they finally could—and Lily heard the faucet running in the hallway bathroom. She caught Romeo's gaze and nodded. "I'll be right back."

"Sure. Is everything okay?"

"Yep. All good. I got a question for my mom." *Like why she slipped off into the bathroom and what she doesn't want anyone else to hear on the other side of all that running water.*

TWENTY-SEVEN

L ily pressed her ear up against the bathroom door, followed by her fingertips. A quick combination of a revealing spell plus the simplest one for enhancing her senses flashed beneath her fingertips, and the young witch heard her mother loud and clear on the other side of the door.

"Not in Mexico anymore, huh?"

"Obviously not."

Her eyes widened. *I know that voice. How did Mom get Melissa Bore in the bathroom with her?*

"So what happened?" Greta asked the other woman who somehow happened to be having a conversation with her in Julian Stephens' bathroom. "It sounded like you had things basically all resolved."

"Yeah, very funny. I'll tell you what, you...troublemaker."

"Good one."

The other woman snorted. "Things down south went... well, south, okay? The pack essentially turned on me when they heard about the High Seat falling. So no, things weren't completely resolved. Of course, Hugo thought I had something to do with it, based on my colorful history with virtually everyone."

"Right, well, no one ever said that pack's alpha was an idiot."

"He sure as hell isn't. So now it's only little ol' me all on my own again, and then I get these messages from you talking about the Council and Carmichael and trying to rip this whole thing out by the roots. When's that all going down, by the way?"

"Tonight," Greta said. "Seven-thirty. And I really hoped you'd get your country-hopping self back into Charleston to meet us there."

"Sorry, lady. I've been a little busy trying not to die. It sounds like you might be in the same boat right about now too."

"Please. Everyone already thinks I'm dead. Seriously, though, I could really use those wards of yours as backup in case things don't turn out exactly the way I hope. Plus, there's that whole situation with the stone and all the magic we—" Greta stopped short and her voice dropped a little lower. "Hold on, Mel. I have a surprise for ya."

Before Lily could react to the sound of her mother's footsteps heading toward her, the bathroom door jerked open. Greta grabbed her daughter's arm and yanked her into the bathroom before she closed the door again quickly. She spun the girl toward the bathroom mirror and grinned.

"Would ya look at that." Melissa Bore's image shimmered in the mirror next to their reflections. The woman looked tired and a little dirty, but her smile made all of that seem inconsequential. "Were you spyin' on your mama, girl?"

Lily raised her hand to give the woman's reflection a little wave. "Hi, Melissa."

"You know what, Lily? Before I run out of chances to say this to your face, I'm proud of you. You did exactly what that woman standing behind you knew you would. There's a lotta people all over the place who owe you for what you've done. Don't forget that."

The young witch glanced at her mother and shrugged. "I only did what I had to. And we're not quite done yet."

"Huh. That's what your mom was trying to tell me too."

"Are you coming to the meeting?"

"I'll..." Melissa lifted the baseball cap on her head enough to scratch her scalp a few times. "I'll see what I can do."

"Now you're simply avoiding the whole thing altogether." Greta put a hand on her hip and raised an eyebrow. "You already know how helpful it'd be to have you and your skills with us. Maybe even share your perspective on a few things—"

"Okay, let's make this clear." Melissa pointed at them through the mirror. "If I do end up crashing your little party with those thick-skulled, aristocratic...council members, it'll be to offer my support with wards and keep you from blowing yourself up, Greta. And everyone else around you. But I'm not saying a damn thing about anything to the Council. You know where I stand on that."

The woman inclined her head toward the mirror. "Fair enough."

"All right." Melissa turned her gaze onto Lily, and her features softened into a playful smile. "How's that no-good, reckless werewolf of yours, Lily?"

"Romeo's doing great. He still has your handprint on his chest, but it's not nearly as weird as it used to be."

The woman threw her head back and laughed. "I'd tell you to stay outta trouble, girl, but your mama's standin' right there next to you. So I'll wish you luck instead."

"Or you could make it to the meeting. That'd be even better."

"Would you listen to this one?" Melissa pointed at them both. "It sounds like someone's tryin' to take your place in the stinging-witticism department, Greta."

"Yeah, we'll see about that. Let me know if you can make it," Greta retorted

"Uh-huh. Gotta go." In an instant, Melissa Bore's image shimmered again and disappeared completely from the mirror.

Lily turned to face her mom and shrugged. "You can't blame me for wanting to find out why you disappeared in here."

"Of course not, Sweets. I also don't blame you for eavesdropping. It's exactly what I would've done." Greta put a hand on her daughter's shoulder and gave it a little squeeze.

"You're worried about the stone, aren't you?"

With a sigh, the woman closed her eyes and tilted her head from side to side indecisively. "Yes and no. It's better to err on the side of caution. And believe it or not, having Melissa around with her wards is essentially as cautious as things can get."

She nodded. "And we still have to bring the stone with us."

"That's part of our evidence, sweets. We gotta be able to prove everything we know and everything we've done."

"Well..." She smoothed the hair back from her forehead and turned the faucet off. "No one said meeting with the Council was gonna be boring."

Greta laughed but with more sarcasm than humor and opened the bathroom door. "Actually, I think that's been said about every Council meeting for at least as long as I've been alive. Except for maybe when they meet with me."

"You give yourself way too much credit, Mom."

The Antony witches stepped out of the bathroom together with smiles on their faces. They had both put in considerable effort to learn how to hide their emotions whenever they needed to.

Something doesn't feel right. Lily watched her mother step into the living room to join Darius in casting ridiculous spells to gauge how much Julian and his friends could handle with the aid of the wolfsbane they'd consumed. *I don't think Mom even knows exactly what it is either, but she feels it too. We're missing something.*

The only problem now was that they had neither

enough time nor resources to determine what that was before they stood in front of the Council of Magic to deliver what the council members would have to be idiots not to believe.

TWENTY-EIGHT

G etting everyone ready at 6:45 pm was the easiest part. They split up and took two cars—Maxwell's and Chris', at their insistence—and headed toward the location Bentley had texted to Lily's phone half an hour before that.

At 7:10 pm, both cars stopped in the parking lot of the Gaillard Center on Calhoun St. The surrounding street lamps were turned off but the lights in the building were already on, which was a fairly good sign. Bentley met the group outside the building and before they headed inside, he asked them all to wait while he dug around in the trunk of his car.

"You might want these." The man shoved an oversized black hoodie and a plain black baseball cap into Greta's arms.

She huffed at the clothes. "Do you want me to dress up like I'm trying to rob the place, Bentley? I'd be better off simply casting a glamour charm on myself and calling it good."

"You could." He closed the trunk and regarded her with a half-amused expression. "But their detection wards would go off the minute you stepped inside. It's a slightly different way to handle the element of surprise, but if you'd rather they found out about your return from the dead and all that before we actually step into the conference room, by all means, glamour away."

Greta stared at him, then snorted and handed the baseball cap to her daughter. "Will you hold this for a second, Sweets?"

"Yep." The girl took the hat, distinctly aware of Darius, Romeo, and four other werewolves who watched them with varying degrees of anxious expectation.

Her mother tugged the hoodie on over her newest outfit—it honestly looked more like she'd taken a few things out of Julian's closet and left it at that, although Lily didn't want to even bother asking—snatched the hat again and pulled it over her blonde hair. She jerked the sweatshirt's hood up until it covered the hat, her head, and most of her face. "Is that anonymous enough for you?"

"Quite." Bentley's mouth twitched and he turned and motioned the group forward across the parking lot. "Until the Council members offer us the floor to say what we came here to say, the only thing you folks should remember is to let me do the talking. At first."

A round of muttered agreements met that warning as they reached the entrance to the Gaillard Center. The accountant opened the door and gestured for everyone to step inside first. "Stop right here in the lobby, if you will. I'll go and let them know we're here."

Without waiting for an answer, he hurried down the hall and left the group standing in silence.

Lily slipped her hand into Romeo's and gave it a quick, reassuring squeeze. "How are you doin'?"

"I'm, uh...I'm doin', Lil." He gave a wry chuckle and swept his gaze across the lobby. "I know the whole episode with Cadre Europa was supposed to be a practice run, but this feels a heck of a lot different."

"That makes sense. You did everything you needed to do in front of Cadre Europa, and they were definitely impressed."

"Uh-huh."

"So do the same thing here. You'll be fine."

He glanced down at her and chewed on the inside of his cheek. "And you're not even a little nervous, are you?"

"I wouldn't say that." She took a deep breath and smiled. "Maybe not as nervous as you."

"Hey, thanks." He shook his head but she felt the tension loosen a little inside him.

Lily watched her mom and Julian talking to each other in low tones. The man seemed even more nervous than his son, which really didn't take very much and was perfectly understandable. Romeo had far more practice standing in front of magical officials in situations like this. The part that bothered her was that Greta also looked nervous and that was definitely new.

Almost as if she'd heard her daughter's thoughts, the

woman looked up from her hushed conversation, met her gaze, and nodded.

"Okay, everyone." Bentley stood at the end of the hallway and gestured for the group to follow them. "They're ready. It's time for us to be ready too."

"Here we go." Greta wiggled her eyebrows and strode after him.

The remainder of the group followed soundlessly until they reached the double doors into a room labeled *Auditorium A*. Bentley nodded at them and pushed down on the handles before he yanked both doors out toward the hall. He left them open and strolled into the venue like he owned the place.

I guess he might have if we were here fifteen years ago.

The auditorium was brightly lit. A long table and seven chairs had been set up on the stage, and a member of the Council of Magic sat in each seat. None of them spoke to welcome or even greet the magicals who'd scheduled this meeting with them.

"They don't look too happy about this, Lil," Romeo whispered.

"They don't need to be happy. They only need to listen."

The accountant led their entire group down the center aisle of the auditorium, then gestured for Romeo, Lily, and Darius to take their seats in the front row. He'd told Greta to wait just inside the auditorium doors, where the council members might have more difficulty recognizing the world-renowned archaeologist witch who'd been pronounced dead six months before. Julian and his werewolf friends were shown to their seats a few rows behind Lily, although a few rows back wasn't far enough to hide the disdain on the seven council members' faces when they noted the five werewolves in their presence. Fortunately, the meeting didn't start with that.

Bentley inclined his head toward the officials seated at the table. The stage almost gave the impression that it was a throne put together at the last minute simply to make them feel important. He gestured toward the front row of auditorium seats one more time. "Lily Antony, Romeo Stephens, and Darius Balsur."

"Thank you, Mr. McClure." The older gentleman seated in the center chair nodded somewhat disdainfully and didn't bother to hide his smirk as the accountant sat, apparently unperturbed by the lack of enthusiasm from the Council.

Lily tilted her chin and waited for the witch's gaze to settle on her. *There he is. Councilmember Brast. These people are gonna flip when they see Mom standing here.*

"We hear you have valuable information to share with us tonight." Brast looked at the front row over the bridge of his aquiline nose. His short gray hair was as neatly trimmed as the thin, graying goatee on his chin. "Please, let's get this started."

After a quick deep breath, she stood. "Thank you, Councilmember Brast. Councilmembers."

She nodded at the other magicals seated behind that table, which made the situation even more awkward as all she could see of them from where she stood were their faces. Brast couldn't completely hide his surprise at the fact that she knew his name—or his satisfaction. *It's like he doesn't remember me at all. That can't be real.*

"First, I want to say how much we appreciate your willingness to meet us on such short notice."

A thin witch with purple-gray hair puffed up by too much time in curlers tittered at her statement. "And our apologies for only being able to secure this space on such short notice."

"There is no need to apologize." Lily held her head high and forced herself to smile. *So I gotta start this off by groveling, apparently. Well, it won't be for long.* "I'm sure you all know what we came here to discuss with you tonight."

Councilmember Brast stroked his goatee and glanced at the other council members on either side of him. "We have some idea, Ms. Antony. But we would very much like to hear it all directly from you. So, whenever you're ready."

The man swept an open palm over the edge of the table toward her.

It's like he's tossing gold coins to a group of beggars. I guess it's a good thing I already have enough of those.

"Thank you. I'd like to start by bringing to the Council's attention the existence of a widely unknown and unrecognized organization of magicals who call themselves the Black Heron Society."

"Oh!" The weasel-faced man at the far-right end of the table widened his eyes and leaned forward. "More stories. We've heard something like this before, haven't we?"

The other officials nodded and mumbled some form of agreement or annoyance. Lily fought not to clench her fists or give any indication of how much of a headache she now expected this entire meeting to be. "I may not be the first to bring this up with the Council, but I do know that I'm the first to tell you everything you're about to hear tonight."

"And the first to bring a whole werewolf pack in front of the Council of Magic." This time, it was an old council member seated on the purple-haired witch's left whose hair looked like he'd modeled it after Einstein. "You'd better make this good, Ms. Antony."

"Well, I'll do my best."

A round of disappointed sighs and a few more titters from the purple-haired witch was the Council's only response. She risked a quick glance at Bentley seated across the aisle from her. To anyone else, the nod he gave her looked like another formal way to encourage the young witch forward with whatever she had to say. Fortunately, she knew him better than that. He was telling her to keep her cool and keep going, no matter what.

At least, that's what it looks like he's trying to say. Which is good advice anyway so I'm gonna go with that. And I guess we'll see how long it takes before Mom feels like she needs to interrupt and cue the big surprise for everyone.

TWENTY-NINE

I t was like their meeting with Cadre Europa all over
again, except for the fact that Greta hadn't inserted
herself into the conversation yet. The Council of Magic
didn't seem remotely interested in listening to a thing Lily
had to say and the response remained unvaried every time
she presented a new piece of information. She recounted
her travels with Romeo, listed the countries where they'd
personally seen magicals kidnapped or murdered by the
Black Heron Society, and related her meeting with Darius
in Romania and hearing everything he'd told them about
what he and Greta had discovered before she was taken.

Occasionally, one council member or another had a
biting quip or ridiculously bullheaded question. They
constantly derailed her story, and after forty-five minutes
of trying to take them more seriously than they apparently
wanted to take themselves, she somehow still managed to
keep her cool through all of it.

"What I don't understand, Ms. Antony, is how you can possibly prove any of these claims to anyone."

She settled her attention on the overweight witch seated beside Brast and while she she'd given up on trying to force a polite smile, she hadn't yet fallen into scowling at any of them. "I can prove it, Councilmember. If you'll simply let me finish—"

"You can, huh? My dear girl, you've brought us a very large witch from Romania, however impressive he may be, and five werewolves. That's hardly proof of anything but your apparent desperation for someone to pay attention to you."

Did he really say that?

Beside her in the front row, Romeo shifted uncomfortably in his auditorium seat. Darius merely folded his arms and remained as quiet as usual.

"Yes," Lily began and fought the natural response to inject a snide edge to her response. "I brought these werewolves with me because they're part of what I'm trying to explain. They've all agreed to—"

"I don't remember ever needing an explanation for why we don't allow their kind into common establishments in the first place, let alone meetings with the Council." Brast raised an eyebrow and stared at her, almost as if he tried to goad her into some kind of outburst.

"Excuse me?" That was as much as she could manage without completely losing her carefully maintained control.

"They seem to be handling themselves fairly well so far," the man at the center of the table continued. "But we didn't have as much time as usual to prepare our more effective security wards. Tell me, Ms. Antony, what would happen if all of us on this stage—or even only one of us—cast a few spells with real power to them? These friends of yours wouldn't stand a chance, and we'd have the rest of this conversation after they'd been apprehended and detained for the kind of behavior werewolves have always and will always continue to exhibit."

For a few seconds, she was completely speechless. *This jerk was Mom's mentor? Seriously?* She cleared her throat. "With all due respect, Councilmember Brast, I think you've missed the point."

"Oh, I highly doubt that."

"This is ridiculous," Romeo muttered.

"Wait, hold on a sec." Lily put out her hand in a weak attempt to stop him, but he had apparently made his mind up.

"You did your best, Lil. Which was actually really good." He stood and nodded at her. "But it's not getting through to them."

She pressed her lips together and sat in her chair. *Please, be careful.*

"Ah." Councilmember Brast smirked and stroked his goatee again. "I hit a sore spot, I see."

"Not really." The young werewolf shrugged. "None of what you said actually applies to me anymore. Or to the other werewolves we brought with us today."

"Really?" The purple-haired witch snorted. "And why is that?"

"Well, I'm part of the proof." He spread his arms and

summoned spouting fountains of purple and blue sparks in his palms. They illuminated the front of the auditorium in dancing flashes, and the council members on the stage exploded in outrage.

"How in the name of source did you come to learn that?" one demanded indignantly.

"Stop it. Stop it right now!"

"Whatever game you're trying to pull, Mr. Stephens, we won't have it."

"It's not a game." Romeo ended the simple spell that was really only for show and took a step toward the stage. "This is what she's been trying to explain to you the whole time. This actually happened. To me. And the Black Heron Society is responsible for all of it."

"The Black Heron Society does not exist!" The weasel-faced councilmember pounded a fist on the plastic table. "And I, for one, am rapidly growing tired of hearing about them over and over again. This proves nothing."

"And what about them?" The werewolf turned slightly and gestured toward Julian and the other three werewolves a few rows back, all of whom looked completely caught off guard by being brought into the argument at all. "I tossed a fair number of sparks around and they haven't so much as blinked."

"We should never have agreed to this," the purple-haired witch protested. "Werewolves in a Council meeting? There's something else going on here."

"Oh, come on!" Lily leapt to her feet and pointed at the werewolves now too. "We've told you exactly what's going on and you've seen it with your own eyes. These werewolves took wolfsbane before we came here, and they're fine. That's what we're trying to get across to you here. We need everyone's help if we want to stop the members of the Black Heron who are still out there trying to perform this Transference spell again—"

"Which is even more ridiculous than civilized werewolves!"

"You merely refuse to see what's right in front of you," she retorted angrily.

"These are lone wolves," Romeo added. "They don't have a pack and they don't have any incentive to come together and sit here while you say all this to their faces—except for the fact that they're here to help me to show the Council what's possible."

Brast uttered a sharp, sardonic laugh. "I don't know what you called this meeting to achieve, Ms. Antony. Is it to convince us that the Black Heron Society is real and capable of such an outrageous thing as a widespread Transference spell among thousands of magicals? Or is it that werewolves aren't really a menace to magical society and can be tamed with a little poisonous petal?"

"Tamed?" Romeo gawked at the council members on stage. "You've gotta be kidding me."

While the argument escalated by the second, Bentley slipped out of his seat in the front row and darted up the aisle toward the auditorium doors. When he reached Greta —who'd merely stood in silence for the duration and watched from beneath the shadow of the sweatshirt's hood —it seemed he wouldn't be able to find the words he wanted to ask her. Finally, he caught his breath. "So, is there something specific you're waiting for? Because now looks like a really good time to stop this mess and cut to the chase, don't you think?"

Her frown deepened and she squinted at the council members on the stage, most of whom were not engaged in a shouting match with her daughter. "Something's wrong."

"That's ridiculously obvious, Greta."

"No, I mean this isn't the meeting I expected. It's like they've already made their minds up about writing us all off before the conversation even started."

"What are you thinking?"

She rubbed her lips a few times and shook her head. "I don't know. But I'm gonna find out. Don't worry about introducing me or anything."

With that, she strode down the aisle toward the stage, leaving Bentley McClure to simply stand and stare after her in surprise. "It's not like you need an introduction anyway, is it?"

No one noticed the magical in the baggy sweatshirt and baseball cap until she stood beside Lily. The young witch stopped when she noticed her mother and she couldn't decide whether she should say anything at all.

"And who else have you brought to sell us these ridiculous stories?" another official demanded and gestured abruptly with his hand toward the woman none of them had yet recognized.

"We're not trying to sell you anything," Greta said. "But I would really love it if the Council in all its wisdom would wipe the stupid out of your eyes so you can see the truth."

Someone gasped, but that had to have been at the insult because she hadn't even pulled the hood down or removed the baseball hat. When she did, though, the auditorium fell completely silent. The overweight councilmember at the end of the table wobbled a little on his feet and lowered himself slowly into his chair.

Greta Antony stepped forward toward the stage and fixed her gaze on all seven members on the Council of Magic individually before she spoke. "It's easy enough to ignore everything these young people have tried so hard to tell you, whether or not you even want to try listening. So I feel like I should ask if any of you would have a different opinion of how to categorize this new information if it came from my mouth instead."

The purple-haired witch uttered a startled squeak of surprise. "How is this possible?"

"Do you mean how am I alive?" She shrugged, then set her hands on the edge of the stage and leaned forward to force the council members to mirror the action so they could actually see her over the edge of the table. "That's very simple, really. I never died."

"And this has to do with the rest of this nonsense...how, exactly?" Councilmember Brast asked in a hard tone.

Greta gave her former mentor a pained smile. "Come on, Alexander. I'm here. Someone's obviously tried very hard to cloud your judgment, but this is me. I'm here because we can't stop any of this without the Council first recognizing everything that's happened. And everything that will happen if we don't take a stand right now."

The goateed council member raised his chin and gazed

at his former apprentice with a raised eyebrow. "We've been down this road before, Greta."

"And this time, I have even more to bring you. How can you not see this?"

"I see a group of magicals severely desperate to satisfy their own agenda," the weasel-faced official added.

"Alexander." She took a deep breath and didn't look away from her mentor. "You know what I am. You helped me get to where I am today. Because of that, I felt I could come to you with something important. Please. Help us do this."

Stroking his goatee again, Councilmember Brast walked around the table, stopped in front of her, and lowered himself into a squat at the edge of the stage. He tilted his head, frowned at his former pupil, and released a sigh that sounded more wounded than anything else. "I understand the illusions you've always had of yourself, Ms. Antony. But let me assure you, there are no Optatus witches left in this world and you're wasting our time."

Greta stared with wide eyes at the man who'd turned her away completely, leaving no room whatsoever for things to be set right again.

Lily held her breath. *What's going on?*

Her mother took a sharp breath, seemed to lose her train of thought, then looked at the other council members on the stage before her gaze settled on Alexander again. "Did someone pay you to say that to me?"

The minute she finished that question, the auditorium exploded into chaos, not the least of which came from the outraged shouts and furious denials of the six other officials. The real trouble, however, came from the double doors of the auditorium's entrance, which burst open after Bentley had quietly shut them for privacy.

The one-eyed leader of the crippled Black Heron Society stepped through into the auditorium.

THIRTY

"This is a private gathering," the purple-haired council member protested from behind the table.

"So I've heard." Carmichael strode calmly forward down the sloping decline of the auditorium's center aisle, his hands seemingly clasped behind his back. "This won't take long, I assure you."

One of his hands moved forward to slide into the inside pocket of his teal smoking jacket. He removed a small, bone-white object, raised it toward Greta with a nod, and put it in his mouth.

"Stop him," she muttered and stared at the maddened witch with wide eyes.

"Ms. Antony, there's not much we can do if this man has come to either support or refute your claims. If he's here as part of our discussion, he is allowed entry and the opportunity to participate."

"He's not here for either of those things, you idiot," the woman snapped and whirled toward the weasel-faced council member who'd tried to rationalize the intruder's presence. "Are you blind? He swallowed a runic—"

"Mom!" Lily pointed toward Carmichael, who had now withdrawn both broken pieces of the copper rod that had once been the Varelos from behind his back.

"Damnit, stop him!" Greta lunged toward the Black Heron Society's leader but before she reached him, a large group of magicals flooded through the double doors that were still wide open at the back of the auditorium. The council members reacted with immediate consternation to the crowd that had apparently decided to disrupt the meeting.

"What is the meaning of this?" one of them bellowed.

Lily summoned her sparking red attack spell. "To stop anyone who doesn't—"

The venue exploded with spells from the two dozen mutant society members who had streamed through the doors. She fired her spells and glanced quickly to where her mother attempted to reach Carmichael. The man stood in the center of the aisle and muttered a spell in a low voice as he slowly drew the broken pieces of the Varelos together in front of him.

Romeo snarled beside the young witch and in the next moment, a blur of shaggy black fur streaked over the front row of seats away from the stage. He almost reached the man but a mutant witch with shimmering purple skin and hair that looked like it was constantly on fire jerked her hands toward him.

He narrowly escaped the blast of whirling dark-purple magic that surged toward him. When he tried to push toward his target again, he was bowled over by one of the abnormally large white wolves of the Black Heron Society. It's glowing red eyes revealed its true mutant nature as it darted out of sight behind the many auditorium chairs.

Julian and his friends weren't far behind. They all shifted in a matter of seconds and left a pile of their clothes on the floor as they joined the fray.

"This is unacceptable!" One of the council members pounded a fist over and over on the plastic folding table onstage. "We will not have such uncivilized behavior during this—"

A ball of churning green flames exploded against the side of the table and hurled it across the dais. The Council of Magic scattered and they were now forced to enter the chaos and defend themselves. Lily didn't miss the fact that most of them cast defensive spells only and none of them seemed to pay any attention to Carmichael at all.

"Lily!" Greta blasted a hulking werewolf hybrid very much like the one the young couple had fought in Oitylo, only this one's skin was a bright, sun-burned pink mottled with white. The woman werewolf shifted, snarled, and grew another three feet as she advanced toward the woman, still on two legs while her eyes wavered between silver and black.

The young witch hurled a few volleys of her inextinguishable blue flames at the mottled were-mutant, which only made it stumble sideways into the closest row of seats.

"Forget about me," her mother shouted again and thrust a hand toward Carmichael. "Stop that!"

The young witch spun toward the man, who still stood

in the center of the auditorium, his focus completely consumed by his muttered incantation and the pieces of the Varelos he'd almost drawn completely together again. She leapt away from two snarling wolves entangled in their own battle—one of them a dark-gray and the other pure white, both splattered with blood. She only made it two steps up the incline of the center aisle as she dodged the spells that came from all directions around her. Ingrid sneered at her from a few rows back with a malevolent expression on her face.

The necromancer muttered a sharp curse and hurled dark energy and swarming black projectiles toward her. Lily raised a warded shield barely in time and the energetic jolt of the curse pinged away from her. Her arms tingled with each successive burst against her magical barrier.

"Lily!" Greta shouted again.

"I'm...trying!"

Her adversary gave her no respite. Lily pushed against the force of the other woman's dark spell but it took way too long to gain any traction up the center aisle. *If I let this shield down to get to Carmichael, I won't make it.*

An earsplitting thunderclap shattered the air behind her. Darius bellowed and shoved both hands across the auditorium toward the necromancer. A burst of red and orange flames erupted from his hands and rocketed over the upholstered seats accompanied by the same roar as the witch who'd cast them. Lily saw a fiery mane around burning eyes and a mouth open in rage while four powerful legs of flame churned the air, and a lithe tail tipped in a tuft of flame whipped ominously. Whatever spirit Darius had conjured was enough to interrupt the necromancer's constant stream of attacks on her. Ingrid shrieked and fell back beneath the whirling flames that bore down on her.

The girl spun to thank Darius, but the massive bearded healer gestured up the center aisle and shouted, "Go!"

Her focus immediately restored, she ran and ducked a scattered blast of searing green embers like fired buckshot that careened across the aisle. Carmichael merely continued to recite his incantation, his one eye wide with growing anticipation. The glass eye swirled with silver energy she was sure didn't belong there at all. Before she could reach him, a short, stunted-looking fairy—mutated by what could only be a warlock's stolen and transferred magic—leapt from the next row of seats between her and her target.

"Not this time," he challenged and raised both hands. Despite the fact that he was most likely laughing, the magical mutations inside him made it look as if he had lost all control of his face, which folded and melted around his features like he was made of soft, warmed playdough.

Lily blasted him with her red attack spell and followed it up with another burst of her perseverant blue flames. The mutant shrieked and his spiraled blast of pea-green magic shot harmlessly toward the auditorium ceiling. A huge tan wolf pounced onto her would-be attacker and dragged the screaming mutant down one row of seats, tugging fiercely a few inches at a time.

Carmichael almost had the ends of the Varelos pressed

together, and his low muttering had increased its pace. She thought she saw him start to smile. *My time's up.*

She clapped her hands together and drew them apart. The billowing energy of her roiling black cloud grew between her palms and hissed and sparked with silver light. Before she could pull her hands any farther apart than a few inches, Carmichael uttered a startling scream of victory and thrust the broken ends of the Varelos together.

The ground trembled. A bright copper flash burst from the reconnected center of the copper rod. He cackled like a madman and his triumphant shrieks cut through all the other chaos of spells and shouting magicals and snarling, snapping wolves.

Lily's hands moved another inch apart and the black cloud of her Optatus magic reacted almost in slow motion. The Black Heron leader looked at her, both his good eye and the glass orb full of wild fury and anticipation. He shrieked again but this time, his cry quickly morphed into a scream of agony.

"Take him down, Li—"

Greta's shout was cut off by a second massive shudder in the floor beneath them. The Varelos released another copper burst and a blinding white flash. A mind-shattering crack rent the air, exactly as it had when Lily had commanded the magical weapon to destroy itself. This time, however, it was reawakened.

The unfathomable amount of magical energy needed for Carmichael's spell could no longer be contained. The white light exploded from the center of the Varelos and drove a shockwave of magic and force and tingling, rippling power out in every direction. It thrust Lily off her feet and flung her down the decline of the center aisle toward the stage. Every other magical within a dozen feet of Carmichael received the same treatment, no matter who they were fighting for.

Her back struck the hard metal armrest of the aisle seat in the first row, and she toppled onto the floor. Her ears filled only with a high-pitched ring that wouldn't go away. Slowly, dizzy and nauseous from the Varelos' massive power release, she propped herself up onto her side and looked around.

Magic of every color still speared through the air across the auditorium. Another white werewolf-warlock hybrid leapt over two rows of seats to engage someone else in a fight. Darius roared again and a coiling purple cobra longer than the healer was tall snaked from his hands. Bentley McClure had reached Greta's side and now stood back-to-back with the woman to deliver precise, efficient spells in bright yellow and blinding-white toward any Black Heron mutant who came too close.

Lily couldn't hear any of it. Scowling against the pain in her head, she pushed to her feet and stared up the center aisle of the auditorium.

Carmichael lay sprawled along the red carpet of the aisle, his neck twisted at an impossible angle above his shoulders. The man's eyes were still wide and wild, although the silver energy in the white glass orb was now gone. His mouth remained open in his agonized scream, and even though she could only hear the painful ringing in her ears, she knew his torment had already been silenced by death.

For a fraction of a second, she dared to hope he'd failed to restore the broken pieces of the Varelos and his spell had backfired and destroyed him in the process. Her gaze fell on the copper rod in the center aisle at his feet. It glistened in one long piece of smooth, seamless metal.

No...

Her legs wobbled beneath her as another wave of nausea and dizziness surged over her. All around her, the fight continued unabated. Her friends and those who'd always believed in her and her mother fought the bastardized society members who obviously stopped at nothing to remove every obstacle from their dark path.

A shadow fell over the curved, inverted-U shape of the Varelos' staff head and the sharpened tines at each end of the U. Shiny black shoes stopped beside the magical weapon and a hand stretched down to take the copper rod in a firm grasp.

Lily steadied herself against the cold metal armrest beside her and stared at the only magical in this entire bizarre battle who'd noticed and understood exactly what Carmichael Cantus had sacrificed.

Councilmember Brast, head of the Council of Magic and former mentor to Greta Antony so many years before, straightened where he stood and turned with the Varelos in hand. A thin, cold smile spread across his face as he looked away from the restored weapon to the violence that still raged. She still couldn't hear but she saw the witch's mouth move and understood his words perfectly.

"That's quite enough."

The weapon released another rapid burst of shimmering copper light and the entire auditorium fell still beneath its power.

Cast spells froze mid-air. A snarling wolf hung suspended in the middle of shaking his head with a mutant's arm locked in his jaws. Bentley had one arm outstretched toward an attacking society member while behind him, Greta had already turned fully to face Brast. Her eyes were wide in shock and fearful understanding, but no one could move, not even Lily.

Only he retained his control over his own body and he turned the Varelos so it hung vertically in his hand. "Now that I have everyone's attention, I would very much like witnesses to this fateful event."

The weapon flashed again, and every magical in the auditorium fell free of the magical suspension. The fighting had stopped completely now, and all eyes turned toward the witch who wielded the powerful weapon most of them didn't even know existed.

"That's much better."

"Alexander," Greta whispered and took a step up the center aisle toward him. "What are you doing?"

"What this blind idiot could never have done all on his own." Alexander turned toward Carmichael's body and kicked the dead magical's shoe as if he were merely scuffing aside a pile of trash that had tumbled toward him. "He was so sure of himself, so intent on taking everything into his own hands because of how much he thought he understood you. For years, Margaret, he thought he understood you better than I did. That he'd been closer to you than I ever was. How silly of him."

The woman stepped forward again and reached her hand out calmly. "Don't."

"Trust me, my dear, I don't hold any claim to jealousy or wounded pride or a warped sense of proving myself to anyone, least of all you." Councilmember Brast chuckled. "I do, however, wish to see things change in a world that has fallen so far from its original design. That was perhaps the only thing Carmichael and I had in common, and his ignorant perseverance has made this far easier for me than I expected."

Lily narrowed her eyes and lowered herself into a crouch beside the front row's aisle seat. she stretched her jaw from side to side as her hearing returned enough to follow the tense conversation in front of her.

"This isn't what you really want." Greta lowered her hand again and stood tall, braving her former mentor and all the power he now wielded with the Varelos in his hand. "I found the doorway. Did I tell you that?"

"Hmm. I seem to recall very little opportunity for you to tell me anything." Alexander raised his eyebrows in a mocking attempt to feign sympathy. "The doorway isn't that difficult to find."

"I opened it." The woman inclined her head and gazed at her former mentor with a burning, unwavering stare. "And now, I'm standing here. There's so much beyond this realm and I can show you how to access it."

He snorted and lifted the Varelos a little higher. "So

can this. I'm rather tempted to listen to an entity who only answers the questions I ask and doesn't talk back."

Lily swallowed. *He's obviously never had a chat with the Varelos.*

Behind her, Romeo padded on silent paws until he hunkered below the front row of seats. In the next second, he'd shifted into bare skin and dark, curly hair. Lily heard him rustling through his clothes and wondered why he thought now of all times was the right moment to get dressed again.

"You won't get what you need from that weapon," Greta continued. "And the Transference spell doesn't work the way you think it does."

"But I'll find out exactly what it does do, won't I?"

Romeo nudged Lily's shoulder, and she turned to look at him with wide eyes. Before she could say a thing, he lifted the mirror charm on the silver chain he'd worn around his neck since she had put it there herself at the Black Heron's High Seat. His eyebrows raised and she immediately understood everything he meant to do.

"In the meantime," Alexander continued with a dreamy little sigh, "I'm far more interested in seeing exactly how well the Varelos stands up to a seasoned Optatus."

He pointed the tip of the weapon at the center of Greta's chest, and Lily thought her heart had stopped.

THIRTY-ONE

"Mom—" Lily knew she'd spoken but she couldn't hear the words over the new rushing in her ears. Or maybe it was the crackling hiss of the black, spitting magic that erupted from the tip of the Varelos to wind itself in less than a second around Greta Antony's neck.

Her mother stared at Councilmember Brast with wide eyes and clutched the quickly tightening magic with both hands. She uttered no sound and instead, raised both hands and aimed them shakily at her former mentor.

"Not quite." The council member sneered and the Varelos flashed again. The black tendrils of magic around her neck flared as well and now, they were the same bright copper color as the weapon itself. Two whips of energy lashed out and caught her wrists to force her hands down at her sides while the rest of the spell created entirely for an Optatus witch's demise curled tighter and tighter around her.

"You may have convinced the world you were something special, Margaret." Alexander flicked the Varelos into the air and the spell under his command lifted Greta Antony off her feet and raised her slowly above the red carpet of the center aisle.

No one in the auditorium moved and all seemed to know they wouldn't stand a chance against the magic empowered by the restored weapon. There was, however, another Optatus witch Alexander and the Council of Magic as a whole had failed to recognize.

"And now we can put these myths about you to rest, my dear." The man snarled at Greta as she finally started to choke when her body betrayed her willpower in favor of trying not to suffocate. "Margaret Antony can, in fact, die. Let's show them, shall we?"

"Now," Lily whispered.

Romeo gritted his teeth and clutched the mirror charm in a tight fist. He scrunched his eyes shut, and she could only hope the last forty-eight hours were enough to reset the cooldown on the magical artifact. It was the only thing that could reverse the most powerful setback before the Varelos could accomplish its purpose to kill her mother.

For a second, it seemed she and Romeo had misjudged the timing and their own abilities. Her heart sank but before she could even begin to fight the feeling of despair, the Varelos flashed with another earsplitting crack. The coiling copper tendrils that had tightened around Greta's throat, waist, and arms shuddered and vanished. The woman fell five feet to the red carpeting with a gasp.

Alexander hissed in irritation and shook the weapon. "Of all the—"

Lily stood and clapped her hands together. This time, when the roiling black cloud of her Optatus magic formed between her palms, she had sufficient time to finish the spell. She walked forward up the center aisle and the cloud grew quickly and sparked silver light between her hands. She jerked her arms apart and vaguely registered somewhere in the back of her mind that she might have screamed. Her focus, though, was on the Varelos in Alexander's hand and the one thing she understood about such a powerful weapon. *It doesn't belong here.*

"You're finished!" Councilmember Brast shouted and moved toward her, raising the Varelos to target her instead.

A second before he could cast his next spell, she finished hers. The black cloud erupted ahead of her and seared toward Alexander. He stopped short and stared at the dark energy that barreled toward him, but the black cloud funneled into the Varelos instead. With a crack and a muted flash of light, the entire copper rod vanished from the council member's grasp.

The dark witch stumbled forward, struck dumb for a few seconds by the Varelos' sudden disappearance.

"That doesn't belong to you either," Lily said as she fought to catch her breath and stay on her feet after having cast the spell all on her own this time.

Alexander screamed with rage and spittle sprayed from his lips as he charged down the center aisle. She raised her hands toward him but couldn't find the strength to do any more than that. The next thing she knew, her head thumped against the red carpet behind her. Alexander fell on her, snarling and roaring in fury. His thin, gnarled hands clawed around her throat and squeezed. The mad witch's shoulders hunched around his neck as he bore down with all his weight on the young Optatus witch who'd snatched his power.

"Lily," Greta gasped, although the woman was unable to do much more than crawl across the carpet toward her daughter.

Choking and fighting for breath, Lily stared at the crazed face above her own and wondered if things would be any safer for the people she knew she was about to leave behind. Her pulse pounded in her head, her entire face hot and tingling while her chest burned. Whoever moved around her would be too late to stop Brast, she knew that.

A dark-gray blur leapt over the closest rows of seats. The air filled with a ferocious snarl and the hiss of air knocked out of someone else's body. She was sure of that because now, she drew in raw, searing gasps of breath and cried out at the pain of it.

Jaws snapped and claws slashed at Councilmember Brast's deceptively thin frame. A loud crack, a sickening crunch, and a heavy thud were followed by nothing but a high, slow whine.

Cool hands settled on her forehead and she struggled to focus on her mom's face as it hovered over her. Greta's blue eyes studied her daughter's with terror and desperate hope. The young witch clutched the woman's wrists, barely able to hold onto them before she was drawn into a frantic embrace. They lay in the auditorium's center aisle, holding one another as tightly as they could. Their chests heaved with the effort to regain breath and strength and a confirmation that this really wasn't the end.

Then Lily remembered the wolf.

She tried to sit up and could only twist herself sideways to see the gray wolf seated at the edge of the aisle. He panted and his silver eyes were steady and fixed intently on the bundled heap of black clothing and gray hair in front of him.

"Mom," she croaked. "Is he—"

The gray wolf whined again, stood, and backed away a few paces as footsteps raced up the incline of the center aisle toward him. The remaining members of the Council of Magic moved past the Antony witches huddled on the floor. The purple-haired witch bent forward and stuck her hand inside the heap of black clothing. When she straightened again, her eyes were wide and she shook her head at her fellow council members.

"He's dead."

Lily couldn't quite put all the pieces together in her own head. The officials launched into another conversation she couldn't logically follow before a shout cut through their frantic voices.

"Hey!" Romeo jogged up the center aisle, barefoot and bare-chested as he finished fastening his pants again.

"Stand back, Mr. Stephens," a council member warned. "We don't need anyone else involved in this."

He dropped to his knees beside Lily and brushed her hair away from her face to study her intently. "You okay?"

"Yeah—" She winced as the single word seared through her almost crushed throat and managed a few weak nods.

The hybrid wolf glanced at the council members and took a deep breath. "I'm very sure everyone in this room is involved. And we all saw what happened."

"Stay out of this, young man—"

"It was an accident!"

A fresh wave of sparking, crashing spells rocketed across the auditorium toward the gathered council members. The acting Council of Magic moved as one, raised their hands, and fired spells at the errant Black Heron mutants who still seemed determined to fight for something. More shouts rose along with screams of pain and surprise and growls of frustration. Lily's vision blurred as the short, messy end of this entire battle drew to a close.

It seemed like no time at all before the Council of Magic had effectively incapacitated every member of the Black Heron Society who now acted without an organized leader. Hybrid mutants twisted and jerked within flashing, sparking bindings of powerful, warded magic twisted around them in a similar way to how the Varelos spell had wound around Greta Antony. The difference, of course, was that none of the society members would die there or any time soon.

The woman council member patted her airy purple hair into place, turned toward Romeo, and caught her breath. "None of us expected a fight. Or a betrayal like this."

She nodded at the pile of black suit on the floor, and Lily's mind finally caught up to her. *That's Alexander. He's gone.*

"Neither did we," the young werewolf replied. "And we have almost ten witnesses to what happened. You can't seriously think it's right to punish him for what he—"

"Romeo." The voice was scratchy and thick with bewilderment, but it was undoubtedly Julian's. The man crouched buck-naked where the gray wolf had been, although he now raised his head to meet his son's gaze. "It's okay."

"No, it's not—"

"We obviously have much to discuss and considerably more action to take after tonight." The weasel-faced magical snapped his fingers and produced a thick gray cloak seemingly out of thin air. He draped this over Julian's back, nodded, and turned to address everyone else in the auditorium. "In light of the disturbing discoveries made tonight—especially regarding the head of the Council of Magic and one of our own falsely beloved fellow witches— the Council has decided to lend credence and viability to the claims offered by Ms. Lily Antony, Mr. Romeo Stephens, Mr. Darius Balsur, and, although previously unannounced, Ms. Margaret Antony. Now, if you'll excuse us, the criminals we have apprehended must be taken into secure custody and we have an empty seat on the Council to fill."

The man nodded toward his fellow council members,

who silently fell into step behind him. Their next spells were far more understated than the few seconds of battle with the society members they'd finally agreed to fight, however belated their decision. Three of the officials strode toward the auditorium doors and streamed tethers of pulsing magic to draw the captured mutants and dark society members behind them.

Somehow, the two Optatus witches managed to help each other to their feet. Greta pulled her daughter swiftly into her arms again, and Lily buried her face in the blonde hair that spilled over her mother's shoulder.

Romeo offered Julian a hand and helped his dad to his feet. The older werewolf wrapped the conjured cloak tighter and stared at the body of Councilmember Brast. "I was only tryin' to get him off her."

"I know, Dad."

"He was gonna... That bastard woulda..." The older werewolf sniffed.

"I know." He moved to put his arm around his dad's shoulders but they were interrupted by the overweight council member with a mop of stringy, dull blond hair matted across his forehead with sweat.

"Mr. Stephens." Both werewolves turned toward him until the sweaty witch finally nodded at Julian. "We'd like a word with you as well, please."

"Wait a minute," Romeo protested. "What are you gonna do with him?"

"That is what we'd like to discuss."

"But you won't take him away or anything, right? Lily

almost died and my dad was the only one who managed to keep that from happening. You can't simply—"

"Hey." Julian placed a hand on his son's bare shoulder and clutched the cloak tightly with the other hand. "It's all right, son. I'm willing to face the consequences of what I did. I don't regret it, but I ain't gonna run from it, either. Y'hear?"

He clenched his jaw and stared at his dad. "Yeah."

"Good. Now take them home"—the older man nodded toward Greta and Lily—"and make sure your phone's on. If I get my phone call, it's gonna be to you."

With that, he turned away and nodded at the council member, who gestured for him to walk ahead of him up the center aisle toward whatever awaited him beyond.

"He'll be fine," Greta muttered, her voice hardly more than a harsh, raw whisper. "They have to decide what to do with him after this, but it's not nearly as bad you think. He'll be back. Trust me."

Romeo sighed heavily and approached silently to wrap his arms around Lily now, who looked like she could barely stand on her own. She melted into him and was more than content to simply press her face against his bare chest and try not to think about anything else.

"Do you know what they'll make him do?" he asked her mother.

"I honestly have no idea." She swallowed and raised a hand toward her raw throat but thought better of it. "Whatever they decide is fitting for the man who killed the head of the Council of Magic. Who also happened to be a traitor leading all of them blindly into the darkness. Nothing too severe, if I had to bet."

"I hope so."

Chris, Maxwell, Donnie, Darius, and Bentley made their way toward the center aisle from wherever they'd been when the fighting stopped. The auditorium had cleared completely now except for the group who'd come to appeal to the Council. Instead, exactly what they had predicted had happened before they had even finished their meeting.

"Let's call it a night, huh?" Greta squeezed Lily's shoulder and said nothing more. She let her daughter walk with Romeo as the group moved up the center aisle.

Before they reached halfway to the back of the auditorium, the entrance doors burst open. A flare of brilliant red light darted through the double doors and circular runes twisted and rotated in the air in front of a witch in a denim jacket and a blue-and-white baseball cap. She raced down the aisle.

"I made it!" Melissa Bore shouted, lifted her wards away from her face, and stopped in front of the startled group. "I'm here. So where's the—"

The woman glanced around the empty, silent auditorium and lowered her hands. The red, swirling wards faded from around her, and she exhaled a heavy sigh of disappointment.

Greta walked to her friend, nodded, and leaned slightly toward the other witch to mutter, "You really need to work on your timing."

"Well, I didn't expect everyone to take care of the

whole thing without needing a little help. Do you have any idea how far I came to be...what? Only a few minutes late?" Melissa eyed Lily, Romeo, and the others who passed her on their way out of the auditorium, then puffed out a dejected breath. "All right. At least let me buy the beer, huh? Every single one of you looks like you could use a few beers."

THIRTY-TWO

One week later...

The cool breeze rushed over Russel Creek and onto Edisto Island where it brushed through the Palmetto fronds studded across the peninsula. Lily leaned back on the old, rotting picnic bench against the table and turned her face up to the salt air and the sunlight that spilled between oak branches. The Winnie's side door clicked shut, and Romeo stepped out with a cooler in hand.

"Okay. I put everything together for literally the best barbeque for two you've ever had." He lugged the cooler onto the table and bent to kiss her on the cheek. She hummed in approval. "Now we only need to wait for the grill to heat up."

"So come sit with me." She patted the picnic bench beside her.

With a chuckle, he complied and draped his arm around her shoulders. "Yeah. This is nice, huh?"

"Yes, it is." She caught his hand where it dangled over her shoulder and laced their fingers together. "I like being all the way out here. There are no TV's broadcasting everything about Greta Antony, famed archaeologist, returned from the dead."

"Yeah, the news kinda went wild over that one." He made a face and uttered a wry laugh. "I'm only glad there isn't a media conglomerate focused only on covering magical news stories. Wait, there isn't, right?"

She laughed. "Not that I know of."

"Okay. That's partially reassuring."

"What, you don't think your dad would be super-proud to have his face plastered all over some magicals-only news channel?"

"Well, sure." Romeo ran his fingers through his dark curls and stared at the sun sparkling off the creek at high tide. "Think about it. 'First werewolf to hold a seat on the Council of Magic' is a heck of a lot better than, 'Crazed werewolf murders head of magical council in cold blood.'"

Lily elbowed him lightly in the stomach, and he chuckled. "No one would have said that anyway. And it's not what happened."

"I know. I can't tell you how glad I am that the rest of the Council saw it that way too."

"You know..." Lily squeezed his hand and leaned closer to him. "I'm very sure that night officially took care of every part of our deal."

"Please, go on." He took a deep breath. "I'd love to hear how you put all that together in your head right now."

"No, seriously. We got the Council to believe us—

finally. Okay, yeah, it took my mom and me almost dying and Carmichael killing himself with the Varelos for them to open their eyes, but it worked. They've already snatched most of the other random Black Heron members."

"Plus the ones who turned themselves in."

"I know." She frowned and shook her head. "That's a little too weird for me to wrap my head around. But they're done. And your dad got a seat on the Council as a thank you. That plus the recognition his friends got for having been a part of the whole thing... Sure, it's not total freedom for werewolves everywhere, but it's the biggest step I've seen anyone take before this."

Romeo grinned. "Do you think we should go back to that art museum in New Mexico and rub it in their faces?"

She shot him a 'don't push it' glance, and he laughed. "I don't think that's even worth the trip at this point."

"True. You know what I really would have liked to see, though?" He grinned when she raised her eyebrows. "The looks on the Council's faces when your mom showed up to hand over that magic-stuffed stone in a freakin' fanny pack. Right before Gabriel and Cadre Europa offered their full support in cleaning up the whole mess."

Lily burst out laughing, covered her face with a hand, and groaned. "My mom and that fanny pack."

"I know!" His eyes crinkled when he laughed with her before he turned to gaze over the creek. When they finally recovered themselves again, he pulled her closer and released a long sigh. "I can't believe what we've done in the last few months."

"Yeah. We finally got our super-grand adventure all over the world, didn't we?"

He shook his head. "You had no idea it was coming."

"Hey, neither did you."

"Maybe. Maybe not." Romeo turned toward her and leaned away a little so he could study her face.

"What?" She wrinkled her nose and grinned at him.

"Well, it's only that I always kinda knew we'd have our adventure together. Okay, not this exact quest laid out by your mom and all the weird stuff we had to do to see it through. I mean us. You and me. Since we were kids, Lil. I always knew I wanted my biggest adventures to be with you. And I don't ever want that to change."

The young witch pursed her lips and raised her face toward his. "Exactly what are you trying to tell me, Mr. Stephens?"

"That I love you." He shrugged. "That, oddly enough, you make a wolf wanna settle down."

With a silent laugh, Lily cupped his cheek with her hand and pressed her lips against his long enough to make sure he knew she meant it. Then, she pulled away and glanced coyly behind the picnic table toward the Winnebago parked beside Julian's cousin's old cottage on the creek. "You know, we could settle down anywhere we want."

"Oh, yeah?"

"Totally. We have a Winnebago and a couple of bags of gold and all the time in the world."

Halfway across the world, a fair distance away from the place Lily Antony and Romeo Stephens had reached in the Sahara Desert, the pyramids of Egypt held their own secrets. Deep beneath the architecture designed by the brilliant minds who'd created them and miles below the surface, a hidden, undiscovered crypt illuminated after centuries of darkness. One after another, the dried, almost crumbled torches that lined the walls burst into flame to reveal the hieroglyphs of stories and legends unseen for centuries. Optatus witches were featured in all of them—heading off to battle, leading magicals to victory and achievement, and building civilizations from the ground up to watch them rise and fall, prosper and decay.

A low stone altar at the back of this untouched crypt shimmered under the flickering torchlight that filled the undisturbed haven. Upon its surface, surrounded only by empty space and eons of dust, sat the Varelos. Whole again and once more restored to its original purpose, the shimmering copper rod pulsed once beneath the firelight. It had returned to the place of its origins and would spend another timeless age exactly where it belonged.

The End

This series may be over, but there's new series coming your way this year and they're coming sooner than you think. Goth Drow will be out in February 2020. Leira, YTT, Correk and more are returning this year. Then there's The Never Ending War series and universe as well as the

Terranavis Universe series continuing and expanding! If you aren't keeping an eye on www.MarthaCarr.com, you should! We post new releases there as well as teasers to upcoming books!

Get sneak peeks, exclusive giveaways, behind the scenes content, and more.
PLUS you'll be notified of special **one day only fan pricing** on new releases.

Sign up today to get free stories.

CLICK HERE

or visit: https://marthacarr.com/read-free-stories/

For Hire: Teachers for special school in Virginia countryside.

Must be able to handle teenagers with special abilities.

Cannot be afraid to discipline werewolves, wizards, elves and other assorted hormonal teens.

Apply at the School of Necessary Magic.

AVAILABLE AT AMAZON RETAILERS

Austin robbery detective Maggie Parker knows how to run down a felon. Now add in magic.

When she finds a gnome breaking into her garage to steal a favorite wooden puzzle box everything changes. Did she just see a compass fly?

Can she learn how to use the magic of bubbles to chart a new course in time? It's a lot harder than it sounds.

Join her on her quest to rescue passengers on an ancient ship – a big blue marble called Earth – and save herself.

<u>AVAILABLE ON AMAZON AND IN KINDLE UNLIMITED!</u>

A little background. The Oriceran Universe started in July of 2017 and now has about 150+ books in it. In 2018 fans wanted to write their own stories in the universe and two anthologies were created. Out of that our crackerjack Leader of Editors, Lynne spotted one fresh voice.

Lynne tapped me on my virtual shoulder and said there's a writer you guys should take a closer look at. He's really got something to say. That's how I met TR Cameron who loves all things Oriceran almost as much as I do. He even went and got himself his own troll in Federal Agents of Magic!

Turns out Lynne knows what she's doing – we already knew that – and Mr. Cameron has been a fan fave from the start. His books open with a twisty, turny plot and the occasional guns blazing and keep going from there. Best of all it's with characters that suck me in right away.

But wait, there's more. I mingle, mingle with a lot of writers and most bring some amount of small dramas about whether they can hit a deadline or find the motivation or wonder if the readers will like the book. TR Cameron is more of a steady, reliable, creative soul who keeps putting out a good story, while working a full-time job, quietly working away. Imagine how much meditation this guy has to be doing!

Now he's knee deep in another Oriceran story, The Scions of Magic telling more delicious tales and introducing more Atlanteans with a New Orleans flavor. Makes me wonder what he might come up with next... Stay tuned!

-Martha Carr

1. Tell our readers a bit about yourself.

I'm in my fifth decade and can't believe how fast the last one flew. I'm a husband and a father, and have a day job I usually enjoy. My happy places are at home, at amusement parks, or in movie theatres. I write in a variety of places – on the track at the gym by narration, at home, on the bus, at Panera, in the bleachers while my kid does sports. It's kind of like a common thread that weaves into all my stuff.

2. Tell a little bit about your history with writing.

Like many authors, it's one of those things I always wanted to do. Dabbled in a little fan fiction way back when, but the need to make it a priority wasn't there, until the day it was. Literally something just clicked, and I was like, "Okay, time to write some books." I had an idea that had been banging around in my head, and started on the first book. Ten thousand words in, I realized I had no idea at all what I was doing. The next three months I devoured courses and texts on writing, plotting, marketing, and publishing, and then I started again. Early mornings were my key writing time, walking the track at the gym and talking to myself. Since then, some things have become easier, and others harder, but I still get people looking at me like I'm abnormal when I wander past them with my rock-star microphone wrapped around my head.

3. What genre(s) do you write?

I write Urban Fantasy and Military Space Opera, so far. I'm open to doing other genres in the future, but right now UF is my zone of happiness.

4. What genre(s) do you read?

Pretty much everything except romance (and some-times even romance). I'm partial to UF, Fantasy, Sci-Fi, Thriller, and Mystery. Horror if it's really good.

5. Do you have hobbies?

Writing doesn't leave me time for many! But I get to mix family time with fun time for videogames, board games, bowling, movies, and amusement parks. Hopefully hiking more soon as well.

6. What is one of your goals for the new year?

Come up with a killer idea for the series to follow Scions of Magic and convince Martha and Michael to work on it with me!

7. Do you have a website you want to share?

www.trcameron.com

OTHER BOOKS BY MARTHA CARR

Series in the Oriceran Universe:

SCHOOL OF NECESSARY MAGIC
SCHOOL OF NECESSARY MAGIC: RAINE
CAMPBELL
ALISON BROWNSTONE
THE DANIEL CODEX SERIES
THE LEIRA CHRONICLES
I FEAR NO EVIL
FEDERAL AGENTS OF MAGIC
THE UNBELIEVABLE MR. BROWNSTONE
REWRITING JUSTICE
THE KACY CHRONICLES
MIDWEST MAGIC CHRONICLES
SOUL STONE MAGE
THE FAIRHAVEN CHRONICLES

Other series:

THE LAST VAMPIRE
THE WITCH NEXT DOOR

OTHER BOOKS BY JUDITH BERENS

OTHER BOOKS BY MARTHA CARR

**JOIN THE ORICERAN UNIVERSE FAN
GROUP ON FACEBOOK!**

CONNECT WITH THE AUTHORS

Martha Carr Social

Website: http://www.marthacarr.com

Facebook: https://www.facebook.com/ groups/MarthaCarrFans/

Michael Anderle Social

Michael Anderle Social
Website:
http://www.lmbpn.com

Email List:
http://lmbpn.com/email/

Facebook Here: https://www. facebook.com/TheKurtherianGambitBooks/

www.ingramcontent.com/pod-product-compliance
Lightning Source LLC
Chambersburg PA
CBHW031617100726
47898CB00006B/1833